Neon Revenge

Book One of the Neon Lex Trilogy

Graeme J Greenan

D1681010

To Francisco

All the best

Graeme J Greenan

Copyright

ISBN: 9781688076853

Contents

For mum and dad

Prologue

Malcolm Jacobson watched the procession amble along the dimly-lit tunnel against the backdrop of their tall, shuffling shadows. Their heads were bowed low; their demeanour that of defeat. High spirits were scarce within the hollow tube they marched through. They all knew where they were headed; the destination was more or less spelt out for them during their interrogation. It was an inevitability which would have had them fighting with every fibre of their being under any other circumstances. But now, Jacobson thought with mild amusement, his lips twitching into a satisfied grin, they almost looked like they welcomed it.

He found the whole spectacle sad, especially since this group in particular, at one point, would have been the definition of defiance. Not now, and if he was being honest with himself, he'd probably feel the same way if he'd played host to the attentions of the bleeders for as long as they had.

He shivered at the thought.

He leaned forward, taking hold of the grubby rail, and gazed down. He began to feel pity for them in their current state; their torn, sodden clothes hung off their frames in tattered strips; wounds varying in severity, haphazardly patched up or left open for all to see; their pathetic faces painted the perfect picture of persecuted misery. The initial emotion brought on a wave of anger which swept away his absurd bout of empathy. He clenched the railing, his skin stretching his knuckles white. These pathetic creatures were outcasts, firebrands, and troublemakers. They were enemies of the state who, if given the opportunity, would pull down order with their disillusioned ambitions to wreak havoc and chaos.

They were reaping what they'd sown, it was as simple as that.

He'd been tasked with the 'necessary exodus' – as it was officially labelled within the inner circles of government – for the last couple of years now, and as he stood above the sorry group, he still knew it was a matter of self-preservation that the rose bush was trimmed from time to time. It was better for everyone that a few bad apples were thrown away before their rot spread to the rest of the orchard; to maintain the Prime's vigilance to keep humanity safe from those who would do her harm. And if that meant expunging those who'd decided to fight against society into the barren wastelands, then so be it.

He watched, stoic, the initial sympathy for the way these traitors had been treated already fading, his focus returned, as their pathetic squalls and cries echoed down the tunnel. He should have brought earplugs. In Jacobson's eyes, they'd brought this on themselves. Prime Vonn had given them the best possible chance to thrive, and how did they repay this gift? He shook his head, feeling repulsed as their stench invaded and insulted his senses.

If it were up to him, he'd line them up against a wall and spray them in a hail of lead and be done with it. It was how the task had been carried out before, that was until… He grimaced, pushing the memory to the back of his mind before it could rear its ugly head and plague him with shit, he was more inclined to repress. Six months ago, this whole operation had been placed in jeopardy by his inability to keep one of his own from stepping out of line. Luckily, it had been taken care of; the threat dealt with before it had cost him his place – though, his reputation had suffered because of it.

Good riddance, he thought, gritting his teeth and letting go of the rust-pitted balustrade and walking away from the scene below. He marched along the narrow balcony fixed on stanchions to the cylindrical wall of the tunnel, his boots clunking against the thick steel of the floor. A few guards stationed below – overseeing the exodus of prisoners – glanced up at the sudden noise above their heads. He paid them no heed, feeling the need to be out of this wretched place. They knew who he was, and thus quickly returning their attention to the prisoners.

Very few knew of this place's existence. It was deep below the city, only accessed via an elevator within a dull, well-guarded warehouse in a section of the city rarely frequented by citizens. A series of corridors led away from the elevator through multiple doorways and checkpoints. The tunnel itself was strewn with the remnants of a bygone era; of times when war reigned supreme. Old cruisers – or cars as they were once known; primitive vehicles which ran on petroleum-based fuels, long-gone from the world – lay piled against the outer walls like a scrapheap graveyard; dust and debris lay so thick upon the twisted, battered metal, it was like a layer of skin.

He reached the end of the walkway to the exit stairwell and began to descend, leaving the cacophony of footfalls and the stench of their march behind him. He wanted to be as far away from the tunnel as possible before the outer doors were opened; the reek of the barren wastelands, beyond the outer walls of the city, was an unpleasantness he could do without.

Halfway down the creaking stairwell, the lights failed. His heart thumped against his ribcage as he squinted in the gloom. The only source of light came from the faint glow of the tunnel, which given its distance from his position, was almost useless. Cursing, he reached into the inside pocket of his overcoat and fished out his lighter – the lighter he'd received as a gift from the Proxy on his ascension, solid silver with his initials emblazoned in gold on its front – and ran his thumb down the small wheel sparking it into light, casting the narrow stairwell in a soft orange glow. The small flame flickered and danced as he continued down the steps. He took each step with caution so as not to accidentally slip or stumble and risk the chance of dropping his only source of light. If he fell and broke his ankle, he'd never hear the end of it from his fellow comrades – he was on thin ice as it was.

He sighed with relief when he reached the bottom, his boots crunching on the gravel-strewn concrete. A metallic clang rang out, breaking the silence, causing him to flinch. He wheeled around, raising his lighter up in a feeble attempt to shed light up the stairwell where he thought the noise had come from, but the light emitted from the flame only cast its glow a few feet in front of him.

He remained where he was, rooted to the spot, waiting for a follow up to the sudden noise. He took a step forward, trying to attune his senses – all the while feeling utterly ridiculous. Was there someone on the balcony? Stupid, he thought. The stairwell he'd just traipsed down was the only way in or out. He could still make out the steady hum of the outcasts, their slow rhythmic march thumping its beat. Maybe it had come from the tunnel and the sound had just carried, the practical part of his mind suggested – a guard, perhaps? Maybe one of the prisoners had stepped out of line? He couldn't be sure; the acoustics in this claustrophobic shithole made it difficult to determine the origins of certain sounds.

Then a thought occurred to him. The guards had seen him leave. Maybe one of those asshole's had thought it hilarious to play a joke on him. "If I find out this is all part of some elaborate joke, mark my words the perpetrator will find themselves strapped to a bleeder's table so fast it'll make their head spin," he bellowed, but there was no reply.

He waited a few more moments until he was satisfied it was quite probably his tired mind playing tricks on him. He shook his head, managing a half-hearted chuckle. He turned around and made for the exit, deciding he'd earned himself a decent measure of scotch when he got home.

The second his fingers touched the chipped paintwork of the battered door, another clang resounded once more, freezing him in his tracks. This time it sounded closer, a few feet away, maybe halfway up the stairwell.

He slowly turned on his heels, fear gnawing at his insides as his mind tried to work out if there was an entrance onto the walkway he wasn't aware of; the place was a warren of old service networks, it wouldn't be entirely improbable if there was more than one way in and out of the tunnel. He could feel his bladder weaken, threatening to vacate its contents. The tunnel freaked him out at the best of times, the last thing he needed was random noises ringing out around about him, exasperating his unease. He raised his hand, the lighter trembling in his grasp, as he took another look up the stairwell. Beads of sweat were beginning to surface on his forehead. Again, there was nothing there. He sighed, his breath causing the flame to wobble, relieved to find he was still alone.

He yelped involuntarily as the lights began to strobe on and off. He squinted from the harshness of it. Spots began to form in the corners of his vision. He had to suppress the urge to scream when, for the briefest of moments, the silhouette of a looming figure stood watching him from above, sinister, wreathed in shadow.

The lights suddenly stopped flashing, dying for a few heart-wrenching moments, before kicking back into life once more, bathing the area in artificial light – presumably powered by the backup cells. He looked with bulging, fearful eyes to the spot where the strange figure had stood.

There was no one there.

He closed the lighter and turned. Fuck this, he thought. The sooner he got to his cruiser – and his security detail – the better.

Before he'd taken his first step, an echoed, haunting voice called out to him, chilling his very bones. "Jacobson," it called.

He stiffened, his lighter slipping from his paralysed fingers, as he recognised the voice. It was a voice he'd remember for the rest of his days. A voice he'd listened to as it wailed and screamed for mercy; those cries falling on the deaf ears of the bleeders as they'd set to work on her.

It wasn't possible, it couldn't be, could it? He scanned the area with frightened eyes. Where was it coming from? He took a step towards the foot of the stairs. "Hello, who's there?" he called out, his voice betraying the abject terror he felt.

There was no answer. The silence dragged on for an excruciatingly long time. His overcoat suddenly felt too heavy, claustrophobic. He searched for the source of the voice, but all he could hear was the thump, thump, thump of the exodus in the tunnel.

The silence was broken by a soft hiss, followed by an almighty crack as one of the lights, fixed to the wall, exploded in a spray of sparks and broken glass, the pieces showering the metal steps like confetti. Jacobson stumbled back, wishing he'd brought his pistol.

"You know who this is, Jacobson," the voice called out, its tone cold and cruel.

"Y… you're dead," he cried, not sure where to direct his gaze as he wasn't a hundred per cent sure where the voice was coming from. He pulled out his scribe – the small handheld tech allocated to all Sanctum-One citizens – and held it aloft. "Whoever you are, if this is some sick joke, know that you're dealing with a member. I have armed security at my disposal. One call and you're dead."

A sadistic laugh cackled, the awful sound reverberating all around him. "You *had* armed security, Jacobson. They're currently lying in pieces in front of the smoking ruin that used to be your cruiser. You're all alone…"

What remained of the light died. Before he could even attempt to comprehend what was going on, he felt a thin coldness slip into his back and out through his stomach, piercing the fabric of his shirt, followed by a warmth trickling down his torso and down his crotch.

The lights flickered on once more. He shuddered, his legs suddenly growing weak. He glanced down at his midsection where three inches of sharp steel protruded – poking out from a crimson mess that looked very much like his stomach. A hand grabbed him roughly from behind. He felt a warm breath against his ear. "…and you're all mine," said the cruel voice.

Jacobson jerked forward as the blade was pulled from his body with a wet slop. He turned his head just in time to see a shadow wielding the blade; swinging it with expert precision towards his neck. The razor-sharp blade cut through bone and sinew like it was cutting water.

13

The slice was so fast, and so clean, his head – whose face still retained its expression of shock and horror – remained where it was, perched on his neck, blood gurgling out of the thin line which circled its circumference, until his legs finally gave way and his body crumpled to the ground, pitching the head a few feet away.

The dark figure approached the corpse as it continued to spew its contents from the fleshy mess where the head had been attached, and bent down to examine her victim. She searched the body until she found what she was looking for. A gold pin which bore the image of a golden dove, wings outstretched as though in flight, lay against the black backdrop of the man's lapel. She unclipped the silver clasp that fastened the pin to the dead man's coat and pocketed it.

It had begun.

I

Jared ran through the precinct, his breath laboured, his thighs burning as his debilitating terror was barely kept in check by the constant waves of adrenaline that coursed through his veins. Keep going, he told himself, keep going. His shirt stuck to his chest; the mixture of blood and sweat pasting the silk to his skin like film; the expensive material stretching with every breath he sucked in, all the while, his lungs felt as though they were on fire.

He took a quick glance behind him to see if his pursuer was close. There were so many neon lights, it was all a blur to him; people, market stalls, and the ever-present strobe of the shop lights. His head beat with its invasiveness.

Too busy glancing over his shoulder, he collided with an elderly woman, laden with shopping bags. They both fell in a tangle of limbs and groceries onto the tiled floor, quickly drawing a multitude of onlookers to the sudden spectacle. His shoulder screamed in protest; the bullet wound raw and burning.

He scrambled to his feet, knocking the woman into a man in the process of pulling her to her feet. He ignored the shouts, and cries of outrage as more people came to the old woman's aid. He felt a hand grasp at his coat. He slapped it away. They didn't concern him. All that mattered was escape. All that mattered was sanctuary.

He reached the end of the precinct, and the scene he'd caused. He maintained the speed of his flight as he burst through the doors and out into the street. Another wave of pain and nausea swept over him. He fought with all he had not to pass out.

A few startled citizens stared at his bedraggled state. He ignored them, too busy trying to find his bearings; he'd been so engrossed in fleeing from the maniac, he'd forgotten where he was.

The welcome sight of a nearby street sign told him where he was; he was on the west side of the market district. His apartments – and security personnel – weren't far. He'd made it this far; he'd be damned if he was going to be caught now.

The whine of a bullet whipped past his head, so close he felt it on his cheek. It ricocheted off the pavement, smashing the light fitting fixed to the side of the door he'd just burst through. He was showered with glass and small shards of metal which nipped his skin.

He screamed in terror, sprinting north, not waiting for the next bullet to find its mark.

Rain lashed the dimly-lit street as he barrelled down it. His feet kicked and splashed through the puddles that pooled by the kerb, soaking his shoes and the bottom half of his trousers. The smell of shit and waste from the filthy water crawled up his nose, invading his senses, threatening to make him vomit.

He reached an intersection and made a left. He ducked as another bullet smashed into the brickwork above his head. He overshot the corner, careening onto the road, straight into the path of an oncoming taxicab. He stood, transfixed, waiting for it to mow him down. Luckily, it blared its horn as it just managed to swerve out of his path. He heard it collide with something, followed by screams from a few surprised bystanders.

He ignored it as the entrance to his apartments lay ahead. The blue and neon sign fixed onto the lintel was the only thing he focused on – a beacon of salvation.

Rodic and Marr – his two doormen – whipped their heads round in his direction as he splashed and staggered towards them; their eyes widened in shock at the bedraggled figure sprinting straight for them.

Marr pulled out a stun-baton from inside his jacket and held it high, ready to swing it at the crazed stranger. His arm relaxed the moment he realised it was his employer.

He had just enough time to slip it back into its holster as Jared threw himself into the burly man's arms.

"Sir, are you alright?" he asked.

"Does it look like I'm fucking alright?" Jared screamed at the idiot. "Just get me the fuck inside."

Marr, his intellectually-challenged brain finally grasping the fact something was wrong, lifted Jared up as though he were a baby, and carried him inside.

Rodic, who had watched in stoic silence, held the door open as they hurried past. He remained outside baton at the ready.

Once inside, Jared felt his fear subside, though it was replaced with a weariness that was threatening to overwhelm him.

Marr jabbed at the button to call the elevator at the end of the lobby. He still cradled Jared in his arms. Jared thought about telling the big ape to let him down, but he didn't have the energy, and his shoulder hurt like hell.

As they waited for the numbers on the digital display to reach zero, he leaned in close to Marr's ear. "When we're safe in the apartment, I want you to call Faulks." He paused, still struggling to catch his breath. "Tell him I've been attacked by the woman, that he's to send a doctor and ten of his best. Make sure they're armed to the teeth."

Marr smirked, which enraged him.

He leaned in closer, his lips brushing Marr's earlobes. "Did I just make a fucking joke?"

"I think me and Rodic can handle one little girl, sir," Marr said.

"Just make the call. I'll feel better when there's a dozen of you and a doc between me and that psycho. I'll be fucked if I'm going to end up butchered like the others."

~

The elevator doors opened in the middle of Jared's apartment – though 'apartment' was an understatement, to say the least. A hundred square foot of quality real estate, filled with the best furniture and antiques money could buy. It was the one place he truly felt at home, safe from the

18

outside world — though, it was a feeling he guessed was about to be truly tested.

Marr carried him over to the ridiculously large sofa; high-backed, hand-stitched leather whose cushions were stuffed to almost bursting. The lights flickered on as the sensor picked up their presence. He was dropped unceremoniously onto the thick leather, jarring his shoulder.

He cursed as Marr — who appeared to be less than sympathetic for his obvious wounds, which he hadn't enquired about — pulled out his scribe and began to jab at the screen in an effort to find Faulks' number. To Jared, he worked the phone like a caveman who had just discovered something wondrous but hadn't quite figured out its purpose.

He put the cell up to his ear. "Get me Faulks," he demanded. He paused, listening to whatever was being said to him, which wasn't to his liking. "I don't care if he's asleep. Wake him up. The boss is hurt, he says it's the woman."

If the recipient on the other end of the line had a retort, it was stopped dead in its tracks at the mere mention of the woman. Marr grunted as he was put on hold. He looked down at his employer, slumped on the couch. He pursed his lips and gave him a nonchalant shrug.

'The woman', whose current identity was still unknown to the Inner-Sanctum, but a thorn in its side, all the same, had been spent the last six months killing members of the organisation; members that included colleagues, business acquaintances, and a couple of close friends. And with every death, she took the same trophy: the silver pin which bore the golden dove of Sanctum-One – a particular pin worn only by members of the Inner-Sanctum. The thought made him bring his hand up to his own pin as he sat on his sofa, in pain and miserable.

While they waited, Jared glanced to the window where the glow of the city shone. Hundreds of screens, fixed to skyscrapers, flickered with advertisements and government messages – each fighting for the attention of the citizens below. Many of them belonged to Jared. A constant display of his wealth and social standing, which usually gave him immense pleasure whenever he cast his eye to them; what he'd achieved, always reminding him he was a king amongst men – he was having trouble finding that pleasure in his current quandary.

Looking down at himself, it was hard to believe he was king of the gutter rats. Made to run and hide by that bitch. She'd pay, he promised himself, she'd pay.

Before he could wallow any deeper into self-pity, Marr grunted, breaking the silence. He began to pace back and forth as information was relayed to him. He cut the call, slipping the scribe into a pocket.

"They'll be here in ten minutes," Marr said. "Faulks said to sit tight until the cavalry arrives."

Before Jared could answer, the lights died, descending them into darkness. She was here, and all of a sudden, ten minutes may as well be ten hours.

II

Through the scope of her rifle, Lex watched as Jared Trammel was carted into the building by one of his security guards, shouting and screaming in complete terror. He didn't realise he was only alive because she allowed it.

In truth, she could have shot all three of them multiple times as they'd dithered on the front steps, rendering them dead in an instant. She'd almost succumbed to the urge and squeezed the trigger; the leather of her gloved finger creaking from the tension of her temptation.

She'd relented, however. The will for inflicting the most miserable of deaths had won over in the end.

It would've been too quick.

The men she hunted deserved to feel every moment of their doom. Right to the last wail of agony, to the last drop of blood. She'd promised herself that from the very beginning.

I vowed to answer for your death with every ounce of my being. I promised that the moment your little blue eyes became dull and lifeless. The spark gone forever.

But not my love…

Amusingly, Trammel had thought he'd been pursued from the ground. The image of his face, crazed and sweat-soaked with fear, as he'd charged through the precinct brought a thin smile to her lips.

She lowered her rifle and peered over the edge. The street was washed in the neon glow of the lights lining the sidewalk. The citizens passed in all directions, the tops of their umbrellas floating by like leaves in a stream. Cruisers ripped through the steadily increasing water levels on the smooth tarmac of the road; their tyres splashing the rainwater onto the sidewalk.

To most eyes, it appeared to be nothing out of the ordinary; people going about their lives, oblivious, harmless. To Lex, she saw subjugation, bondage in plain sight. You just had to look *that* bit closer, a few seconds longer, then it became all too apparent.

It was in their eyes; like cattle, fear most prominent when a government cruiser rolled by. Their heads bowed low, not from the rain or a need to mind one's own business, but for the desperation to blend in – to avoid drawing attention.

Lex didn't just see it in the herd, but in the street itself; the ragged, torn posters of political insurgency; faded spray paint, bearing messages of encouragement to rise up and fight back... against crimes committed by the cream of society, by those who should know better...

She holstered the rifle onto her back, swinging it over her shoulder with practised ease, and ran towards the fire escape.

She descended down the fire escape, her rubber-soled boots barely making a sound on the metal stairwell until she reached the bottom – ten feet above the alley.

She vaulted over the railing, landing catlike onto the hard concrete. She made her way towards the end of the alley, keeping her body close to the wall; near the sanctuary the shadows provided.

She was a ghost.

The rain pattered against the roof of her hood, running down her suit in beads. The material was thin which aided manoeuvrability in combat situations, black for stealth, and waterproof. It had cost a small fortune from the underground market; bought from individuals who had a tendency to look the other way if the price was right. It was a little on the tight side, but it served its purpose.

She peered around the edge of the building towards Trammel's apartments. The guard he'd left behind was scanning the street, alert and coiled like a spring. He had a face whose resting position settled on barely concealed rage, with the promise of violence. His nose sat flat, taking centre stage above a lantern jaw peppered with stubble. His little piggy eyes darted from side to side, nervously.

He held a stun-baton down by his side. The tip glowed a faint blue, the promise of a few thousand volts. She had no doubt he carried a pistol or two within his long overcoat, which fell to just above his knees.

Lex made a quick check of her weaponry. She had two sidearms holstered on each hip, the rifle on her back, and an array of knives and small blades strewn about her person. She also had a small collection of grenades because… 'you never know'.

The street was fairly quiet. Those that passed the opening, where she waited, kept their heads down. Obliviously unaware the strolled mere feet past death incarnate. The streets could be a dangerous place at night. Gangs and a whole host of crazies roamed the streets in search of prey; ready to strike from the darkness.

She looked up to the sky. Several Zeps floated above, advertising their wares, or broadcasting government messages on the sides of their massive bodies. Above the floating monstrosities, the sky was black. There was just too much cloud cover and light pollution to see the stars.

He used to love the stars.

She closed her eyes, pushing those thoughts to the back of her mind. She fixed her gaze across the street. She had a job to do. Men to kill. Another trophy to acquire.

The distance between her position and the thug outside the apartment building was roughly fifty yards. There were a few citizens in the vicinity, but that couldn't be helped. She hadn't been naïve enough to expect to get in and out without attracting some sort of attention. Given the high stature of those she hunted, it was unavoidable.

She waited for the guard to give her the best opportunity to attack. She slowly slid a throwing knife out from its sheath, her muscles taut, coiled like a spring ready to pounce. Her world narrowed to tunnel vision – her and the guard.

The guard turned his head to gaze down the street, in the other direction, away from where she was hidden.

Lex bolted from cover without the slightest hint of hesitation. She could feel the adrenaline, the anticipation of combat already building within her. Her heart hammered in her chest pumping blood through her veins.

She made it halfway across the street before the guard cast his gaze in her direction.

That's all I need.

She threw the knife, her arm a blur. The small blade left her hand and soared through the air. It struck true, the knife embedding itself into the guard's neck. He grunted in surprise, staggering back. There was surprisingly little blood; the blade ironically acted as a plug for the hole it had created.

Lex sprinted across the road, closing the gap, her only focus on the guard. She was disappointed her throw hadn't dropped him. He had also managed to keep his grip of the stun-baton, which he raised above his head, the thick metal glowing.

He swung it down as she reached him, aiming for her head. Lex found no difficulty avoiding the blow. As much as it was impressive, he'd remained on his feet, he still had a throwing knife sticking out of his neck.

She pivoted to the side, pulling a dagger out of its sheath. She twisted around his outstretched arm and dealt him two cuts with the razor-sharp steel; one to the lower side, near a kidney, and another to his upper thigh.

Blood spattered the concrete as he fell to one knee, dropping the baton, which clattered onto the sidewalk. She grabbed him by the collar and dragged him inside – it wouldn't do to have a dead guard lying outside for all to see.

She pulled him along the lobby, towards the elevator, her boots squeaking audibly on the polished tiles.

He weighs a fucking ton.

Halfway, he began to struggle. He kicked, trying to gain purchase on the slippery floor tiles. She let him go, his head thumping against the white, tiled floor.

She thumped the handle of her dagger to the bridge of his nose before he had a chance to recover. He reached around to where she had a grip of his collar. The fight left him as he spluttered and cried. Blood flowed over his mouth and down his neck.

The gaping wounds she'd inflicted on his body had created a thick trail from the door. she was surprised he was still conscious. His eyes scrunched in pain and his teeth clenched tight within his bloody mouth.

She grabbed him by the shirt. "What floor is Trammel on?" she hissed. "I'll only ask once."

The guard heaved, his breath coming in quick gasps as his body struggled with Lex's violent onslaught. His broken nose had also caused his breathing to come in an irritating, high pitched wheeze; burbling out of his nostrils with every exhalation.

He spat a mixture of blood and spit in her face. Enraged, she drew the dagger across his throat in one smooth slice. Arterial spray washed over her.

She rose, the guard looking up at her in disbelief; his expression suggested he'd expected

26

some sort of drawn-out interrogation. She shook her head at him as he twitched. "I told you I'd only ask once."

His eyes glazed over, then became vacant. She waited until the twitching ceased until she removed her throwing knife from his neck. She wiped it on the dead man's jacket before sheathing it.

Now, she had to think. There were ten floors to this apartment building. She assumed Trammel would be on the top floor – he seemed the type to want to sit at the top of his castle. It would have been good if the guard had told her, saving her a little time.

She looked down at the dead guard. "Asshole."

She decided her only sensible option would be to head directly to the penthouse. But, just in case Trammel assumed she would do this, and was skulking on one of the lower floors, waiting for her to pass him by… she needed to cover the front door.

She pulled a portable-cam from her belt and placed it on the floor, facing the front door. The small piece of hardware was equipped with a sensor. If it was triggered, the camera would spring to life and send the image to the small high-def screen on her wrist.

If that slimy worm thinks he can escape the building without me knowing about it…

With the entrance covered, she approached the elevator. She was about to press the call button when something caught her attention. A door towards the back corner of the lobby. A sign above it read 'Electrical cupboard'.

She smiled.

Perfect.

III

The silence seemed to drag on for an age. It felt like his heart was beating in his ears. Jared could make out Marr's silhouette, his head turning from side to side. Eventually, it was the security guard who broke the silence.

"Shouldn't the back-up generator kick in?" he asked.

Despite the woman's notoriety within his social circle, Marr hadn't really grasped who they were dealing with. Aside from this, Jared was somewhat assured that his security guard didn't appear to be as shit-scared as he was.

Jared sighed a long, tired breath. He looked down at his shaking hands. His shoulder pulsed uncomfortably. He slowly pulled himself to his feet. Marr tried to help; Jared slapped his outstretched arm away. If Marr was hurt, he didn't show it. He merely shrugged, taking a few steps back to allow his boss to rise unaided.

"Well, clearly she's thought of that," he snapped.

To further dampen his mood – quite literally – the emergency sprinkler system kicked in – ironically one of the only things in his building with an external supply; a mandatory government policy.

He watched the spray wash over his possessions, ruining most of them. Thankfully, they were insured and the pay-out for the items were worth more money than what he'd paid for them. If he managed to somehow pull himself out of this disaster, he could take solace in the fact the crazy bitch had made him some money.

Marr walked past him, towards the open-plan kitchen. He picked up a food tray, raising it over his head, shielding him from the downpour. Jared wondered what the big oaf was doing until he pulled the vibrating scribe from his coat and placed it to his ear.

While he waited for Marr to finish his muted conversation, Jared squelched through his sodden carpet to his bedroom. Every wet slap his shoes made was another insult from that interfering bitch from hell. Though scared out of his wits, the fact she was skulking somewhere in his building made him seethe with anger.

He entered his bedroom, already soaked through, his mind a blur of all the things he would do to her if they somehow managed to subdue her.

The thought drew his eye to the king-size bed, which took up a fair majority of his sleeping quarters, already had a sizable puddle in its centre. The sheets alone had cost him over two thousand credits. He brought his gaze up to the wall, eliciting a groan at the state his telescreen was in; a small waterfall cascaded down its sides.

At the far corner, he was relieved to find the touch-screen, which gained entry to his panic-room, was still operational. He'd had the foresight to have it hooked up to an external power supply, just in case the need for its use surfaced – though in the back of his mind, he really didn't think he would need it. The pad emitted a soft green LED, ready for his thumbprint.

Satisfied he had a Plan B, he hurried into his bathroom and grabbed one of the towels from the rail. He shrugged off his jacket and wrapped the towel – though wet, was still warm – around his shoulder. He winced as a lance of pain shot down his arm. He gritted his teeth, eventually managing to fix it in place. Blood was already beginning to show through the white cotton.

A wave of nausea swept over him. Unable to suppress the bile from climbing up his throat, he vomited. He quickly turned to face the toilet bowl, but it was in vain. The toilet seat had been left down. Yellow bile sloshed over the smooth surface and spattered onto the tiled floor. Tears streamed down his cheeks.

Not all of them were due to his retching.

IV

Lex stood in front of the large electrical panel – which powered the building – admiring her handiwork. The metal box was a charred ruin; the outer casing had bent out in great winged shards, exposing its innards. After the blast, the charred cables had crackled and sparked for a few seconds, before dying.

I'm going to enjoy this.

The standby generator box was in a similar state of oblivion. She'd noticed it as she was placing the explosive tape on the electrical box, which was a stroke of luck; functional practicality had clearly taken precedence over likelihoods of vengeful woman seeking blood when the engineers had installed the equipment.

In the dark, she smiled grimly, as the automated sprinkler system came on. She removed her hood, letting the cool water wash over her head.

Feeling refreshed, she turned and made her way back into the lobby, pulling her cowl back over her head.

The dark wasn't a problem for her as she splashed on the tiles. The patch she wore over her one remaining eye, switched to night-vision. The long hallway was now a collage of varying shades of green.

She made a quick check of her portable cam, switching on her wrist-pad to make sure the angles were correct and made a dash for the stairwell.

She pushed through the double-doors and stopped, surveying her surroundings. The sprinklers had only been on a few minutes, but already, the stairs looked as though a river had broken its banks on one of the upper landings; it trailed in small waterfalls off each step, finally disappearing down a strip of grating, a foot from the first step.

She drew her pistol and crept to the centre of the stairwell. She looked up, ready to take a shot at the first hint of security personnel, or Trammel, himself. Sadly, there was no-one there.

Did Trammel think he was so untouchable, he only needed two or three guards?

The thought was both a relief and a concern.

Easier to get to him. But why so few?

Trammel knew who hunted him, of that she had no doubt. Which meant that either himself or his stooge, would have already called for reinforcements. It was more than likely it would be from within the Inner-Sanctum, rather than the police – though, the force had a few of their creatures secreted within their ranks. She knew that from experience.

They only use their own when their secrets are at risk of being exposed. That's how I lost you, my love. Whose beautiful face I'll never see again.

They will all answer for their sins. Even if it kills me.

All the better.

Then we'll be together again, my darling.

33

Satisfied the coast was clear, she ran up the stairs, gun raised, keeping to the outer wall, all the while attuning her senses in preparation for battle.

When she reached the first floor. She edged closer to the glass pane on the door. Through the pane, she could see an array of potted plants in a row along the corridor, and expensive artwork lining the walls; most depicted images of great men leading the way or overcoming impossible odds. She surmised Trammel saw these heroes in himself.

Fucking asshole.

She slowly opened the door and took a peek. It looked empty. Her suspicions of Trammel being situated on one of the higher levels was beginning to feel more likely. She closed the door and turned back to the stairwell.

Before she had placed a foot on the first step leading to the next floor, a crash sounded from the lobby, followed by raised voices.

She rushed up to the half-landing and glanced down to the ground floor. Beams of torchlight flashed through the windowpane. She grinned.

The cavalry's here.

V

Jared trudged back through to his living room, the very epitome of misery, as he wiped the remains of vomit from his mouth with another of his towels. His legs felt wobbly from the dry-heaves, his stomach muscles were still contracting from his efforts to expel his stomach from his body.

Marr had ended his call, the scribe tucked within the confines of his coat. Though Jared couldn't see it, he knew the security guard looked at him with something resembling pity. It was at this moment he was glad the room was pitch black. The acrid stench of bile emanated off him like cologne, contaminating the room.

"They've just arrived," Marr announced, thankfully choosing not to comment on the smell that had just wafted into the room. "They'll either pick her off down in the lobby…"

"…Or chase her up here," Jared finished.

"Is the panic room operational, or has the power been cut to the entry-pad?" Marr asked.

Not wanting to be standing out in the open, and at the mercy of that bitch, Jared turned and rushed back into his bedroom. He wiped his wet fingers on the towel draped over his shoulders to remove any dirt, vomit, or dried blood from them.

He heard Marr enter the room as he placed his thumb over the screen. A strip of red light moved from one side of the screen to the other, quickly followed by a bleep of approval.

The rectangular panel, built into the wall to the side of the entry-pad, moved back a few inches, then slid up to reveal a small room.

Light bathed Jared and Marr. They both stepped into the panic-room, finding the lack of indoor rain a welcome relief. The room had a larder filled with enough food and water to last him at least six months – the thought of spending six months in this glorified cupboard didn't sound all that appealing, but he supposed that was a damn-sight better than dead. It was also stocked with an array of wines and beers.

Marr pushed past Jared to a safe fitted into the back wall. He pressed a few keys on the electronic pad, unlocking it. The door swung open automatically. Inside were a couple of handguns, a shotgun, and an array of nasty looking knives, all in their sheaths. Marr picked up one of the handguns and threw it to Jared.

Jared dropped it, cursing as it clattered to the ground. He picked it up, feeling like a fucking idiot, the object foreign in his manicured hands. He glared at Marr. "And what the fuck am I supposed to do with this?"

Marr smiled. "Just in case."

Jared raised his eyebrows. "I'm not going back out there with you."

Marr blinked, stashing the remaining handgun in his coat. "I know you're not," he said, as though it were obvious. He was enjoying this, Jared thought, he just knew it.

He strapped the knives to his belt, looping the leather tags and clipping them in place. He picked up the shotgun. A small box of shells lay at the bottom of the safe. He picked it up and emptied the shells into a pocket. He threw the box aside.

"So, why are you giving me this?" Jared asked, waving the gun.

Marr walked past him, and back into his bedroom. He turned back. "Close the door. I'll call when I'm done. This shouldn't take too long," he said, confidently. "It'll be fine."

Without answering, Jared pressed a button on the wall, finding it difficult to believe the big man's assurance the situation was under control. The door began to slide down, locking him inside.

He had a bad feeling about this.

VI

Lex had to think fast. Her wrist-pad sprang to life as the sensor on her portable cam picked up some new arrivals. And though she wasn't worried – elated more than anything – the situation had become a little more complex. She could hear them; their voices growing louder as they drew closer to the stairwell door.

It would be suicide to fight them on the stairwell. She needed to turn the situation to her advantage. She went over her options. She couldn't go down, but neither could she go up until she'd dealt with the new arrivals.

She slowly stepped back from the rail she'd been leaning on, and pushed through the doors which led to the first floor, deciding it was the best option available to her.

A long corridor spanned from one side of the building to the other. Along its length were dozens of doors, presumably leading to offices usually manned by Trammel's employees, during the daytime, before curfew.

She heard a crash as the new arrivals burst into the stairwell, the noise echoing all the way up the multiple flights to the very top of the building; their radios crackled with barked orders and updates. They would sweep each floor until they found her.

She had every intention of being found, but it would be on her terms.

She pulled out the last of the explosive tape from her belt and strapped it to the door-frame. She armed the trigger on her wrist-pad, and ran to the end of the corridor, toward the front of the building.

She tried the door and was thankful it had been left unlocked. She opened it ajar, turned back, and waited. From where she stood, flickers of torchlight shone through the windowpane on the stairwell door. She pulled out a flashbang from her belt and pulled the pin.

This'll draw the bastard's attention.

She threw the flashbang to the other end of the corridor. It bounced a couple of times, finally stopping just below the window.

She entered the office so as not to be affected by its blast. It exploded with a crack. She heard the stairwell door burst open, followed by heavy footsteps and raised voices. She turned and made her way around several tables and chairs to the window.

She slipped her fingers through the two brass rings, fixed onto the window, and pulled. It wouldn't budge. It must have a lock situated somewhere on its frame, but she didn't have time to look. Instead, she drew her knife, quickly glancing over her shoulder to see where the assault team were. They were still searching the area her flash-bang had exploded.

She twisted the tip of her blade into the small gap she'd pushed it through and heard the satisfying sound of something snapping. The window frame suddenly eased. She slid it up and peered down to the street below.

A white van sat outside the building, mounted on the kerb. Two men stood between it and the front door. They were gazing into the lobby. They look almost disappointed to be assigned sentry duties, instead of where the action was happening. Occasionally, one of them would relay something over their radio; she couldn't make out what was said, but from his tone, he was far from happy.

Let's turn that frown upside down

She looked from side to side, to see if there was anything that would aid her ascent to the next floor. A drain pipe ran down the building from the guttering on the roof, within touching distance of the window.

Torchlight suddenly beamed into the room. Instinctively, she grabbed the pipe and threw herself out of the window. She almost lost her footing on the wet brickwork. Her boot scuffed noisily as she scrambled to gain some purchase.

It drew the attention of the two guards below.

Before they could cry out a warning, she unholstered her handgun and shot them both in the forehead. They dropped to the ground like puppets who'd just had their strings cut.

Her attention was drawn back inside, as the door to the room she'd just vacated was kicked open. "This window's open," a voice called, as a beam of light shone through the window. "I'll check it out, watch my six."

Lex rolled her eye at the ridiculous bravado and tapped the screen on her wrist-pad.

An explosion boomed from within the building, followed by cries of pain, surprise, and anger. She felt vibrations through the drainpipe, as the stairwell door was blown off its hinges, reduced to a smoking pile of splinters.

She began to climb.

~

A muted rumble, followed by heavy vibrations, shook throughout the panic-room. What in god's name were they doing out there, Jared thought? As much as it was the woman, it was still at least a dozen against one.

He looked down at the gun. He hadn't let it go since Marr left. If the situation showed itself, and he found himself standing in front of the woman, he had some serious doubts if he had the balls to fire – more likely he'd drop the fucking thing. He was a man of business, not a common soldier. Weren't men in his position supposed to be the ones barking orders from a distance, instead of being on the front lines?

He jumped, almost firing the gun in terror, as the call-screen – situated above the small desk in the corner of the room sprang into life. He shook his head, laughing grimly at himself, and got up. He picked the phone up and looked at the screen.

It was Faulks.

"Trammel?" Faulks' dry tone asked from the other end of the line. He expected to be met with the weathered face of the Proxy, but it remained blank – the fucker must have left it off.

"Who the fuck else is it going to be?" Jared replied, a little more tartly than he'd intended.

Faulks paused a moment. Jared thought he could hear the older man sigh. "Well, it could've been the woman answering as she stood over your bullet-riddled corpse."

"Is that supposed to be fucking funny? It sounds like that witch is attempting to blow my fucking building up." He rubbed his forehead with the barrel of the gun, then quickly lowered it as he remembered what he was holding. "Tell me you sent a doctor; it feels like a fair majority of my own blood is anywhere but in my fucking veins."

Faulks ignored his sullen tone. "He's there. He should be on his way up as we speak."

"I'm fine by the way. Thanks for asking."

"I wasn't. Though, there is one thing I'd like to know." Faulks said.

"And what's that?"

"Before you ran to your panic-room – pissing your pants like a little girl – did you check to see if you left anything incriminating that might lead back to us? Anything in your apartment that might give the woman access to the Inner-Sanctum?"

Jared stood there with his mouth open. Did he? He quickly scanned his surroundings. He felt what little blood he had left in his face drain away, leaving him with an ill feeling in the pit of his stomach. "My scribe… it's in the apartment."

VII

Lex climbed the drainpipe as though it were on fire. The rain beat down on her as she ascended to the third floor, where the pipe disappeared into the wall. She grabbed onto the window frame to her left and craned her neck to see below her.

Two figures emerged from the main entrance – presumably to see why their two comrades had suddenly dropped to the floor. It didn't take them long to gather where their death had rained from. They looked up, immediately spotting her. They raised their weapons and fired.

Bullets whipped past her head, some of them smashing the brickwork around her. She flinched as she was peppered with masonry. It wouldn't be long before the men inside were alerted to her whereabouts.

She tried to pull the window open, but it was locked. She cursed, drawing her handgun. She spun it around so she was holding the barrel, and drove it through the glass like a hammer. The pane splintered, but the glass remained intact. Several cracks snaked out from the impact point like thin tendrils.

A fresh wave of bullets split the wall around her. She was a sitting duck; she was lucky the two idiots below were lousy shots.

The firing ceased as they reloaded their weapons. Using the momentary respite from their assault, she pulled her arm back and swung the butt of the gun against the glass. This time the pane shattered, sending a hail of broken shards down to her two admirers. They ran for cover, giving her enough time to drag her body through the empty frame.

As she hauled herself inside, she felt her suit tear from some shards jutting out of the frame. She winced as it gouged her thigh. She felt a sudden warmth as blood coursed from the wound.

She landed awkwardly; her head clattering off a nearby desk. She pushed it aside and ran for the door. She tried the handle, but it didn't move an inch. She stepped back and fired a couple of rounds, destroying the lock.

She pulled the door open just in time to receive a fist to the jaw.

It seems they're more competent than I gave them credit for.

She stumbled back into the room. Her assailant wasn't giving her time to regroup. He rushed in after her, charging low. She felt the air escape from her lungs, as he tackled her, taking the two of them over a desk.

She landed on her back, cracking the back of her head against the unforgiving floor-tiles. All the while punches rained down on her. Her vision swam as her body was pounded from multiple angles. She weathered them, waiting for an opening.

It didn't take her long to realise the man attacking her had clearly heard of her skills and was trying to subdue her with sheer strength alone.

He must not have been listening well enough.

44

She endured the assault, timing his blows until she found an opening. She found it soon enough. He began to tire; the pause between each punch becoming longer as time went on.

At the correct moment, she moved her head out of the way from a strike aimed to her jaw. She heard his knuckles break as they crunched into the tiles, followed by a pained gasp.

She turned and whipped her forearm into his elbow, snapping the joint at a sickening angle; the way it unnaturally bent reminded her of a flamingo's leg. His high-pitched squeal was cut off, as she drew her knife and slipped it into his ear.

She felt all of his weight suddenly drop onto her as he spasmed the last vestiges of life he had in him, his eyes rolling into the back of his head.

Another heavy fucker.

With a heave, she pushed him off. He rolled over, the knife – the handle of which was still in her grasp – slipped out of his ear, his blood spurting out of the wound, spilling down his neck in a flowing cascade of crimson. She pulled it out and wiped it on his shirt.

Shouts rang out ahead. She kicked one of the desks over onto its side as two more soldiers burst into the room, weapons raised. Their bullets punched into the thick wood of the desk, one passing through only inches from her head.

She sprang from cover, throwing her knife. It struck one of them on the arm sending him sprawling to the side. She raised her handgun and shot the second man before he could get his shot off. His head whipped back, blood washing the wall behind him.

He toppled back, tumbling over a desk, discharging a few rounds into the ceiling as he fell.

The other man barely had time to look away from his fallen compatriot, before Lex shot him through the eye.

VIII

Lex left the two men where they were; broken, bloody, and unmoving amidst the wreckage of what was once a normal, functioning office space. She approached the door with caution; not prepared to be left wide open again. Satisfied there was nothing sinister awaiting her, she slipped into the next room.

This floor, she noted, was designed differently to the first floor. There was no main corridor with potted plants and fancy paintings. This floor was one big space. Rows and rows of computer panels and telecommunication boxes ran in neat columns, from one end of the room to the other. She wasn't surprised to find that none of them were operational due to her handy-work.

A few service droids roamed the room, pushing at buttons, chirping and beeping their disapproval as their workstations weren't responding to their commands.

They seemed not to notice her presence as she passed them by; their attention taken up by their current operational predicament. She found it amusingly ironic that even Trammel's own service droids were in it up to their eyeballs.

She jogged halfway along until she found a suitable alcove within some of the computer banks. She knelt down, using the momentary respite to catch her breath.

As she tried to figure out what her next move was, her eye was drawn to a tear in her suit, on her thigh – presumably torn as she'd hauled herself in through the window. She noticed it was darker at the edges. She winced as she pulled it back to inspect the damage. She must have dragged her leg over a shard of glass as it had left a deep gash on her thigh. The blood had already begun to clot; it felt tacky to the touch. She picked out a few small pieces of glass that glittered through the dark red of the gash, before closing it with some gauze and surgical tape from the medi-pack strapped to her belt.

She made an attempt to tally the body-count. She'd taken down four of the new arrivals – that much she was sure of. The explosion she'd caused on the first floor would have, at the very least, incapacitated a few more, though without going down there and wading through the wreckage, any number would be a guess.

She noted that Trammel had been carried into the building by his guard, she'd left the other one in the lobby – another figure for her tally. With Lex on his tail, he wouldn't have let the guard out of his sight, so she could only presume he was still with him.

She tapped at her wrist-pad to check the status of her portable-cam, suspecting she wasn't going to like the answer. She wasn't disappointed, the feed had been cut.

I can't waste any more time picking my way through mercenaries and floors. Someone will have heard the gunfire outside and alerted the authorities.

Time was not on her side. She was beginning to regret her recklessness at taking pot-shots at Trammel earlier. She should have done what she'd done with the others and killed the bastard.

Her problem was that her confidence in her abilities had got the best of her; she'd grown complacent. Killing the other members of the Inner-Sanctum had become monotonous, almost too easy.

For six months, she began to systematically pick off high-ranking members of the city's true rulers one by one and, for a time, she thought she was making progress.

Brick by brick.

As time dragged on, and the body count had risen, she slowly came to the realisation that the Inner-Sanctum was like a weed. As the bodies piled up, she found it wasn't making a blind bit of difference. It seemed the level at which each member she'd slaughtered could be replaced easily. She needed to delve deeper into its rotten core, to find out who was the one who'd pulled the trigger.

She felt like a fly bothering a lion.

I woke from the murky depths with a purpose. To avenge you, my love. Whatever the cost. But it has to mean something. It has to cause them unimaginable pain, and unrepairable damage.

She rubbed her eyes as she felt the beginnings of one of her headaches lurking in the background of her mind. She needed information.

I'll start with Trammel. I'll root the bastard out and find a way.

She looked up, startled from her reverie, as torchlight and hushed voices filled the room. She pulled out her two curved blades and made her way toward the voices.

There was more to add to the tally.

IX

Jared stood a few feet from the door as it slid up. The light from the panic-room spilt out into his sodden bedroom. He was thankful the sprinkler system had shut off. He had the handgun raised in front of him, as he slowly ventured out of the only safe place in his building.

His hands were shaking. His shoulder throbbed, and he felt weak. He was still angry at the tone Faulks had used as he'd called him every name under the sun. He would bide his time with the Proxy. He was beginning to show his weakness in his old age. Jared would wait for the perfect moment to exact his revenge.

Soon, he would answer for his disrespect. He was equally irritated at having been cut off from the call, before he'd had time to fire back an insult or two, as much as anything, he grudgingly admitted.

He made his way around the bed and peeked his head around the door. There was no sign of Marr. Where the fuck was he? He breathed out an exasperated sigh, frustrated his guard wasn't close; it was exactly what he was being paid for, to stay close and keep him safe.

Adding another annoyance to his ever-growing list of grievances he had for this nightmare, he glanced around the room in search of his scribe.

He could barely see anything. His living-room was too damn dark – in spite of the fact it sat in front of one wall made entirely of glass.

He had to take a closer look, which meant leaving his bedroom. For all he knew, Marr was lying dead and the crazy bitch was waiting for him.

Still shaking, he managed to steel enough courage and walk over to the centre of the room, all the while expecting that fucking witch to jump out at him. He could feel the water from his wet carpet seep into his shoes.

"Sir?" Marr called from the shadows.

Jared yelped, dropping the gun onto the coffee table. It clattered onto the varnished wood; the noise it made seeming louder to his shattered nerves.

"Get back in the panic-room," Marr said, the guard's tone struggling to suppress his disapproval.

"As soon as I find my scribe, I'll go back into my hole, just try and stop me." He took a closer look at the coffee table, where he usually left it. It wasn't there. He looked up at Marr. "Have you seen it?"

"How the fuck should I know where it is… sir" Marr snapped, realising who he was talking to. "No, I've been watching the door."

Jared glowered at him. "Faulks' men? Have you heard from them?" he asked, striding over to the breakfast bar. Though irritated at his man, he felt a little easier having him close-by.

"They gave me an update when they raced up to the first… but nothing after she blew something up down there."

"Found it," Jared exclaimed, triumphant.

His delight was short-lived as a spray of bullets ripped across the room. Holes were punched in his sofa, sending puffs of interior stuffing into the air. He heard the crack of his kitchen tiles as they were reduced to mangled shards. Marr fell to the floor, though Jared couldn't see if the guard had been shot.

Deciding his panic-room was now the only sensible place to go – now that Marr was out of sight, and for the moment, currently out of the fight – Jared ran back towards his bedroom. He only made it a few steps as he tripped over the coffee table, landing face-first onto its surface. Searing pain lanced across his mouth, feeling one of his teeth cut through his bottom lip. He suddenly began to taste copper as he rolled off the table and onto the floor.

Lying in misery, he heard something heavy clatter into the room… then nothing. He wondered if Marr had managed to get a shot off. He hoped he had and that bitch was lying in a pool of her own making.

His hopes were dashed, as something exploded. He knew it wasn't a grenade. If it was, he'd be dead.

For a second after the explosion, all he saw was a blinding white light, then everything descended into darkness. His hearing was consumed with an unbearably high-pitched whine, and his head felt as though it had been crammed full of cotton wool.

He writhed in terror and disorientation. Which way was the fucking panic-room? Where was Marr? And most importantly of all, where was the woman?

His question was answered as he felt something heavy strike his chest, as though a sledgehammer had been brought down with significant force onto his ribcage. He tried to scream, but he didn't have enough air in his lungs to expel anything other than a strangled wheeze.

Thin fingers snaked their way through his hair before he was yanked to his feet. He was dangled in the grip of his assailant, his vision slowly knitting itself back together.

Looking him dead-in-the-eye was the woman. She glowered at him from the confines of her hood, her one eye boring into his with unforgiving malice. Her face was covered in blood – most of it he presumed wasn't hers. He felt his bladder give up the good fight as warm piss ran down his legs – his humiliation complete.

"Please," he screamed, holding his hands up. "Don't kill me."

He thought that was it, she was going to dismiss his begging and end his life. But surprisingly, she didn't. Her attention was on his hand, or to be more precise, what he held in his hand. He realised, to his surprise given his rough treatment, he was still holding his scribe.

"Turn it on," she growled, throwing him onto the sofa. He bounced awkwardly, sending splashes of cold water up into his face. "And you better hope the sprinklers haven't fucked it."

Despite the fear that was crippling his insides, like shards of ice being pushed in and out of his guts, he recognised the face staring down at him.

"You died," he exclaimed. "I watched them hold you under… after they killed…" He knew the Proxy was struggling to control the situation, but he never thought in his wildest dreams the woman was… This revelation was gold to Trammel. If he managed to somehow get out of this alive, he could use the information to his advantage – an opportunity for further advancement.

With lightning speed, she grabbed him by the shirt, pulling him back to his feet. She wrenched him forward, so their noses were almost touching. He could smell death on her; death and blood.

She arched her head back and drove her forehead forward into the bridge of his nose. His vision became a field of stars as he heard the unmistakable sound of cartilage splintering. His face seared in agony. He burbled a whimpering cry through bloodied lips.

She held him steady. A great warmth ran down his lips and chin, cascading down to his shirt. "Don't you dare say his name," she screamed.

His head swam. They killed her. He'd watched as her thrashing had stopped; all life was gone. It was maybe why nobody had suspected their tormentor was her. They'd left her body for the fish. There was no one else there.

Thinking about it, since she'd emerged, what little CCTV there was of her, none of the footage contained her face. Just a shadow – a reaper plaguing their every step.

He pressed his thumb against the screen of the scribe and opened his eyes, the effort causing fresh lances of pain down his swollen features. He looked into her cold, blue eyes. She looked different; her hair was black – it had been blonde before; shorter too.

His scribe chirped into life. Relief swept over him as the scribe hadn't failed. They both looked down at the hardware.

"Log in, and hand it over," she said, coldly. He blubbered his acquiescence and did as he was told.

"Are you going to kill me?" he asked, suspecting he knew the answer. It didn't matter, either way, he'd find out soon enough – though, from her previous exploits, the odds weren't in his favour. He hoped she took pity on his pathetic state and spared him.

His scribe lit up, casting their features in a soft green hue.

She grabbed it from him and took a step back. His legs struggled to keep him upright. She glanced at the screen; a thin smile spread across her lips.

"On your knees," she commanded.

"Please, I beg you. Don't do this," he pleaded, feeling a fresh gush of piss run down his legs.

"On your fucking knees,"

He slowly lowered himself onto his knees. He felt shame as tears began to stream down his bruised cheeks. This was it. He was going to die.

"Drop the fucking gun," a voice said, coming towards the breakfast bar.

Marr stood; gun aimed at the woman's head. If his mouth didn't hurt so damn much, he could've laughed – hell, he could've kissed the big man.

The woman remained where she was; her lack of concern couldn't have been more evident. She rolled her eyes... eye. "Can't do that, I'm afraid. Drop your weapon or your boss gets it between the eyes."

Marr stepped forward and shrugged. "Makes no difference to me. You can't shoot Mr Trammel without dying yourself. You're quick, but not that quick."

Anger coursed through Jared. The two of them were discussing his death in this fucking scenario as though they were playing chess. "Just shoot this fucking bitch," he tried to shout, but it came out as an incoherent wail.

Marr ignored him. "What's it to be?" he asked the woman.

The woman sighed, closing her eye. "I choose you," she said, spinning around, her arm a blur.

They both fired at the same time. Marr ducked for cover after he got his shot off. The woman ran towards the window after she'd discharged her own.

She leapt over the sofa and shot the window. The glass cracked and splintered, but never smashed. Before Marr could regain his composure and fire at her, the crazy bitch jumped through the window, disappearing into the night.

Time stood still for a moment. He listened for the sound of a body hitting the sidewalk. There was nothing. All he could hear was the rain falling outside his open window.

He raised himself to his feet and limped over to the window. He looked down. There was no sign of her. the only activity outside was the approach of several police vehicles, an armed response van to the front of the convoy.

"Can you believe that?" Jared asked, turning to his security guard.

It was the last thing Jared Trammel would ever ask. The last thing he would ever say, as the bullet from Marr's gun passed through his brain, and out the back of his skull in an explosion of blood and bone. His head snapped back as he crumpled to the floor in a heap.

"Yes, I can," Marr said, walking away from Jared's corpse.

X

"Today, police teams were called to the city's financial district as gunfire and explosions caused panic and destruction to the area, resulting in multiple deaths and at least a dozen casualties.

Our sources suggest it may have been instigated by the notorious terrorist cell, Sapien-Republic – known for their anarchistic views towards our government. If this is the case, it means they have ramped up their efforts to violence in their machinations to compromise our Prime's wise vision of society.

Government contributor, Jared Trammel, is believed to be among the victims. The respected businessman is rumoured to have been the terrorist's prime target.

At the scene, is Hanna Ves. Hanna, are there any updates? is there any news on Mr Trammel's condition? Has there been a statement from government officials at NewHaven?"

"Good evening, Hanna Ves reporting. The scene of the attack is the private residence of Mr Trammel. We believe it's also where he conducts some of his more lucrative projects. As of yet, there has been no word from the paramedic crews, currently working at the scene, on the condition of the businessman. As of yet, we're still waiting on an official statement from NewHaven."

"Is there any information on how many perpetrators took part in the attack?"

"At the moment, investigators are keeping tight-lipped on the matter."

"I see. Has anyone come forward with information that will shed light on what happened?"

"I've spoken to a few eyewitnesses who've stated they'd seen Mr Trammel running through a local market precinct, not long before the attack took place. According to some accounts of the events leading up to the violence, Mr Trammel appeared to have been running from something, or someone. We can only assume it was from the perpetrators of this devastation, behind me..."

"...We'll have to get back to you Hanna. Government Proxy, Samuel Faulks, is ready to give a statement to the citizens of Sanctum-One."

"Fellow citizens, let me assure you our investigators will have all the resources available to them as they search for the perpetrators of this senseless act of violence.

Prime Vonn has instructed me personally to state that the pillars in which this society stands will not crumble from cowardly acts of terrorism carried out by a small minority – who hide their wanton destruction behind clever, and convenient ideals – would have all the hard work and accomplishments, achieved by the good people of this city, reduced to ashes.

The Prime, as well as myself, worry for the safety of his citizens, therefore, curfew will commence two hours earlier until further notice, starting tomorrow evening.

Be assured, we will find those responsible, and deal with them accordingly.

60

The government will report progress as new information comes in. Thank you for your patience. Sanctum stands as one."

XI

Lex seethed with rage as she watched the lies spew out of the media puppet's mouth. It was something she'd never noticed before – during her old life. Lex could see the clues as blatant as the sunrise, whenever they doled out government messages of reassurance; the eyes went slightly vacant; their tone almost not their own like someone had flipped a switch and the robotic slave appeared to indoctrinate the masses.

Lex noticed it now. It shone like a beacon to her eyes; eyes that were fully awake to the world. The realisation of the horrible truth infected her with scorn and cynicism.

They willingly go to the butcher's block, and they're grateful for it.

She switched the monitor off, descending her cramped room into darkness once more; her vague, wraith-like silhouette barely visible in the gloom.

She ached from head to toe; pain throbbing from her many wounds, each one fighting for supremacy to be heard. The jump from the window had almost killed her – she almost had the obscure notion of thinking she was lucky to be alive. It was luck; the devil had deemed that she was to linger in this nightmare that little bit longer.

She limped through to the bathroom and switched on the light. Bathed in the soft blue glow of the lamp, she looked at herself in the mirror, surveying the damage. The thing that stared back at her was a battle-weary, wound-scattered mess. She lowered her head to examine her current state. Her suit was torn to ribbons; what little integrity it had was now ruined from the shards of Trammel's living-room window.

She peeled off her suit, one ragged piece at a time until it was a bloodied pile on the floor. It was beyond repair – it didn't matter, as she had a few spares, hanging up in her wardrobe.

She turned her battered body, scrutinising her injuries. Her pale skin was mottled with bruises; angry blue and red welts that were sore to the touch. Red streaks ran down her torso from the various cuts she'd received, which had now clotted.

She removed her eyepatch, placing it on the shelf above the sink. She still hated looking at the raw scar tissue that used to be her eye.

She turned on the shower. It spat out a few spluttering jets then flowed consistently from the shower head fixed to the tiled wall.

She sighed and stepped under the stream of warm water. She winced as it ran over her wounds. It felt like sharp pins were viciously pricking her skin, unseen to the eye. Pushing the pain to the back of her mind, she began to clean herself. She felt tired and weary.

I should have killed him. I would have been fast enough to shoot them both.

It was a problem she would soon remedy, though her efforts weren't entirely in vain. She'd acquired Trammel's scribe. It could be a way into the Inner Sanctum.

To unearth the truth; to find out who pulled the trigger.

She arched her head back and let the warmth wash over her. She ran her hands through her hair, finding a couple of more cuts to her scalp, and a few small pieces of glass. She flicked the small shards onto the shower tray to be washed away.

She stood underneath the shower until the water at her feet lost its red colouring and began to run clear. She switched it off, climbed out, and wrapped a thick towel around herself.

She was startled, as a thump came from the front door.

Her senses heightened, she quickly ran into the living room and picked up her handgun. She screwed on the silencer and approached the front door.

She waited until it thumped again, then slowly opened it a crack, her finger tensing on the trigger.

She eased the tension on her finger as Jeff, her neighbour, stood in front of her.

"Hi Lex, just to remind you, the payment for the cleaning droid is due," he said, rolling his eyes melodramatically. "I thought it was our turn to pay, but Edward said we paid last month. I forgot… you know what I'm like."

Lex smiled and nodded. Jeff and Edward lived across the hall. She liked the couple. As much as she tried to segregate herself from society, she felt being in the company of her neighbours tempered the rage that threatened to consume her.

"Are you alright?" he asked, peering at her.

She shook her head. "Sorry, Jeff. I was a million miles away. Yeah, I'm fine. Just been a long day."

You have no idea.

He looked at her with sympathy. "Working you hard, are they?"

She rolled her eye and faked a yawn. "Like you wouldn't believe. About the droids, I'll send some credits first thing in the morning."

He smiled and was about to leave when he spotted a couple of the cuts on her face.

Shit.

"My God, Lex. What happened to your face?" he asked, raising a hand towards her cheek.

She quickly held up a hand. "It's nothing Jeff, really."

"What happened? Doesn't look like nothing. Is there anything I can do?"

"No. I fell off my bike on the way home from work," she said, hoping he'd buy it.

His look of sympathy had changed to that of pity. "Well okay. Give us a knock if you need anything," he said, turning.

She gently closed the door behind her, waiting for the sound of Jeff's door closing, behind him.

She waited a few more seconds, before returning to her bedroom, discarding the towel, and throwing it into the laundry basket.

She opened the first aid kit on her dresser and pulled out the array of bandages and tape; a collection she found depleted at an exponential rate, always requiring replenishment. She patched up the worst of her wounds, thankful she didn't need to staple any of them.

I'm wasting away one wound at a time.

She wiped away a few stray trickles of blood that had seeped from her wounds, then threw on a shirt. She ventured into the living room, settling on her sofa.

Like most citizen apartments, it was small, filled with the bare essentials; sofa; dining table; state-issued flat-screen. The bedroom consisted of a bed, a dresser, and a walk-in wardrobe, adjacent to the bathroom. The large apartments were reserved for Inner-Sanctum members, and the minority who held the majority of the city's wealth – Though, Lex knew from experience, the two generally went hand in hand.

She'd rented it using an identity acquired from a dubious individual – from her underground contacts – who'd wished to remain anonymous. Lex suspected he/she worked within NewHaven, so she understood the need for secrecy. At the same time, it was also possible they were part of Sapien-Republic – the crackpot revolutionaries.

To maintain the façade of being a normal, functioning member of society, loyal to Sanctum-One, she worked four-hour shifts cleaning a local office. It suited her needs. She didn't want to be immersed in an environment where there was a possibility of making a 'work friend'. It was the perfect cover; nobody paid any attention to the cleaner.

She poured herself a scotch, quaffing the measure in one, burning, satisfying gulp and lit a cigarette. She booted up Trammel's scribe and began searching through his files, hoping she'd find the breakthrough she needed to delve deeper into the Inner-Sanctum's network in the hope of finding something, anything that would lead her to the truth, and bring it all toppling down.

With me underneath it, if need be.

XII

Marr pulled his cruiser into the empty carpark. He slowed as he approached the only other vehicle in the vicinity. He flashed the lights three times; it was quickly reciprocated. The harsh succession of beams made him squint. He continued at a crawl until their bumpers were almost touching.

Marr knew who was in the other car, but it was always a good idea to stick to protocol when conducting secret meetings – off-the-books and away from the prying eyes of NewHaven.

Thankfully, the rain had ceased in its attempts to aid the sea in claiming back the land. As he got out, he found it didn't make the docks any less depressing. There was something oddly cold and characterless about it; its drab collection of square warehouses; the dirt and grime which appeared to spread to almost every surface like a skin rash; an inevitable symptom caused by the fumes spewing out of the endless number of outlets, coating the area in a perpetual state of filth – no matter how many cleaning units patrolled the area.

Above him, there was no Zeps hovering above. The area was regarded as a black zone; the perimeter stretched around the harbour five miles out – land, sea, and air. All harbour personnel were either mechanoid or vetted down to the last cell. Employees were paid a handsome salary and were certainly aware of the consequences of discussing what went on at the harbour to the public.

He strolled to the other vehicle and climbed in. The overpowering scent from Samuel Faulks' cologne invaded his senses, which induced a coughing fit.

"Nasty cough you have there, Marr," Faulks said, unaware his aftershave was causing Marr to react the same way a person would if they'd had a blast of pepper-spray to the face at point-blank range.

Somehow, Marr managed to compose himself. "We have a problem," he said, getting straight to the point. He wanted to get away from the offensive odour as soon as possible.

Faulks raised an eyebrow. "Problem? Trammel's dead, what more could that idiot do in death?"

Marr clasped his hands together. "The woman got away."

Faulks waved a hand dismissively. "A minor inconvenience. Despite that slippery little bitch being a thorn in our side, her hit and run tactics to low-ranking members are but piss in the wind." He lit a cigarette which Marr appreciated. He wasn't overly keen on the smell of cigarettes, but it was a damn sight better than the cloying musk Faulks liberally doused himself in.

"Suffice to say, the thorn in our side may cause us bigger problems," he said.

"Your meaning?" Faulks asked, twirling his fingers for Marr to elaborate.

"She escaped with Trammel's scribe. She got him to unlock it before she took a dive through the window."

"A dive that must surely have killed her?" Faulks asked.

Marr shook his head. "I searched the area for her body, there was none to be found." Marr took a deep breath. Faulks had lost his air of indifference and was beginning to look pissed off. He wasn't going to like the next bit. "I managed to get a look at her before she fled."

"Who is she?"

After Marr said her name, he silently weathered the torrent of verbal abuse from Faulks as he got himself into such a frenzy, Marr thought he'd collapse in a state of apoplexy.

"How in the world of fuck is that fucking woman still alive?" he bellowed, his face scarlet with anger. "After the boy, I held my boot on her head until she stopped fucking struggling."

Marr hadn't been there when they'd 'killed' the woman, but he was one of the select few who had seen the recordings. The first time he'd watched it, he'd been thankful he hadn't been there. The years he'd spent doing what he did, he felt he had a pretty high tolerance level where his stomach was concerned. But the images of the woman's torture had him struggling to keep his stomach contents down.

The brutality of what the woman was subjected to was a perfect example of the consequences of anyone foolish enough to take on the Inner-Sanctum. In Marr's opinion, Faulks had taken the situation too far. If they'd just shot her in the head on that dock, they wouldn't be in this mess – he kept that thought to himself.

He sat patiently, as he waited for Faulks to calm down enough for him to speak. In the years he'd worked for the Proxy, he'd never seen him blow his top, not once. He found it disconcerting; to let personal feelings get involved was to lose control.

There was another matter that had been niggling him for a while. He decided to broach the subject to help temper the Proxy's mood. "The Prime? We haven't seen him in some time…" He trailed off as Faulks narrowed his eyes.

"Don't change the fucking subject. The Prime is fine… a minor infection. He's quarantined himself to help recuperate. He's still aware of everything that's going on." He paused, almost daring Marr to prod the subject further. Marr remained silent. "Now, that bitch?" he asked.

Marr sighed. He wasn't happy with the Proxy's vague explanation as to why the Prime hadn't been seen as much lately. He had several more questions to ask Faulks, but in the end, Marr was his subordinate, so he decided to drop it for the time being. "I'll take care of it," he said.

"And how are you going to do that? She slipped through your fingers tonight when she was barely ten feet in front of you."

Marr ignored the barb. If they knew the woman was going to go after Trammel tonight, they could have come up with a plan, but they hadn't. Faulks was just directing his ire to the nearest person. Aside from the driver – safely ensconced behind the privacy glass – Marr was the only target available.

"You won't like this, but I think it's the only way. She'll find her way to us, whether you like it or not. We'll need to help her along the way. We need to lure her out; give her a trail of breadcrumbs so that it'll be on our terms."

"Are you fucking insane? We find her, and eliminate her," Faulks said, pointing a finger at him.

"We haven't been able to find her these last six months. Up until now, her kills had been quick; efficient."

"What makes you think this will be any different to all the others."

Marr smiled. "Her hit, tonight, was sloppy. She's becoming reckless, desperate. She doesn't know Trammel's dead, we've kept his death water-tight. Hell, most of the emergency services on duty don't know he's dead." He paused. "We need to give her an opportunity she can't resist."

"Fucking Trammel," Faulks said, slapping his thigh. "I advised Prime Vonn against his advancement. When that was ignored, the little prick had barely been in his position five minutes, before rumours of his ambitions began to fill my ears. I placed you within his security personnel to keep an eye on him. And look how that turned out."

"Pretty well, I'd say. He is dead."

"Don't split fucking hairs, Marr," Faulks snapped. "If some of this shit gets out, it could cause us some serious problems." He rubbed his eyes in an effort to rid himself of the beginnings of a migraine. He looked Marr in the eye. "Well, enlighten me. What do you propose we do?"

So, Marr told him.

XIII

They dragged her along the rough ground, her feet leaving a trail of blood in their wake. The cold numbed her bare skin, which she was thankful for, as it dulled the pain. What little vision she had left through the narrow slit of her eye, came in waves; each one threatening to descend her into oblivion. She longed for it... but it never came. She could hear voices all around her, but not clear enough to know how many there were. They boasted and mocked at her expense.

She'd lost consciousness several times during her torture. She felt liquid run down from her eye and down her cheek, knowing it wasn't tears.

They had broken her into a thousand pieces, put her back together again, and started all over. She'd been betrayed by a system she had sworn to protect. She'd found out, too late, that it was a system rotten to the core.

She managed to look up. There were no Zeps; no clouds. Only stars, shining brighter than she had ever seen before. They dusted the night sky like glitter scattered across a pool of oil. She focused all her attention on its beauty.

She was being carried to her end – that much she knew. But she didn't care; the pain she was in, she welcomed it. She'd managed to find a safe place for the only person who mattered; her blue-eyed boy. Despite the fact she'd been betrayed by those she'd trusted most in the world; she knew

74

they wouldn't harm her son; he was innocent in all of this.

She smiled as she let images of him flood her mind; memories that took her far away from this terrible place. Her last thoughts would be happy ones.

They came to the edge of the docks where the water sat a few inches below the concrete. Two silhouettes grew larger as she approached; one tall, the other significantly smaller.

Her smile died on her lips as her gaze settled on one final betrayal that killed her soul.

A rancid smell, like cheap cologne, emanated from the two figures. The tall one was holding a gun to the shorter one's head. To her blue-eyed boy's head. She began to wail in protest before her cries of anguish were silenced by something heavy striking the side of her head.

"Citizens should know to obey and know their place. You left us no choice," the tall one said, and fired.

The resounding boom filled the night's sky, as she screamed out the last of her will. Her blue-eyed boy dropped to the ground without a sound.

Lifeless.

She was held above him. Those blue eyes looked up at her but through her.

The spark had gone.

"Put the bitch in," a voice commanded.

~

Trammel's scribe vibrated against the bedside table, startling Lex from her darkest thoughts. She picked it up, squinting from the bright light of the screen. It was a message from an unknown sender. Intrigued, she opened the file.

Member info:

Subject: The Woman.

As you are no doubt aware, the attack on the Trammel building, tonight, has claimed the life of member 20461-5 – J. Trammel. Like the other 'incidents', his I/S pin was taken by the assailant. Media and SPD are on a strictly need-to-know. Clean-up of the scene will be conducted as of tomorrow morning.

Addendum: After analysis of member 20461-5's personal files, there is a distinct possibility there may be sensitive information at the crime scene. If found, all necessary documentation is required at NewHaven.

Sanctum stands as one,

Proxy.

Lex stared at the message, speechless. Trammel was dead? He was definitely breathing when she last saw him. Was it possible his guard's bullet – meant for her – had accidentally got Trammel? It was possible; they were close enough. A small part of her mind told her it had the rank odour of a trap.

She reached over and picked up a small wooden box that lay on the centre of her coffee table. Inside, were the Inner-Sanctum – or I/S – pins she'd taken from her previous victims. If Trammel was dead, she needed that pin. The message had stated it had been taken, giving voice to her suspicions of the message being a trap. It was possible they knew she was in possession of Trammel's scribe.

When she'd started her killing spree, she didn't really know why she felt the compulsion to take a souvenir. Her mind had been so preoccupied with killing as many members as possible until she found her son's killer. But as the body-count had grown, she'd come to the conclusion she needed those pins. It helped to remind her why she had to go on; to prevent her from putting the barrel of her gun in her mouth and pulling the trigger.

On its own, the lure of another bauble for her macabre collection might not have been enough to draw her back to the scene. But the possibility of there being information – maybe evidence – she could use against the Inner-Sanctum was too much to resist.

She closed the box and returned her attention to the message. An attachment was provided. It contained a list of names of those who would be in attendance to this aforementioned 'clean-up'.

The scribe bleeped, indicating the message would self-delete in thirty seconds. She grabbed her own scribe and took a photo of the names. Then the message disappeared.

She knew the Inner-Sanctum had members within the police force. The scene would be swarming with SPD. As an organisation who worked via secrecy, it was highly unlikely they had enough resources to pull the investigating teams off the scene to carry out their 'clean-up' without raising suspicions. That meant they would probably use a high-ranking member to direct the line of enquiries; someone maybe already working the investigation into her antics.

But all she had to go on was a list of names.

She tried to access Trammel's business accounts and wasn't surprised it was encrypted with facial recognition software, using the scribe's built-in camera. A window appeared, asking her if she wished to proceed. She declined; she wasn't Trammel, and she couldn't be sure she wouldn't get locked out if she tried.

She inserted a chip into the side of the scribe's side port – another item she'd acquired from an underground source. It contained bypass files which skipped these very security protocols. She lit another cigarette and waited as the chip did its work.

Once she was inside, she was able to access Trammel's itinerary. It ranged from audit meetings to receipts from escort services. Staring at the vast selection of avenues, she wasn't sure where to start. She could be sitting here until the end of time if she went through everything.

What else can I do?

For an hour, she trawled through his logs of business dealings, making attempts to cross-reference anything linked to Inner-Sanctum. He was careful; there was no mention of them.

However, she did manage to glean some information on a certain, Mr Trammel's, ambitions to climb the Inner-Sanctum ladder – via subterfuge, and a copious amount of backstabbing. She decided to leave that path of digging, promising herself she would return if it would help accelerate her plans.

She was about to lose all hope when one particular file caught her eye. It was labelled: PL. When she hovered her finger over it, it read: Police Liaison.

She opened the folder. It revealed a list of names, matching those included in the Proxy's message. As she dug deeper, she found each name represented a police investigator. There were also numbers attached to each name and the names of companies. It didn't take Lex long to figure out it was a bribe list.

Trammel kept a note on all the officers he'd bribed, presumably to turn a blind eye when they sniffed a little too close for comfort. The companies had one thing in common. Jared Trammel seated the board on each and every one of them.

You slippery little bastard.

Trammel hadn't been working alone. It seemed he'd been tipped off by one officer in particular.

Alon Reid.

On her scribe, she hacked into the police network. She found Alon Reid. He'd been an investigator for twenty-three years, with honours. For the majority of his career, he'd mainly worked tax crimes.

That was until six months ago.

He'd been moved to homicide not long after Lex had begun her reign of terror against the Inner-Sanctum. He'd been assigned to every case she'd been responsible for.

He stinks of Inner-Sanctum.

Of all the names attached to the clean-up crew, Reid was the most senior. Serendipitously for Lex, he was logged in for duty on the Trammel building in the morning. She knew she was veering dangerously into reckless territory, but it was an opportunity too tempting to resist. She needed that pin. She had to see if the scene held more information; information that could lead to her finding her son's murderer. And the one person she thought could aid in her aspirations was Alon Reid.

XIV

Alon Reid stood amidst the ruin that used to be Jared Trammel's living-room. The thick, expensive carpet was peppered with glass and soaked through. Priceless antiques were shattered or in irreparable condition. But his gaze wasn't on Trammel's ruined trinkets and baubles. It rested solely on one piece of carpet in particular; a small piece, about a foot in diameter, stained black with blood… Trammel's blood.

The sight didn't make him want to throw-up his breakfast like some wet-behind-the-ears rookie – twenty years on the force eventually desensitised an officer to such things – nor was it the horror. It was the fact that the blood staining the carpet had belonged to someone he'd known; someone he'd spoken with; had drinks with. He'd stood where he was, rooted to the spot because his brain was having trouble processing something that was completely alien to him.

Only a few forensic scientists remained from the vast team that had descended on the scene at the beginning of the clean-up. Reid ignored them as they carried out their monotonous task of bagging and tagging.

He could still see Trammel's corpse in his mind's eye; pale, lifeless – the back of his head missing. The bullet had caused only minimal damage to his forehead but had reduced the rear of his skull to a bloodied mass of pulp.

His eye flicked to the wall at the far left of the room, between the window and the door which led to his bedroom. Traces of bone and brain matter were scattered across its surface – more evidence to add to the ever-growing pile logged in the forensics van parked out front.

This was a nightmare. It was worse than all the others combined, he thought morosely. This fucking woman was going to be the death of him. As of yet, despite painting the building in blood and carnage, forensics hadn't found a single piece of compelling evidence that would shift the advantage his way.

To add to his frustration, there was next to no CCTV footage of the attack – aside from the two minutes it had taken her to cut the power. He'd viewed the grainy images several times. The lack of a decent shot of her face rendered it virtually useless.

He knew why the Proxy had placed him in charge of the operation to find her, with assurances he had the full support of the Inner-Sanctum – via members who worked within the SPD, hidden in plain sight. It still didn't make it any easier. For six months he'd been chasing a ghost; like trying to catch smoke with his bare hands. What worried him the most, was the longer the investigation dragged on the more his position was put in jeopardy – he was under no delusion he was irreplaceable.

Looking at the scene before him, he hoped there would be a small chance of apprehending her; in this crime-scene, there was a piece of evidence just waiting to be found. This had been the most visible she'd been, he felt he should feel confident. But standing amidst the mess in front of him, the only emotion he seemed to be feeling was despair.

"Where do we start, sir?" Hall asked.

He turned to find his subordinate gazing up at him, note-screen at the ready, eyes filled with enthusiasm that only came from being fresh out of the academy.

He was getting too old for this shit. He was fifty-one years old, but Hall's irritatingly chirpy optimism made him feel seventy. Over the last couple of years, he'd noticed his hair sat a little thinner above a short forehead. Below thick, bushy eyebrows were small green eyes resting on top of heavy bags brought on by years on the force.

Hall, stood before him, a complete contrast to her superior. She was half a foot taller than Reid, garbed in the SPD-issued investigator trouser-suit. He noted the starch hadn't quite been washed out of the material as it sat stiffly on her slender frame. Her dark hair was tied tight into a ponytail. Her brown, intelligent eyes sat above a slightly upturned nose and thin mouth. She waited eagerly for orders.

"Well, we know what happened, Hall," he said, raising his arms, inviting her to take in the room. "She came in, cut the power after she opened the guard's throat. Then she made her way to the top, blowing the shit out of everything in her path until she reached Trammel." He pointed to the dark stain on the carpet. "Where she blew the back of his head off."

Hall nodded, thinking. "Doesn't make sense," she said.

Reid raised one of his eyebrows. "What doesn't?"

Hall walked over to the window, which had been covered with strips of crime-scene tape. "There had to be someone else here." She looked down to the street below. "I mean, why jump out the window?"

Reid sighed. She was still so green. "Did you read the initial report?" he asked, as though he were talking to a simpleton. "Our assault team were arriving as she pulled the trigger on Trammel. I would say she had no choice."

She pursed her lips, clearly not convinced. "There's an emergency escape on the landing, isn't there?" she said, tilting her head to one side and casting her eye past him.

"Yeah, so?"

"Our boys had only just arrived. Their first move would be to seal the entrance. Given the fact she knows what she's doing, all she would have to do is climb out that way, maybe jump over to the next building. We know what she's capable of."

Reid narrowed his eyes. She did have a point. Although unbeknown to his underling, Reid knew the real reason she'd jumped out the window. Faulks' man had fucked up. If it wasn't for Marr's incompetence, they'd be zipping the woman up in a body bag instead of Trammel. He would have to keep an eye on Hall. She seemed the type to go sniffing where she didn't belong.

He had to divert her attention elsewhere. "I'll assign a team to run a trace on Trammel's personnel, see if there's anyone missing from the body count, or the hospital beds."

"I think that's a good idea," she said.

"I'm glad I have your approval," he said, deliberately asserting his tone to remind her their difference in rank.

She caught his meaning, her cheeks flushing faintly. "Sorry, sir. This is my first homicide. Just keen is all."

"It wears off, believe me," he said, smiling. "I'm going to have another look at the images. Join me downstairs when you're done."

He left Hall at the scene. He had to make a few calls.

~

Veronica Hall watched her superior leave with the distinct feeling she wasn't being told everything. Reid knew something. He probably regarded her as too green, too fresh from the academy. She sighed, wondering how long it took a graduate to be taken seriously – she was new, not stupid.

Reid was wasting his time with the CCTV evidence; she'd watched the footage several times herself, quickly coming to the conclusion it gave them nothing. She didn't know why he felt compelled to view it again – aside from getting away from her probing questions, she suspected.

But wasn't that what good police-work was all about? Asking questions, probing? She remembered one of her tutors, at the academy, telling her the truth couldn't be unearthed until you picked up a shovel and started digging. That little gem of encouraging advice had stuck with her since, and she'd be damned if she was going to be told otherwise.

She pushed her frustrations to the back of her mind and returned her attention to the broken window. A faint breeze blew into the room giving it a chill. The cordon tapes fluttered back and forth; rippling between the frame. The window itself had seen better days. There was ten, or twelve jagged pieces – ranging from a few inches to a few dozen in length – jutting out from the groove cut into its centre. She narrowed her eyes, inspecting them closely. The woman had to have suffered wounds as she'd thrown her body through the pane – the fact she'd done it at all astounded her. More worrying was the tinge of awe and respect she felt.

She glanced down at the carpet. There was no way they'd find an uncontaminated trace of her blood there. They would have just as much luck searching the lower floors; there was just too many bodies, too much blood from multiple sources.

But the window…

As far as she was led to believe, only Trammel and the woman had been present in this room at the time of his murder, and her subsequent escape. There was the possibility one of Trammel's security guards had also been present, but three sources were better than a dozen. Her being was that nobody jumped through a window without leaving blood behind – it was nigh on impossible. She scrutinised each shard until she found a piece with a dark red tip. She smiled, opening an evidence bag.

Gotcha.

As she zipped up the bag, she had the odd sensation she was being watched. A shiver ran down her spine. She turned to find one of the white overall-clad scientists staring at her, face covered by the paper mask.

Then she noticed the scientist wasn't staring at her, but at the evidence bag, she held in her hand.

"Can I help you?" she asked. Something felt off about this figure. For some reason, her instincts told her to edge her fingers close to her firearm. She was also aware they were the only two in the room. She hadn't even noticed the rest of them leaving, as she'd been so embroiled in her analysis of the scene.

"I can take that downstairs for you, mam," the scientist said, taking a step forward. It was a simple enough request, Hall thought, but for the smallest hint of panic wavering the scientist's voice.

Hall slowly began to reach for her holster. "I'm more than capable of bagging and tagging one piece of evidence."

"I wouldn't do that if I were you," the scientist warned, though Hall was beginning to get the distinct suspicion this wasn't a forensic scientist. This was someone else. But who could it be? Was it possible?

The woman?

A sick feeling began to knot in her stomach. Images of a violent blur, dispatching trained mercenaries as though they were mere children, flooded her mind causing her limbs to freeze up. If it was who she suspected – if it was the woman – she couldn't believe her audacity. The place was crawling with police.

Despite her growing terror, accentuated from her lack of experience, she continued to edge her fingers closer to the butt of her handgun.

In one quick flick of her wrist, a handgun slipped down from beneath the bogus scientist's sleeve. She pointed it at Hall's head. "You're going to give me that bag and walk out of here, or if you want, I can blow your head off, take the bag anyway, and then your comrades can carry you out of here in a body-bag."

"You won't get out of here alive," Hall said, trying and failing to sound braver than she felt.

"It didn't stop me last night," the woman said, coldly.

Thankfully, for Hall's sake, they were interrupted by a forensic operative who walked in, his head down, carrying a few bags of evidence. "Excuse me, mam..." He raised his head and froze at the scene before him.

Unlike Hall, the scientist never became apoplectic with fear. Instead, he made an attempt to call for help, but his cries were cut short as the woman spun round at an alarmingly quick pace, driving the handle of her gun down onto the operative's nose, breaking it. He crashed back into the hallway, clutching his ruined face, blood escaping through his fingers.

Hall's training finally kicked in. Using the distraction to her advantage, she unholstered her firearm and fired at the woman. The woman rolled out of the way as the bullet whipped past her head, punching a hole into the plaster wall.

The woman then disappeared down the hallway as Hall fired a few more rounds. She ran after her, raising her comms to her lips. "Officer in need of assistance. The woman is in the building, I repeat, the woman is in the building."

~

This is a fucking nightmare.

Not only was Trammel, his pin, and any sign of new information missing from the scene, her impatience to find her son's killers had made her complacent – reckless – and had inadvertently exposed her.

Now half the SPD were trailing her ass.

Lex sprinted down the hallway as the cacophony of gunshots boomed all around. She skirted around two forensic officers too bemused to know what was going on. She deliberately drove her body into them, creating cover from the intrepid little bitch in pursuit. She almost reached the emergency exit, when a police investigator suddenly blocked her path.

She increased her speed, reaching him before he had time to raise his pistol. Realising this himself, he attempted to strike her with the weapon, using it as a makeshift baton instead. She slapped the clumsy blow aside and whipped her hand across his temple. The chop sent him reeling to the side as he grunted in pain. In no capacity to reply with a strike of his own, she easily slipped around his body to apply a chokehold, as the thumps of the investigator's boots drew closer.

"Stop," the investigator shouted, as she caught up to them. She had her gun aimed towards Lex.

She won't shoot with her colleague between us.

"Hand over the bag, or I'll shoot your comrade," she said.

The investigator shook her head. "Can't do that, I'm afraid. Release him now and give yourself up."

She could hear hurried footsteps growing closer, as police backup made their way up to their position. The young investigator visibly relaxed at the sound of much-needed back-up. Lex let go of the officer and pressed the barrel of her gun to the base of his skull. "As tempting as that sounds, I think I'll pass." She reached inside her overalls and pulled out a flashbang.

"I won't ask you again," the investigator shouted. Lex noted the fear in her voice, coming off her like heat.

Lex was tempted to put a bullet through both their skulls, but they weren't the problem she was fighting. She had enough weight resting on her conscience without adding two dead cops to the load. Contrary to her reputation as a psychotic killer, she was happy killing corrupt officials, mercenaries, and members of the Inner-Sanctum, but she drew the line with cops and civilians – if it was in her power to do so. Her hostage and the investigator were just sheep. She needed to strike the shepherd.

She pulled out the flashbang, flipped the pin, and rolled it towards the investigator.

"Grenade, get down," the investigator screamed, diving into the nearest room.

Lex quickly struck her hostage to the back of the head and ran for the fire escape. She heard the flashbang explode behind her, not looking back, she slipped through the fire escape and descended to the street below.

XV

Reid took the stairs two at a time, pushing past anyone in his path. One officer tried to voice his disapproval as Reid sent him crashing roughly into the stairwell railings. He aimed a multitude of profanities at Reid's back, but the officer's indignation evaporated as he was given a look of barely contained rage. Realising it was a superior investigator, all aggression left his face as he held up his hands and began a torrent of stuttering apologies. Reid ignored him and continued his ascent towards the carnage being wreaked above.

The woman had the fucking cheek to come back barely twelve hours after she'd ripped the place to shreds. She must have been in the same room as him, or at least been in close proximity, for god's sake. He was never going to live this down – himself or his department. How had he allowed the woman to waltz through his crime-scene with impunity? Right under his fucking nose.

The Proxy was going to blow a gasket when he heard. Any career prospects he'd hoped to achieve in the future were now undoubtedly reduced to piss from this calamitous clusterfuck.

On the top floor, he was met by police personnel still in a state of shock and disorientation; a few officers ambled aimlessly, holding their ears to rid themselves of the tinnitus, caused by the flash-bang. Hall was kneeling over another officer, tending to a nasty looking graze to his scalp. She looked up as he approached, an expression of frustration and shame etched upon her features.

"He'll be alright, sir. I've summoned a doctor to examine his head."

"Where the fuck did she go?" Reid snapped. He couldn't care less if the officer's head was hanging off. They needed that audacious bitch – who was running rings around him – in cuffs or a body bag.

Hall narrowed her eyes at him. He wasn't sure whether it was from the flashbang, his sour tone, or the fact the woman had got the better of her. She arched her head towards the fire escape.

Reid stepped over Hall and the stricken officer and peered down the fire escape.

This was going to take some explaining.

~

Officer Grant sat within the confines of his police cruiser, his seat back a few notches, sipping a lukewarm latte laced with sugar. He wiped the foam from his upper lip, quite content to listen to the chatter on his radio as his colleagues pursued the woman. He managed to summon enough energy to crane his neck out the window to look up to the floor where she'd been sighted. He pulled his head back in and sighed.

He knew he should clamber out of his cruiser and make at least some sort of effort to assist his colleagues, but the fact he'd just started his break killed any enthusiasm he might've had in doing so; he'd be damned if he was getting out until his thirty minutes of allocated break time was up. He chuckled to himself – you had to draw the line somewhere.

Unfortunately for Grant, the decision was taken out of his hands. Lex pulled the door open and hauled him out. The cap from his coffee cup popped off as he landed face-first onto the sidewalk; its contents spilling out from its receptacle.

He watched, in stunned silence, as his cruiser sped away from him.

~

Lex kicked the cruiser up through the gears as she careened it around a bend in the road. The corner was sharper than she'd anticipated as she struggled to keep in under control. The tyres screeched as they slid across the tarmac in a blaze of smoke. A truck veered out of her way, horn blaring, as it swerved out of her path, colliding with a taxi cab. The five-foot grille on the truck's front bulldozed into the side of the smaller vehicle, hurtling it into a row of refuse bins, its windows exploding outward from the terrible impact.

She kept the radio on, listening in to any updates from the authorities in pursuit. She had a small head start as police cruisers were fitted with tracking devices; all units in the vicinity would be ordered to descend on her position like locust. She needed to find a suitable spot to dump the police unit before she stood any chance of evading capture – she wouldn't last the night in one of their cells.

The Inner-Sanctum would see to that.

She quickly manoeuvred her ride in and out of lanes, glancing at the rear-view monitor on the dash to see if she had company.

She had.

Fuck.

Two cruisers followed closely behind finding no trouble keeping up with her speed or her erratic attempts to shake them off or force them to stop – they had an obligation to prevent accidents and/or injury, she didn't.

Their lights flashed, painting the street in blue and red as they swerved and weaved with frustrating expertise. She wasn't losing them anytime soon. She needed to think of something, and fast.

She jabbed at the navigation system to load up the route map. It bleeped a few times then informed her she had been locked out. No help there then.

Fuck!

"This is the SPD, stop the vehicle at once," an electronic voice demanded from one of the cruisers hot on her heels.

No shit!

She drifted across either side of the road, trying anything to shake them off. She smashed the rear bumper of a nearby cruiser sending it into a spin towards her pursuers, but they split up, veering around the presumably confused bystander. One of them had to slow down to avoid a public transport shuttle that suddenly appeared from a cross-section in the road. The other had seen the move and adjusted accordingly. Soon they were side by side once more.

She leaned forward to see if there were any Zeps above. She grimaced at the giant floating monstrosity directly above her position, her chances of escape growing ever bleaker.

Need to find a way out of this mess.

She knew she was driving through the financial district. The problem was she didn't know where exactly, or which direction she was travelling in. She sought out anything that could aid in finding out where she was; a landmark; a sign; anything. But all she saw was lights within shops and the blurred images of citizens and mechanoids – the former gazing in slack-jawed surprise at being witness to a police chase, if only for a few fleeting moments.

It was then, between a gap in one of the buildings on her right-hand side, she caught a glimpse of trees and grass; the Metropark. She was travelling north, heading for the centre of the city, towards the Freedom Bridge which sat twenty feet above the river that ran through the Metropark. A plan began to form in her mind. It was risky, but it was all she had – in the end, anything was better than capture.

The road opened up; going from two lanes to four as she entered the bridge. She looked to the monitor. Her pursuers hadn't lost ground on her – if anything they'd closed the gap and tripled in number.

A flashing convoy just for me.

About half a mile ahead, she noticed the traffic was considerably thicker. She pressed the foot down hard on the pedal, the cruiser immediately picking up speed. She flicked the cruiser onto auto-drive and unbuckled her seatbelt.

The auto-drive began to blare a warning telling her there were stationary objects at close proximity. It informed her it was going to reduce the speed of the cruiser. She tapped the override button, then closed its advisory assistance system. It continued its incessant whining, but she ignored it.

She drew her handgun and shot the windscreen several times. The bullets punched through the glass, but the windscreen didn't break. She held onto the handle above her door and began to kick at the windscreen. After a few well-aimed strikes with her foot, it creaked inward, before finally giving up its structural integrity. The cab was showered with glass as she clambered through the empty frame and onto the bonnet.

The air whipped at her face. She squinted, struggling to keep her eyes open. She was growing steadily closer to the queue of traffic, she hoped she'd timed this right. As much as she didn't care for bystanders in her escape, she drew the line at actively using their sacrifice for her own ends – or so she told herself.

A lot of people will get hurt if you fuck this up.

She let go of the bonnet and slowly rose to her feet. She found that standing on a speeding cruiser, whilst balanced precariously on its nose, sent an unbelievable jolt of adrenaline through her entire body; the electricity fuelling her intent.

Once she felt as steady as she was ever going to be, she unholstered her gun, took aim and shot at the police cruisers. It had the desired effect. Sparks flew from the police units as her bullets ricocheted off their bodies. Their tyres screamed; the aggression of brakes being hammered on sent their rear-ends spinning from side to side; their drivers struggling for control.

It was the distraction she wanted.

Without giving it a second thought, she reached inside the cab and tugged at the steering wheel sending the cruiser sharply to the right, towards the railing. The cruiser easily burst through metal sending her over the edge. She jumped off the cruiser and braced herself for landing.

She felt as though she hung in mid-air for an extraordinarily long time before she plunged beneath the ice-cold sanctuary of the river.

And hopefully, escape.

XVI

"Good evening, Sanctum-One. Further chaos has engulfed the city, today, as police made attempts to apprehend a suspect in the Trammel terror attack. However, before an arrest could be made, the assailant managed to hijack a police cruiser and was subsequently chased through the streets of the financial district, by the SPD, causing thousands of credits worth of damage.

The pursuit was soon cut short when the suspect lost control of the vehicle and drove it off the Freedom Bridge into the river. Forensic crews are currently dredging the river as we speak in order to find the police unit and its erstwhile occupant.

At the scene is Hanna Ves. Hanna, do we have any updates on proceedings?"

"Good evening, Hanna Ves reporting live from the Freedom Bridge. As of yet, there has been no sign of the cruiser, or the suspect. The authorities are working tirelessly to recover the wreckage, and hopefully, the suspect."

"Has there been official word on the identity of the suspect? Were there any casualties?"

"Luckily, no one was seriously injured; a few police investigators and two officers suffered minor contusions. As to the identity of the suspect, we still don't know whether it was a man or a woman, as the suspect had been wearing a full-body suit, presumably to conceal their identity."

"Has there been an official statement from the Proxy or lead investigators in charge of the operation?"

"Not at the moment. The authorities are using all their manpower on the task behind me... As you can hear, the curfew klaxon has sounded. This is Hanna Ves, signing off."

"Yes, thank you, Hanna. And with that, we shall also sign off. We advise citizens to return to their homes immediately. Any developments on proceedings will be announced over the NewHaven broadcasts. Goodnight. Sanctum stands as one."

XVII

Below the metres of cordon tape, the blare of the blue and red lights, and the cacophony resounding from the mass of SPD investigation crews – scurrying from one end of the Freedom Bridge to the other, like a swarm of flies around a corpse – the river snaked through the park; flanked on either side by trees and walking trails. Nocturnal animals gave out sporadic cries and calls, which gave Sanctum-One's only slice of nature an almost tranquil setting.

A mile, or so, downriver, Lex dragged herself up onto the bank, heaving her tired body up the steep incline. She could hear the muted screams of the sirens in the distance, as she clawed her way through the wet mud, grunting from the exertion, her muscles throbbing from the struggle. Her limbs felt like they were lined with lead, reluctantly obeying her commands.

After the initial shock of the cold that had enveloped her body, and the terrifying disorientation of being temporarily unable to tell up from down, she'd let the current take her into the Metropark. She then fought her way to the edge of the river when she was sure she was far enough away from the bridge to stop and rest.

She was glad she had chosen to wear her combat suit underneath the overalls. It had kept most of the cold out. Though it could have been worse, she was still freezing; her teeth chattered

101
101

uncontrollably and she could see her breath in the night air. She tugged at the remnants of the forensic overalls that still clung to her body. It tore easily; the material not suitable for combat, flights off bridges, and midnight dips in a fast-flowing river.

Midnight dip was putting it lightly, Lex.

She rolled onto her back and stared up at the stars. The view was somewhat spoiled by a couple of Zeps. She had no doubt the powers-that-be would be using their onboard cameras – usually used for collating screen-views from citizens on the ground – to search for her whereabouts. She wasn't overly concerned; the park was massive, and the section in which she lay was devoid of any lighting or paths.

She lay on the wet grass, simmering with rage. She was furious her plans had gone awry – ruined by Reid's overcurious partner, as well as her own recklessness. What made matters worse was the shard of glass with her blood on it, which was now in the hands of the SPD – or more accurately, the Inner-Sanctum. Lex had gone to great lengths to change her identity, but that would mean nothing if the evidence was tested; inevitably leading to her past-self rearing its head for all to see.

The sanctuary of her apartment was now a definite no-go. The moment her face was plastered across every view-screen in the city, it wouldn't be long before someone came forward.

I need to find Reid's partner.

She didn't know whether this inquisitive cop was part of the Inner-Sanctum or not. If she was, the evidence would be made to disappear. If she wasn't and refused to give the evidence up, or saw too much before one of the Proxy's creatures confiscated it, she could be in danger.

From their brief encounter, Lex had the feeling she was the latter. From the way she'd handled their standoff, she looked fresh out of the academy; her hands shaking; voice trembling with fear.

Probably the first time the kid had pointed a gun at a person… But if she is part of it, she'll be dealt with…

The sudden noise of twigs and bracken, breaking under heavy footfalls, above her head, snapped her out of her reverie. She tensed, slowly reaching down for her sidearm. It wasn't there; her belt was missing.

Fuck! I must have lost it in the river!

She reached over to her thigh and slowly slid her knife from its sheath, thankful it hadn't joined her belt at the bottom of the river.

"I know you're quick, 'Woman', but I don't think you could take all three of us. Maybe one or two, but not three," a gruff voice chuckled. "Throw the blade, we only came to talk."

Lex closed her eyes, shutting out the sound of the river and the distant hubbub of carnage she'd left on the bridge. There was three of them, alright; two on either side of where she lay; the one who had spoken, directly above her – maybe ten feet away.

I'm not being taken. I know where that leads – I've got the scars to prove it. If it has to end here, so be it. But it'll be on my terms.

103

She sprang to her feet using her legs and arching her back. She threw the knife at the one who had spoken; her reflexes unencumbered in spite of her current fatigue. She expected her throw to be reciprocated by gunshots, or at least the muted zip of a bullet passing through a suppressor. Instead, she heard two light cracks, followed by a sharp nick to her arm and neck.

Tranquilliser darts.

Sneaky bastards.

Whatever serum had been injected into her bloodstream, began to take effect immediately. Her body suddenly felt heavy; her limbs slow and unresponsive. She watched helplessly as three figures approached her, slowly turning to blurs, growing larger as they drew closer. She felt as though her consciousness was being lifted away from her body, like a balloon slipping from someone's grasp. She fell to her knees, sending her failing vision into somersaults.

A hand emerged from one of the blurs before the blackness took her.

XVIII

Hall stared at the bag containing the small shard of glass. She focused on the blood at the end of it thinking what it could mean for the investigation. She grimaced, closing her eyes, trying to rid her mind of the altercation with the woman at the Trammel building. But it was no use. She kept playing it in her mind's eye in an endless loop – tormenting herself.

She could have ended it there and then if she'd had the confidence to shoot. She knew the woman had used one of her colleagues as cover… but still… She was a great shot; excellent, in fact; the best in the academy. Why hadn't she just taken the shot?

Of course, she knew why, she just couldn't help thinking otherwise; like picking a scab best left alone.

The look Reid had given her as she'd tended to the officer, the woman had assaulted, had made her cringe with failure. If a hole had suddenly appeared at that moment, she would have welcomed it with open arms.

After he'd calmed down, he'd tried to reassure her she'd done the best she could; that anyone would have acted the same if they'd been thrown into the same predicament. She'd nodded her agreement, internally telling him to stick his reassurance up his ass.

Reid was disappointed in her; she could see it in his eyes. He was just going easy on her because she was 'new'. If she wanted patronising she'd go home to her parents. She also doubted his reaction to the situation would have been similar if she had a dick and a set of balls.

She blinked, taking her eyes off the evidence bag to see who was still around. The office was mostly empty. She checked the clock on her desk; it was half eleven. She should have finished hours ago, but she was waiting for Reid so they could discuss the shard she'd bagged.

She hadn't mentioned it to him during their pursuit of the woman; there just wasn't time, as everything had descended into chaos. After she'd smashed the cruiser off the bridge, she'd lost track of Reid, amidst the crowded crime-scene. She hadn't seen him since – which was odd, as he was never away from the office for long stretches of time.

She got up from her desk, deciding she'd waited long enough, and pulled on her jacket. She'd go down to the lab to see who 'the woman' actually was then leave a message with Reid later. She navigated her way through the warren of corridors and stairwells, her anticipation building with every step – each one drawing her closer to finding out the identity of the woman.

When she finally reached her destination, she was oddly relieved to find there was no one in the lab. She strode over to the nearest workstation. She shivered as she sat down and turned on the blood analysis unit. She didn't know how the lab guys stood working in the constant chill of this

106

icebox – maybe they wore several more layers of clothing than herself, she thought.

She slipped on a pair of forensic gloves from the receptacle fixed onto the desk, and carefully pulled the shard out of the bag, placing it on the tray. She keyed in her station identification number and waited. It paused for a few seconds, verifying her clearance, then chirped into life, the tray retracting into the unit for analysis.

The screen flickered, as the analysis unit processed the cells within the blood sample for a match within Sanctum-One's citizen identification database – every citizen was added to the population database, via a blood sample, the day they were born.

Hall was barely aware of her own hand covering her mouth as she gazed at the face on the screen. It was the last thing she'd been expecting.

"Holy shit. She's one of us."

The face staring back at her from the screen was both different and the same. The hair was a different colour and length, and there were two eyes, but it was definitely her.

She needed to find Reid. This was a major breakthrough, though not without certain ramifications; a Sanctum P.D. investigator at large killing high ranking, respected members of society. It would be hard to salvage anything positive from that PR nightmare. There would be mass-investigations across the board which would result in more than a few heads rolling. The sheer scope of it was incomprehensible to her. It felt like the water she was currently treading in had got a whole lot deeper.

What Hall was having trouble piecing together was how the woman had managed to live within Sanctum-One without drawing attention or detection. She couldn't possibly dwell outside of the city; there was nowhere habitable. She had learned from a very young age – like all law-abiding citizens – the outside world was either scorched and barren or steeped in so much radiation, you'd be lucky to last six hours, let alone six months. So, where had she been hiding? Had she managed to obtain false documentation? It was the only plausible explanation… unless she was part of Sapien-Republic?

Deciding to discuss these questions with her superior, she inserted her unit key into the port and downloaded the information. She ejected the shard and slipped it back into its evidence pouch.

She tried Reid's cell but it went straight to voicemail. She thought about leaving a message. She cut the call as the automated voice asked her to leave her details. She considered leaving a message, but he hadn't returned the last dozen she'd left. Besides, it would be better to speak to him face to face.

She rushed out of the lab and made her way back to her department. Her mind was a haze of multiple questions for multiple scenarios; questions lacking answers. A few colleagues she passed tried to strike up a conversation, or make attempts to reel her in for some advice on a case. She barely registered them. All she could see, in her mind's eye, was the image of a dead cop merging into a psychopathic killing machine.

When she reached her desk, she found she was the only one left in the room; the last dregs of officers had finally had the good sense to call it a night. It was common, this late, for the office to be a ghost town; late night and early hours were their busiest time, so most would be out on the streets. She sat down and logged onto the system. She inserted her unit key and loaded up the most recent file. The face of the woman stared back at her from the screen; her eyes cold, expression neutral.

"Let's see who you are," she said to herself.

She typed the name into the SPD search engine. She was desperate to find out everything there was to know about her. How had an SPD investigator become the very thing she'd sworn to fight? A warning label suddenly flashed across her screen, it read in bold black lettering: CONFIDENTIAL – CLEARANCE LEVEL ONE. She typed in her I.D. Another message declared itself: ACCESS DENIED – REPORT TO SUPERIOR OFFICER.

She balled her fist in frustration. What was going on? She needed Reid, but even if he were sitting next to her, he wouldn't be able to open the file either, as clearance level one was the very top of the chain; only the police commander or above were privy to files labelled level one.

She leaned back in the chair and exhaled. What was she getting herself into?

XIX

NewHaven was the crowning jewel of Sanctum-One; a beacon of mankind's newfound purpose. Erected at the very centre of the city during the inception of Prime Vonn's vision, it represented the very heart of civilisation. The walls were a brilliant white, almost angelic, signifying its cleanliness and purity. It towered above the surrounding buildings majestically, its peaks ringed with cylindrical towers sitting a few hundred metres below the Zep epicentre. Inside, its halls, rooms, and the great amphitheatre at its core were crafted and designed to display the evolution of man; how far it had come from the dark days when war had reigned supreme.

Marr hated the place. It gave him a deep feeling of unease, as though he were an interloper unworthy to be present within its walls. A man of sin had no place there, and he knew it. His natural habitat was within the murkier echelons of Sanctum-One – wading through the filth and rooting out anything that could damage the status-quo. His job was to make sure the scales were evenly balanced.

It was the very reason he was marching down the white marble floor, towards the Proxy's command room. His heavy footfalls echoed, his overcoat trailing at his heels. His mind was full of concern. Given his duty, he had every right to be; the scales were on the brink of collapse, never mind imbalance. He felt the eyes of the building's staff – dressed all in white – follow him as he passed. Nobody made eye-contact, they knew what he was.

Though he was only halfway along the ridiculously long corridor, he could still make out the Proxy's voice; loud and vengeful. He also detected hints of his foul cologne – he wondered how his staff put up with the offensive smell on a daily basis.

Marr suspected who the recipient of the Proxy's rage was. He opened the door without giving a sideways glance to the security personnel; who had the good sense to keep their eyes fixed firmly upon their workstation.

Investigator Reid looked like he wanted to be anywhere else from where he currently stood, as he weathered the torrent of abuse from Faulks. The investigator turned to Marr, his face as scarlet from shame and embarrassment as Faulks' was from fury.

"Don't fucking look at him, I'll ask you one more fucking time... how on earth did that bitch get past the majority of Sanctum's finest without anyone noticing?"

Marr opened his mouth, but Faulks held up a hand. Marr was tempted to press the matter but decided it was probably more prudent to let nature take its course and allow the Proxy to vent his ire on some other poor fool. Faulks returned his gaze to the sheepish investigator who was currently fascinated by his reflection on the polished floor.

Eventually, Reid sensed the momentary reprieve from abuse was his cue to explain

111

himself. He raised his head, but could barely make eye-contact with Faulks, so he settled for the Proxy's tie instead. "Maybe she hacked into the SPD servers and acquired false documents?" He shrugged his shoulders – a bad idea in Marr's experience. "I have no idea, Proxy. I've interrogated my officers, who were posted on the cordons. They reported seeing nothing out of the ordinary. The silver lining was her presence was discovered before she got a chance to cause any real damage."

Marr had to suppress a snigger at the absurdity of his defence. Faulks caught his amusement but chose to narrow his eyes at the investigator. "Assaulting several officers and causing havoc on the streets in front of countless witnesses, yes, no real damage, Reid. She didn't take anything that you know of, and I would bet that's a great deal. It was one of your direct underlings who spotted her, wasn't it?"

"Yes, Proxy, it was Hall, fresh from the academy. There was a stand-off between her and the woman. I think she handled it rather well considering," Reid said, his expression proud.

"Oh, do you? The investigator, so green she pisses grass, fresh out of the academy and with thirty years less experience than yourself, 'handled it rather well', did she? Did she apprehend the fucking suspect?" Faulks snapped, wiping the look from Reid's face. He took a step closer to Reid, who instinctively flinched. "What I can't seem to add up, Reid is that barely minutes after you left the scene you were assigned to investigate, the woman emerges from the fucking ether and assaults several officers tasked with bringing her down."

Reid blinked failing to grasp the Proxy's meaning. He stuttered, trying to find words that weren't there. The Proxy held up a finger and stepped closer to the investigator, their noses inches apart. Marr was struggling with the cologne from where he stood, he had no idea how Reid's eyes weren't, at the very least, streaming. He must not have a very good sense of smell, Marr thought. Or worse still, he didn't actually mind the acrid aroma.

"The woman couldn't have just waltzed past half of the SPD unnoticed, could she now?" Faulks brought a hand up to his chin and closed his eyes, as though in deep thought. Marr knew where he was going with this. "…Unless she had inside help," he said, opening his eyes, his accusatory glare boring into the investigator.

Reid took a few moments before the Proxy's meaning dawned on him. He stumbled back, the blood draining from his face. "Now hold on a minute. With all due respect, Proxy, I had nothing to do with this. I left Hall to finish the final sweep as I was going to view the CCTV footage."

"Footage that had been checked several times already, by you most of all. I've read the reports from at least a dozen who were at the scene." Faulks turned away from the exasperated investigator and took a seat behind his desk. Marr noticed Faulks press a call button under his desk, before resting his hands on the varnished oak. He leaned forward. "Six months we've been chasing a ghost. That little bitch has slipped through our fingers at every turn. It wouldn't stretch the imagination to suspect one of her 'ex-colleagues' had reached out to help her, especially one as close to our Inner-Sanctum as you. In fact, it would make perfect sense."

Alon Reid glanced to Marr for support, but Marr merely stared back impassively. He was interested in what Reid had to say for himself. The accusation could be believable, if not for the fact it was directed at a man like Reid. He was useful enough as an asset, but Marr didn't think he had the bottle – or the brains – to get involved with the woman.

Reid managed to find enough self-dignity to look outraged at the Proxy's accusation. He pointed a shaking finger at the Proxy. "You're fucking crazy. You're grasping at straws, looking for someone to blame; a fall-guy; a name to give to the press." Reid pulled his badge from inside his jacket and threw it onto the floor. Marr found himself instinctively reaching down for his firearm. "I'll have no more of this shit; I'm done. Find some other fool to blame for your short-comings."

Marr fully expected Faulks to lose it. As long as Marr had known the Proxy, the only people who spoke to him with as much disrespect as Reid had just done, generally weren't long for this earth. He watched with fascination, awaiting the Proxy's internal fuse to disintegrate completely. Surprisingly, the Proxy simply smiled, his gaze slowly resting on Reid's badge. To Marr, the smile seemed worse than a fit of rage.

114

Realising he'd crossed a line, never to return, Reid marched away from them, towards the door. It opened before he reached it. Reid made a choking whimper at the sight of two of the Proxy's 'Bleeders'; chief interrogators of enemies of the state. They were garbed in red, except for the black surgical masks covering their mouths. Reid backed away from them, almost stumbling. He turned back to Faulks; his face contorted in a grimace.

"You don't have to do this. I haven't been aiding that fucking lunatic." He fell on Faulks' desk, his hands clasped as though in prayer. "Please, I beg of you. I'm telling the tr…"

One of the Bleeders shot Reid with a tranquillizer dart. It found its mark on Reid's neck. He spasmed and drooled on Faulks' desk before falling to the ground unconscious. Without a word, the Bleeders took a leg each and dragged the investigator from the room.

"Was that really necessary? He's not the most competent at his job, I'll admit, but do you think he has the guile to carry that off for six months? He'd struggle to keep his shit together for six hours." Marr said, breaking what had become an uncomfortable silence.

Faulks stared at him with what looked like amusement. "It matters not either way. As much as this fuck-up has been a disaster, it's provided me with an opportunity to rid myself of one more annoyance."

Marr nodded. He didn't really know Reid, but he still hoped his interrogation didn't cause too much lasting damage. He made a mental note to oversee the interrogation, Reid could still prove useful. "I'm here about Reid's subordinate, Hall, the one who discovered the presence of the woman. It would appear she's found something of worth at the crime-scene."

"What? How?"

"I was alerted to a DNA search on the SPD database. I always like to keep tabs on our finest..."

"...yes, yes, very good. Has she been sniffing where she shouldn't?" Faulks snapped.

"The woman appeared to have left a piece of herself at the Trammel building during her first visit. A trace of blood on a piece of glass. She obviously took our bait about the pin and the possibility of 'sensitive information'. One of the forensic officers walked in on the two of them, alone. It's possible the woman caught Hall procuring the evidence and made an attempt to relieve her of it. Luckily the forensic officer interrupted the stand-off, forcing the woman to run... though he received a bloody nose for his trouble," Marr said, his expression darkening. "What I find concerning, is that our intrepid young police investigator has negated to report it to Reid. In fact, she's already run it through the system, without pre-approval from Reid."

Faulks slammed his fist on the desk. "That fucking Reid. That was the reason we placed that bastard in charge of this investigation; to oversee all progress and sweep anything under the carpet which may prove toxic to our presence within Sanctum-One." He paused, struggling to keep his temper in check. "How much does she know?"

116

Marr sighed and shook his head. "Not much. I red-taped as much of the file as I could without raising too many eyebrows. But she's no doubt aware the woman used to be an investigator. If I know her type, she'll keep digging until she finds something we don't want her to see."

"We'll need to get rid of her. Send a team to her apartment and dispose of her quickly and discreetly," Faulks said, waving a hand.

Marr pursed his lips and shook his head, his expression dubious. "It's not like before. The press are all over this. Murdering an investigator, especially one involved in this case, would be counter-productive. We'll have to approach this from a different angle," Marr said.

"Then do what is necessary. Go; keep me updated. The sooner we find the woman – or her body at least – and tie up any loose ends the better."

XX

It was pouring down when Hall finally left the station. It ran down the concrete steps, flowing towards the drains that were nestled at the foot of the kerb. Due to the curfew, the street was quiet; the glow of the streetlights gave the road a glistening sheen as the heavy drops bounced up in great sprays, like a firework display made entirely of water. She stood under the canopy – below the SPD station sign – and looked ruefully to what she was wearing; clearly not adequate for the torrential downpour. She would be soaked through to the bone before she got halfway to her cruiser which was quite a bit down the street.

Sighing at the inevitability of looking like a drowned rat, she made a dash down the steps and sprinted towards her cruiser, kicking up great rivulets as she went. She reached her cruiser and spent a few frustrating moments fishing through her pockets in search of her key. Finally finding it, she unlocked the cruiser and climbed inside, wincing as she realised she hadn't put anything down to protect the seat from her wet backside.

She began to laugh in spite of herself as she placed her index finger on the dash, starting the cruiser; its electric engine kicked into life, humming gently.

She pulled out and made for home, via the city centre, leaving her failed attempts to make further ground on the case behind her. She lived in an apartment complex on the south side of the city, at this hour it wouldn't take too long, maybe half an hour.

After she had discovered the identity of the woman, she'd made several attempts to bypass the restriction on the woman's file, using some dubious hacks she'd picked up from colleagues at the academy. It had all been in vain. It wasn't the same as infiltrating a low-life drugs pusher, or an embezzling trader, skimming off the top. This was SPD encrypted firewalls, developed by the best in the game.

She knew she was at a dead-end before she'd tried, but the image of those cold, blue eyes staring at her from over the shoulder of one of her fellow officers spurred her on regardless. The thought of their stand-off made her feel sick. The feeling brought on shame and anger, not at the woman, but at herself. She was trained for this.

As of yet, Reid hadn't returned her calls. She'd lost count of the number of messages she'd left and she was beginning to get a little worried. It wasn't that she'd known him for years, or they were close friends, but this was the first time he hadn't answered a voicemail from her outside of thirty minutes. From what she knew, he didn't have much of a social life; he had no wife or kids; he didn't meet other investigators for drinks. Policework seemed to be his life.

She shook her head. She was being stupid. Tomorrow, she'd walk into the office and find out there had been a breakthrough in the case, or he'd been called to some other problem from another department. These were all plausible explanations, but the pragmatic part of her brain told her he would have called to let her know he'd been temporarily absconded to another unit.

She felt weary; the day's toil finally catching up to her, seeping into her muscles. She longed for sleep, but at the same time felt the temptation to ditch the cruiser at a convenient location, enter a bar and get shit-faced, but with the curfew, she would have to settle for drinking herself to sleep within the comfort of her own home.

She navigated her cruiser through the city in brooding silence, her mind constantly fighting with the anxiety that came with inexperience, a cold knot in her stomach which refused to untangle no matter how many times she reassured herself she was doing fine.

Blue lights flashed ahead pulling her back to reality. She squinted at its harsh glare, slowing her cruiser to stop in front of a police cordon. She'd been so wrapped up with worry and inner-turmoil, she hadn't realised she'd been driving towards the Freedom Bridge. Two uniforms approached; their body language guarded – understandable given it was after curfew. She noticed she'd also forgot to place her SPD cruiser badge on the windscreen.

She slid the window down, cursing as the wind whipped the rain inside the cruiser, though it mattered, she was soaked through already.

She opened her mouth to explain herself, when one of the officers suddenly leaned in close, his face wet and red from the adverse weather. "You're out well past curfew, mam. The bridge is currently out of commission due to an ongoing investigation." His breath reeked of garlic, an

120

unpleasantness that matched his demeanour. He cast an irritated glance at her cruiser. "So, what I suggest you do, is drive this heap of shit back the way you came and I'll forget I saw you." He leaned in closer. "Unless you want me to book you for obstructing Sanctum mandate."

Hall's blood boiled with rage. After the day she'd had, she would be damned if she was going to be spoken to like a piece of shit by some cantankerous flat-foot, clearly displeased with his late-night cordon duty. She pulled out her badge and pressed it roughly against the officer's bulbous nose. "Is that so, officer?" she said, adding extra emphasis on every syllable of his rank. "Well, I suggest you get your facts straight before running your mouth off at a superior officer. Now get your fucking pumpkin-shaped head out of my 'heap' before I book you for insubordination."

The officer, not expecting this response, pulled his head back a fraction and lowered his gaze to her homicide investigator badge. He gulped visibly. Over his shoulder Hall spotted his partner turn with a smirk spread across his face; the sight of his colleague being dressed down in such a manner was obviously too much for him to bear without bursting into hysterics.

"S...s...sorry, mam, we weren't expecting homicide back tonight. If you'll follow me, I'll lead you to the crime scene," he spluttered.

Hall leaned out the window and looked up at the heavens. "Not without a fucking overcoat; it's pissing down," she snapped. "Do you have a spare?"

He began to nod emphatically, suddenly eager to jump at the opportunity to climb out of the hole he'd dug for himself. He ran off to wherever his police vehicle was situated, almost tripping over in his haste.

She caught the beaming expression still plastered across the other officer's features. "Something amusing, officer?" she asked, finally failing to hide the humour from her tone.

The officer coughed in an effort to compose himself. "No, mam. It's just… we don't have a spare overcoat in our cruiser," he said, laughing. "Though, I think the rest of my shift with him will be less tedious. Do you want a loan of mine?"

Hall shook her head. "It's alright, my coat's on the backseat."

The officer chuckled, shaking his head in the direction of his partner. He looked familiar but she couldn't place the face – due to most of it being covered by his waterproof hood.

She narrowed her eyes. "Do I know you?" she asked.

He took a step towards her, his eyebrows rising in recognition. "Veronica?"

She smiled, recognising a fellow academy colleague. It was Charlie Deacon. She'd studied with him at the academy. They were separated when she'd put in for investigator evaluations. The last time she'd spoken to him was the day they had both graduated. Despite having spent a lot of time in his company at the academy, once students were assigned the training for their respective posts, segregation was inevitable; Hall had chosen Investigator; Deacon had been happy with the uniform. It was a shame because she liked him. "Investigator Hall now," she said.

Deacon nodded, eliciting a whistle. "I'd heard you'd passed the homicide module, after graduation. I didn't think they'd send you to the deep end so soon."

You don't know the half of it, she said internally. "It would appear so," she said. She could feel the stress and anxiety, which had been temporarily alleviated from the altercation with Deacon's partner, begin to resurface. She pushed the feelings to the back of her mind – wait until I'm halfway down the bottle of scotch, she thought.

She realised Deacon was staring at her. Had he asked her a question? "Sorry, what?"

"I said what brings you down here? I thought homicide was done with the bridge. I heard you guys were moving down to the river and the park when it gets light." He paused, turning to look out towards the bridge. "Though if you ask me, you won't find the suspect."

Hall raised an eyebrow, finding herself a little irritated with his attitude; accepting defeat, that they wouldn't catch her. "What makes you say that?"

He whistled, shaking his head. "I saw him… earlier, on the bridge. Standing on the bonnet of the stolen cruiser, shooting at our guys, then…" He made a motion with his hand signifying the woman's descent off the bridge and into the river. "…never seen anything like it. I mean how do you catch that?"

Hall furrowed her brows. "How do you know he's not dead?" she asked, negating to correct his assumption it was a man they were hunting. She didn't want to be the one to let slip sensitive information to the lower ranks – she had enough shit on her plate at the moment.

He shrugged. "Could be, I doubt it though. We've dredged the river on either side. We found the cruiser but there was nobody near it. We're gonna work our way down the river tomorrow; follow its flow."

They were interrupted by Deacon's partner bounding over to them without a spare overcoat. He was panting hard, worry etched across his huge head. "I'm really sorry, mam, we don't have a spare. You could borrow mine, I don't mind at all," he said, nervously.

Hall smiled at the bedraggled officer, her mind already on the bottle of scotch at home in need of some company. "It's alright, it can wait until morning. See you around Deacon," she said, leaving the two officers alone in the rain.

~

Marr waited a good ten minutes after Hall's cruiser had left, before driving over to the cordon. The two officers who'd spoken to Veronica Hall ran over to his window. He rolled it down and showed them his identification. "Banks, special investigation department." Banks was one of several pseudonyms he used for fieldwork. He pointed in the direction of the departed

124

investigator. "The officer you were just talking to? What did she want?"

"What do you mean, sir?" the younger of the two asked.

"It's a simple fucking question, son," Marr barked. From the way this one had spoken to Hall, Marr surmised he probably knew her – possibly from the academy.

"Bit fucking testy, that one." The larger of the two said. "Must be on her fucking period or something."

Marr didn't have time for idiocy. He reached out and grabbed the young officer by the collar and pulled him close. "Are you going to answer me or am I going to have to beat it out of you. I don't have time for fucking games from two flat-foots. What did she want?"

The young officer tried to break free from Marr's grip, then gave up. "Nothing, in particular, sir. She pulled up. We spoke for a minute, then she was gone."

"What did she say?"

"Life after the academy. Where she went, where I ended up. A little bit about the terrorist, then she was gone."

That piqued his interest. "What did she say about the terrorist?" he said, pulling the officer a little closer.

The officer shrugged. "That she thought he was probably dead from the fall earlier. Then she was gone. It was a bit weird if you ask me."

Marr let him go. "I'm not," he said, rolling his window back up. He drove away from the two uniforms, their silhouettes growing smaller in his rear-view screen as he sped away. He would find out what she knew.

Hopefully, for her sake, it wasn't too much.

XXI

Lex rolled over, immediately regretting it. She gasped; her battered body, unprepared for the sudden movement. She couldn't pinpoint a particular wound that was causing her the most discomfort – due to there being so many. It felt as though her entire body was one throbbing haematoma, never alleviating; a constant companion.

There's not going to be much of me left by the time I'm done… if I get the chance to finish what I started.

She appeared to be lying on a soft mattress in a dimly-lit room which was not much larger than her bedroom at home. For the first few seconds, she'd thought she was actually there until she'd noticed the bed was the only piece of furniture in the room.

She sat up, wincing from the pain it caused her. She swung her legs over the edge and touched the coarse carpet with her bare feet. She had no memory of how she'd ended up in this strange room. The last she remembered was being overpowered by superior numbers in the park, after her flight off the Freedom Bridge… then nothing.

She became aware of the absence of her combat suit. Instead, she appeared to be garbed in an ill-fitting boiler-suit a few sizes too large; her captors had presumably relieved her of her scribe and combat suit – or what was left of it when they'd brought her to the room/cell she now occupied.

She pulled the zip down and climbed out of the garment. Fresh bandages lined her body. Whoever had taken her had spent a considerable time patching her up which raised some doubts on her suspicions of the group in the park being members of the Inner-Sanctum.

Those bastards had me chained up, naked as the day I was born when they took me the last time.

All was not as it seemed, she thought, pursing her lips and pressing her hands down onto the soft sheet, covering the bed. This was something different, something new and possibly unexpected. She didn't like it; the unusual feeling of not being the one in control.

She was interrupted from her self-inspection and inner-reflection as the door on the other side of the room opened. Lex squinted at the sudden brightness which filled the room. A silhouette of stood in the doorway, holding what looked like a clipboard. She stood up, her instincts taking over.

"Ah, you're awake," the silhouette said, cheerfully. "Please, sit down, I mean you no harm. My name is Doctor Simon Oliver, I've come to change your dressings and inspect your wounds."

Lex remained silent. She glanced over the doctor's shoulder. He wasn't alone, he slowly entered the room, flanked by two armed men. Doctor Oliver looked to be in his mid-fifties. His hair was a mix of grey and white; cut short. He had an unusually long nose, but it seemed to suit his facial features. she noted he had kind, trusting eyes. Lex nodded in the direction of the doctor's chaperones. "And them?"

Oliver turned to his guards as though he'd just noticed them. He chuckled, raising his hands. "I hope you'll forgive the armed escort. They're supposed to be for my protection. After the altercation in the park, my colleagues insisted I was to be accompanied by..." He paused, struggling to find the right words. "...bodyguards."

Lex snorted. "Altercation? You mean abduction."

He smiled at her. "My dear, you must understand it was for your own protection. The police were closer to your position than you know. If we hadn't intercepted you when we did, you'd be God-knows-where by now." He pointed to the bed. "And not in as much comfort as you are now."

Lex narrowed her eyes in suspicion. "I thought the Inner-Sanctum worked hand in hand with the SPD... not that the police know they do."

The doctor chuckled once more. "Is that who you think we are? The Inner-Sanctum? No, my dear. We fight the same fight as you... just not as brazen as your good-self. May I see your injuries?" He took a few steps towards her.

She waved the offer aside. "I'm fine if it's all the same to you. I'd like to leave."

He held his hands up. "Very well, you are free to leave whenever you wish, though if you'll indulge me, I'd like to take you to our commander before you do. I think we have more in common than you think."

Lex glared at the two silent guards that still held their rifles aimed in her direction. "Well, seeing as I don't exactly have a choice on the matter, lead the way."

He ignored her waspish tone. He turned to leave then stopped abruptly. He gestured to her current state of undress, chuckling. "Would you mind putting the boiler-suit back on? We're not used to having naked women walking around our compound."

~

Lex followed the doctor in sullen silence as they made their way along dimly-lit corridors of dull grey concrete. The two guards followed in their wake keeping a safe distance; out of her reach. She wondered where she was, she noted there were no windows, only ventilation pipes fixed to the ceiling on steel brackets.

"Where are we exactly," she asked, breaking the silence.

"All will be explained," Oliver said. "Just through these doors ahead."

The doctor pushed through the double doors to reveal a massive space, which to Lex, resembled an aircraft hangar. She gazed up at the ceiling a hundred feet above them. Lights hung from thick chains bolted to the concrete, bathing the area in a faint yellow hue. Small wooden shacks lined the floor in columns which resembled little streets. She felt the eyes of the shanty town's occupants scrutinise her with a mixture of fear, awe, and hostility.

"It's like a town," she said, catching the eye of a little girl standing in one of the doorways. Lex smiled at her, but the child scurried inside.

Oliver arced his head in her direction maintaining his pace. "Oh, it's much more than that, my dear."

Lex also noted there was a distinct lack of the technology society was used to. In some ways, it felt as though she'd stepped back in time. Oliver smiled and said a few words to those he clearly knew. They replied to the doctor's comments and greetings with good humour, but their expressions immediately darkened when their eyes settled on Lex. It didn't bother her. If anything, she understood.

They traversed through the small community to a larger shack at its centre. It was raised onto a metal frame which was fenced. Sentries were stationed around its perimeter; all armed with automatic rifles, blades, and resting expressions of hostility. They nodded to the doctor as they passed through the main gate and up to a stairwell, which led to the main entrance to the building. He knocked once and pushed the door open without waiting for a response.

Inside, the walls were lined with screens, all showing areas of Sanctum-One. Hunched over a bank of monitors on the opposite side of the room, stood a small group. They all turned to face her. The man standing at the group's centre smiled at the new arrivals. He looked to be the leader, given the way the others seemed to look at him.

131

"She's finally awake," he said, cheerfully. Lex recognised his voice. It was the one who had spoken to her in the park. "Welcome to our quaint little community. I hope you're not feeling too beaten up from our last meeting. I'm sure the good doctor explained why we had to take you."

One of his entourage smirked at the light jibe. Lex balled her fists. The leader caught her sudden tension and gave a warning look to the perpetrator. He held up his hands in mock surrender. "I meant no offence. If I'm being honest, I was surprised we were able to subdue so easily; you're well known in our little community."

"I'm not surprised," a woman said, behind him.

The leader rounded on the woman who had spoken. "That's enough, Li," he snapped. The woman, named Li, rolled her eyes but remained silent. Lex glared at her, wanting her to say something, to give her an excuse to smash her face through one of the monitors.

Lex managed to take her eyes off Li to address the leader. "And where is this 'little community' exactly? Beyond the city walls..." She paused and turned, ignoring the two guards flinching from her sudden movement, and looked out to the compound, with its lack of natural light, its coldness. "...no, underground?"

The leader nodded, impressed. "Well deduced. We found this bunker amidst the ruins of the old city, whatever it was called before. It seemed the perfect place to base our operations without molestation from the powers-that-be," he said, gesturing above.

132

As she'd walked through the shantytown with Oliver and her chaperones, Lex began to believe the doctor's claims they weren't part of the Inner-Sanctum. There was only one other possibility as to their identity, given the size of the compound and their numbers. "Sapien-Republic," she said as much to herself as the group in front of her.

The leader took a few careful steps towards her, extending a hand. "Jonathon Brooks, I lead this ragtag group of... how does Sanctum-One refer to us? 'Treacherous terrorists'," he said, emphasising the last two words with a hint of mocking.

"Why am I here?" she asked, staring at his hand. "I'm in no mood for extending pleasantries with my captors."

Brooks shrugged letting his hand drop down by his side. "I believe we can help each other. You and Sapien-Republic are the only ones who know what Sanctum-One really is. The only ones with their eyes open to the truth. Prime Vonn is a dictator veiled as humanities saviour, a wolf among the sheep."

"We're doing just fine, Jonathon. We don't need interference from some psychotic bitch with a vendetta," Li said.

Lex took a step forward but stopped at the sound of the automatic weapon being cocked, behind her. Brooks seemed not to notice. He faced Li. "Christ, Li, she's done more damage to the Inner-Sanctum in the last six months than we have in the last ten years." He waved his hand, exasperated. "How many agents have we sent to NewHaven, only to find their broken, bloodied bodies dumped on our doorstep after the bleeders were done with them." Li was about to respond, but Brooks held up a hand. "Have you forgotten about Jennings? Cruz? Alberta?"

Li dropped her head, the fight for an argument draining from her. "Of course I haven't." She raised her head, looking him in the eye. "I'm sorry."

"And where do I come into this?" she asked, breaking the horrible atmosphere that was beginning to settle in the room.

"I want you to join us. To help us free our society from the unbeknown bondage it's in."

It was tempting, there was no denying that. Brooks had a way of inspiring confidence and solidarity. She could see it by the way the others looked at him. Even Li. But she was no freedom fighter. She'd promised herself she would destroy those who had reduced her to what she was. She'd almost made peace with the fact she would follow whoever was responsible for her son's murder to the grave.

"I'll pass if it's all the same to you," she said, coldly. All she wanted was revenge. The image of her son's beautiful blue eyes surfaced to the forefront of her mind, stoking the fire of resolve as to her mission, filling her with a cold rage which could frighten herself at times.

Brooks gave her a hurt, almost disappointed expression. He narrowed his eyes. "I thought you would treat us with a little more gratitude. After all, we've done for you, given you the chance to exact your revenge."

His comment threw her off. She raised a quizzical eyebrow. "Excuse me? I've never met any of you in my life."

Brooks raised his eyebrows, surprised. "You really don't remember?"

"Remember what?"

"We were the ones who dragged your lifeless body from the harbour after they'd killed your boy, and supposedly drowned you."

~

The roar of the gunshot reverberated across the harbour and out to sea like thunder, quickly fading to nothing but an eerie silence. It hung in the air, for just a few seconds, before it was shattered by a primal scream of unimaginable pain and suffering. The terrible sound carried out to the small group, huddled together on a small boat, gently bobbing up and down on the calm swell; their presence hidden by the night.

They watched in grim silence – speechless at what they'd witnessed – as the broken woman who had been made to watch her son's execution was dragged to the water's edge. She kicked and screamed to free herself from their grasp, to get to the boy. The man in the long overcoat pointed to the prone figure, then in a final act of cruelty, she was hovered above the body of the boy.

Brooks and his team were only a quarter-mile out from the harbour. They could hear the woman's sobs as the last vestiges of fight drained out of her. The man in the overcoat pointed to the water. The men dragged her away from her son and submerged her head under the water. The man in the overcoat slowly approached as she struggled and put a boot on her head – not that it was really required, Brooks thought.

"Fucking bastards!" a voice growled, behind him.

"Quiet," Brooks hissed. "She found something, something damaging, and they destroyed her for it. She was our way in. The best chance we've had in years."

The broken woman had stopped struggling. The two men let her go, her body limp and lifeless on the rough concrete. The man in the overcoat spat on her then kicked her in the water. He pointed towards the van they had arrived in and the two men ran over to it. They hurried back with a body-bag and rolled the dead boy into it, all the while the man in the overcoat oversaw, smoking a cigarette.

As the group got into the van, Brooks caught a glimpse of the man in the overcoat's face. There was no mistaking the face of Samuel Faulks. He scrambled in his pack for a camera. He eventually found it, but by that time the Proxy had climbed into the van.

"We've tried taking pictures of these executions before, Jonathon," Li said. "There's no point, NewHaven just turns it around and tells everyone its gang-related."

Brooks wasn't listening to her. He had to get back to base and tell Oliver. For the moment, they'd keep this to themselves until the time was right. Once the van's taillights disappeared from view, Brooks ordered Li to move the boat towards the harbour.

"She's dead, Jonathon."

"Just move the fucking boat, Li."

She grumbled unintelligibly but complied with his order. They cut through the gentle curve of the waves, the engine humming louder than he would have liked, though the quiet of the night may have had something to do with it.

Li slowed the boat down when they were ten feet away from the concrete. Brooks pulled out his torch, clicking it on and scanning the area for the body. He eventually found it, floating face-down twenty feet from the harbour wall. He turned to Adams. "Give me a hand, will you?"

They hauled her onto the boat. They had seen that she had suffered from a terrible amount of torture, but it wasn't until they were this close that they saw the severity of it. Brooks wasn't particularly religious, but he said a prayer for her soul at the image of the injuries she'd sustained – there was no mistake, in his mind, her wounds had been mostly inflicted by the bleeders.

"Throw me a blanket to cover her up," he asked. Li threw him a rough cover, soiled with oil and various other unspecifiable stains. He covered her reverently, feeling like he'd returned a small shred of her dignity. He gazed at her face; pale and gaunt; covered in a myriad of cuts and contusions. Her one remaining eye was still open, the other a pulped, swollen mass. He closed it for her.

Then it shot open and she screamed.

Lex stared at him, suddenly feeling confused and disorientated. Her head began to throb. She couldn't remember the events that transpired that night as a whole, only in fragments.

"We brought you here," Brooks said. "The good doctor treated the worst of your wounds."

"I'm not particularly surprised you can't remember us; you were either in a state of delirium or comatose for the duration of your recovery. Unsurprising... given what you were put through. I had to sedate you when administering medical treatment," Oliver said.

Lex rubbed her temples.

Why can't I remember? I remember being held under the water, then...

"The first thing I remember, after what happened, was waking up in an alley a few blocks from my old apartment..." She touched the patch covering her missing eye.

"As you can no doubt guess, you escaped. We kept you in your room for a few months before the doctor decided your recovery time may be shortened if you were allowed to walk in the park, above ground, in the fresh air."

Oliver gave an embarrassed noise. "A mistake I have apologised for more times than is necessary, Jonathon," Oliver said, failing to hide his annoyance.

Brooks held up his hands. "I didn't ask for one, Simon." He turned back to Lex. "You assaulted the chaperones who'd accompanied you and disappeared. Until your six-month rampage, we'd assumed the Inner-Sanctum had apprehended you… but it seemed we underestimated you."

There was one thing bothering Lex about Brooks' account of the events at the harbour. "Why did you order your colleague to drive the boat to get me? I mean, as far as you were aware, I was dead."

Brooks pursed his lips, considering his words. "I saw evil men kill an innocent child and drown his tortured mother. No one deserves to be dumped into the sea; left for fish bait. I couldn't bring myself to leave you," he said.

He genuinely sounded sad. Lex softened a little, but it didn't change anything. "They deserve it," she said, gritting her teeth. "For what they've done. I'm going to finish this. Do what you want after I'm through with them. Build your new world. Now let me out of this compound, I have work to do."

XXII

Despite the fact the torrential rain had washed through the streets of Sanctum-One, the previous night, lashing the city in a downpour that had caused the water level of the river to rise by a considerable amount – breaking its banks at several of its weaker points – the morning after couldn't have been any more different. The sun shone through sporadic cloud cover; great beams spilling between the gaps with angelic elegance; the day promising to be a lot milder than the citizens were used to of late.

Hall squinted up at the bright sky balefully, the pleasant morning falling short to alleviate her ill mood. What exasperated her cantankerous temperament was the splitting headache she was suffering from, brought on by the copious amount of scotch she'd quaffed to aid in her aims of dreamless sleep; a slumber without images of cold, cruel eyes glaring at her from the other end of a gun.

She'd parked her cruiser a few blocks from the precinct – a deliberate move as she thought the walk may provide her with a chance to, quite literally, shake her shakes. In no rush to get to her stuffy office, she grabbed a coffee from a local café she frequented from time to time. She sipped the bitter brew – she'd liberally doused with sugar in the hope of it boosting her energy levels – and casually strolled past service droids, cleaning the streets, and citizens going about their business in their own little bubbles. She watched them, completely unaware of her presence, as they rushed past her completely oblivious. She envied them, doubting their days would be as unpredictable as her own.

As she was surveying the morning rush going on around her, she spotted a man staring at her from across the street; the fact he was the only in the vicinity not in sort of rush made him stand out from the crowd. She smiled at him, but he didn't reciprocate, instead, he looked away – a little too quickly, she noted. She felt a shiver run down her spine. Had he been watching her? She couldn't be sure – the previous night's alcoholic self-abuse may be causing some increased anxiety, she thought, trying to rationalise her suspicion – of what, she had no idea.

She stopped and scrutinised him a bit more. Everything about him seemed off. He wore an overcoat, a little too heavy for the clement weather. The cruiser he was sitting on looked a lot more expensive than the rest parked on this street. It was also the only vehicle unmarred by bumps or scrapes. She didn't take her eyes off him. He turned his head in her direction once more. She was sure he'd flinched ever so slightly.

Then he did something strange; something that began to confirm her suspicions. He put a finger to his ear and muttered something under his breath. He was apparently kitted out with comm's equipment.

"Hey," she shouted, enraged by this stranger's audacity; his violation. "Can I help you?" She crossed the street, her blood beginning to boil.

He didn't answer. He stood up and hurriedly moved around the cruiser. Hall picked up her pace, her strides quickening to a jog. He opened the door and climbed in, pulling away at speed before she could get a good look at his face. In his haste, he almost collided with a transport shuttle. The cruiser disappeared into the distance, eventually turning a corner and out of view.

But not before she'd got a decent look at the registration plate.

~

She touched her I.D. on the swipe pad and hurried through the door before it had fully opened, clattering her shoulders against the door's edges in the process. Her confrontation with the man, who may or may not have been spying on her, rankled her nerves. He could easily have been freaked out by the deranged woman shouting at him from across the street.

Her logical mind tried to come up with reasonable explanations as to why the stranger had been looking at her. Maybe he was attracted to her; maybe just looking a little too enthusiastically. She caught her reflection on one of the glass panels that walled the corridor, towards the elevator, and immediately discarded that theory – she looked like shit.

She had seen him touch his ear, as though to check-in to a superior... hadn't she?

She called the elevator, waiting impatiently as the lift descended to the ground floor. She tapped her feet on the polished tiles; unable to keep still.

"Hey, Veronica, how are you this morning?" Charlie Deacon said, behind her. She jumped, picturing the face of the man she'd yelled at ten minutes ago. "Jeez, bit jumpy."

She relaxed, a little embarrassed. She forced a smile. "Sorry, Charlie. Yeah, I'm fine."

He appraised her, not convinced she was. "Well, you don't look it. You alright? You look as though you were the one who'd just pulled an all-nighter."

She shook her head, feeling the hangover begin to voice its presence – her brain felt like it was trying to squeeze itself out of her hair follicles. "Just a rough night is all. Couldn't sleep. How was the rest of the shift? Find the woman?" she asked, surprised at her ability at humour given her current state.

The elevator doors opened. She stepped inside, quickly followed by Deacon. "What floor?" she asked.

"Same as you. Need to hand in my report to your boss."

She winced internally at the mention of Reid. "I'm not sure if Reid will be in," she said, hoping she was wrong.

Deacon shook his head. "I'm not handing it into Reid. We got a memo this morning. We've to hand in all shift-reports, related to the woman, to your Captain."

"Why's that? Reid's been assigned with the case," she said, struggling to suppress her mild panic at the news.

Deacon shrugged. "He's on leave, apparently. Not exactly an opportune time to take a break, huh?"

She pursed her lips, nodding. Deacon was still speaking, but she didn't hear him. Her mind was in overdrive. She pulled out her scribe, on the off-chance she'd received a message from Reid, but hadn't heard it. The screen was blank: no messages.

The elevator reached its destination. She muttered something about catching Deacon later, as the doors opened. She stepped out, not waiting for a reply. She slowly ambled over to her desk and sat down.

"Hall," Captain Mercer barked. "In my office, now."

"Be over shortly, Captain."

"I didn't say shortly, Hall. I said now."

All eyes were on her. She ignored them and got up. She was certain today was going to be a shitty one – she made a mental note to get more scotch on the way home, later on.

Mercer's office was dark and stuffy, but at least he had privacy from the rest of the floor – boxed in by four huge sheets of glass. If he wanted some peace, all he had to do was close the door and close the blinds. Maybe one day, she thought. He loomed over his impeccably neat desk; where every pen, pad, and folder had a designated place. She wondered if he used a set-square to align everything symmetrically.

"You look like shit, Hall," he said, failing to hide the pity from his annoyance. He was a stout man, with a neatly cropped beard. His thick, black hair was trimmed short on top of his large head. His dark eyes scrutinised her for a moment before he continued. "Have a drink last night?"

Hall looked down, knowing the question was rhetorical. "Just peachy, Captain," she said, deciding she didn't really give a fuck whether it was rhetorical or not. She didn't feel there was any point in trying to cover up the fact she'd had a few drinks last night; she could still taste the faint tang of the scotch, in spite of the strong coffee.

Mercer tensed, leaning down on the desk with large, hairy knuckles. He looked as though he was about to admonish her for her insubordinate tone, but he didn't. He closed his eyes and sighed.

"Have you spoken to psych? After what happened at the Trammel building?" he asked, almost sounding fatherly. Her expression told him as much. "You know it's the procedure, especially for one as green as you."

Now, he sounded patronising. Though Mercer's mention of the standoff brought those cold eyes to the forefront of her mind. "Where's Alon, Captain? Charlie told me he was on leave," she asked, trying to veer the conversation away from psych.

"Charlie?" he asked. "…Ah, Deacon; the uniform." His expression darkened. "That was the reason I called you in here. I read his report. What were you doing at the Freedom Bridge last night? Without orders to do so from a superior, especially after curfew."

145

"Thought I'd make some headway with the case, sir."

"That's not your call." He picked up his scribe and began to scroll through it. "I've also received a complaint from Deacon's partner. He states you were rude and aggressive."

"He came over to my cruiser and started swinging his considerable weight around. Idiot shit his pants when he realised he was speaking to a superior officer."

"I want a written apology from you by the end of the day."

This was a step too far for Hall. She slapped her thigh in disbelief. "Are you fucking kidding me, Captain? If we're going to start splitting hairs, I could put in a complaint stating that moron was impeding an enquiry into a case linked to that psycho-bitch currently still on the loose."

Mercer, it would seem, had lost his patience with her. He slammed his hand down onto the desk causing her to jump. "Don't you take that fucking tone with me, Hall. I know you went through shit the other day, but don't think that gives you an excuse to start running this case all by yourself. You're new to this department. You of all people should know the chain of command. You were top of your year at the academy. It's the reason I requested you, personally, don't make me regret the decision. At the end of the day, you shouldn't have been on the fucking bridge in the first place."

A voice inside her head told her to shut her mouth, but it was overruled by the stubborn part. She stood up, staring her Captain dead in the eye.

146

"Well if I'd known where my fucking partner was, I would've been able to discuss it with him." She leaned forward. "So, I'll ask you again, Captain, where the fuck is Reid?"

Before Captain Mercer could reply, his door opened and in stepped a tall man, wearing a long overcoat. His sandy-blonde hair was slicked back. He held a folder in his hand. He waved it at the two of them, his blue eyes peering, amusingly from behind a pair of fashionable glasses. "I can answer that before this turns ugly."

"And who the fuck are you?" Mercer snapped, diverting his anger around Hall towards the newcomer.

The man rolled his eyes and brought out his I.D. card. "Banks. Special investigator from NewHaven. Mr Reid is currently in our custody on orders from the Proxy."

Hall felt as though she'd seen Banks' face before, she just couldn't remember where or when. This was the first time she'd met a special investigator.

"Fucking spook," Mercer muttered. "Well tell me, 'Banks', if that's your real name, are you at liberty to divulge the nature as to why one of my officers is currently languishing at the Proxy's pleasure?"

Banks smiled at the Captain. Hall had apparently been relegated to spectator, as the two men were about to engage in some dick-measuring. To be honest, she welcomed it. She knew there would be repercussions for her argument with the captain, and was happy if it could be prolonged for a time.

"Not at this moment in time," Banks said. "This is a sensitive case, and after the shitstorm you guys caused on the bridge, we'll be dipping our toes in the water a lot more frequently from here on in."

"I didn't know you guys had up until now," Mercer said sarcastically. If Banks was aware of the jibe, he didn't show it. He merely smiled at the captain waving a finger at him.

"We wouldn't be doing our job right if you knew we were there." Hall didn't like the man's smugness. He had a self-satisfied expression she wanted to slap from his features.

"When will he be back?" Hall asked, growing tired of the testosterone flying around the room.

Banks looked at Hall as though he'd just noticed she was there. "At this moment in time, he's helping us with our enquiries." He cast an eye to Mercer. "If there's an issue with that decision, I suggest you take it up with the Proxy."

Mercer shook his head, suddenly looking tired. "I won't waste my time. What brings you here?"

Banks looked at Hall. "I've received some intel on the forensic investigation at the Trammel building with regard to bloodwork which may be linked to the woman."

Hall could feel the blood drain from her face. She hadn't mentioned the shard of glass with the woman's blood on it. She hadn't even told Reid. NewHaven must have been running tabs on any system enquiries linked with the case. She had to think fast. She didn't trust this creep, even if he did work for the Proxy. The way he looked at her didn't feel right. It was though he already knew and was testing her.

She cursed herself for using her I.D. to access the system and start the analysis. It was stupid, but how else could she have done it? She now was being presented with an opportunity to offload her burden; to inform the spook of her extra-curricular activities and the new evidence; to pass the evidence to the higher authorities, who might be able to make more ground on the case. But she held back. She thought of Reid, languishing in NewHaven, and the infuriating air of superiority wafting off the spook as he gazed confidently from behind his trendy glasses.

Well, fuck you, she thought.

"There wasn't any bloodwork taken from the scene, at least not to my knowledge," she answered, trying to keep her face as neutral as possible.

His mouth twitched and for a moment, she thought she caught a glimpse of irritation. He smiled and nodded. "Shame. It could've been the breakthrough we so desperately needed. Good day to the both of you." He turned and left them without waiting for a reply.

"Fucking spooks," Mercer said once more. "Hall, just go to your desk. I haven't the energy to fight your insubordination. Make an appointment with psych, that's an order."

Hall closed the door the spook had left open and turned to face Mercer. He raised his eyebrows.

"Didn't you hear me? We're done."

"Captain... what Banks said... about the bloodwork," she said, trying to find the courage to come out with it.

"Yes, what bloodwork? You said there wasn't any."

"There was. I just didn't want to say in front of him," she said, pointing a thumb behind her. "I know he said he works from NewHaven, but I just didn't like the feel of him." She paused, taking a deep breath. "I found a shard of glass containing traces of the woman's blood. I ran it through the system, last night."

Hall had his full attention. He raised his eyebrows and twirled his hand for her to get on with it. "Have we got an I.D. on the woman?"

Hall nodded. "You're not going to believe this, Captain. She was a cop. Supposedly killed in action a few years ago, her body was never recovered."

Mercer's mouth opened in shock. "Alexandra Moretti."

~

Marr watched Hall and Mercer on the screen on the dash-screen within the confines of his cruiser, parked outside the precinct. He was surprised by the young investigator. Her face had paled, and her eyes had betrayed her fear when he'd mentioned the bloodwork. It was subtle, but his vast experience had caught it nonetheless; it was why he was the best at what he did.

Unfortunately, she'd recovered enough composure to maintain her silence, which he found both intriguing and irritating. He could have pressed the matter, but with the captain in the room, he didn't want to reveal the extent of the Inner-Sanctum's surveillance of the case. For the moment, he would keep tabs on their activities.

Mercer wasn't part of the Inner-Sanctum, but he was unknowingly pliable whenever the need arose – usually with the aid of Reid. There was probably a time when it may have been prudent to recruit the captain, but he was about five years from retirement and they'd had Reid installed within the department when the woman had surfaced. If Reid had been more competent, they could have closed the case, dealt with the woman, and waited out the five years, before assigning the job to the hapless investigator, currently residing in one of the Proxy's cells at NewHaven.

"You know her?" Hall asked, incredulous.

Mercer got up and walked to the window. He peered through blinds and gazed at his department, clearly in shock by this revelation. He closed the blinds and turned to face his subordinate, satisfied their conversation would be private. Marr smiled. The idiot had no idea he was being watched.

"Not intimately," he said. "She worked in another department – missing persons. She ignored protocol and followed a lead without backup. It was the last anyone heard of her."

"Where did her lead take her?"

"A disused warehouse. A team were sent down when she hadn't clocked out. Her cruiser's in-built tracking chip situated the vehicle not far from the warehouse's security gate. When the team arrived, there was no cruiser."

"Had the signal moved to another location?" Hall asked.

Mercer shook his head. "The signal mysteriously disappeared. It was like she'd stepped off the face of the earth."

Hall drummed her fingernails on Mercer's desk, thinking. "Was there a follow-up investigation? What about her family?"

Mercer returned to his desk. "She had a son." Mercer paused, his lips twisting as though he'd just tasted something unpleasant. "His body turned up in an alley about a week after Moretti disappeared along with the remains of her burnt-out cruiser. The boy had been shot at point-blank range. We found the murder weapon down a nearby drain with Moretti's fingerprints all over it. He was eight years old," Mercer said, through gritted teeth.

Hall grimaced. "She killed her son? Why?"

"We'll never know. I'd heard she'd had her problems. She had a tough childhood. Her mother died when she was really young, dad left not long after. Then it was years of various foster homes. Given the poor start in life, she buckled down. Got into the academy. As far as I know, she was a decent investigator."

Hall leaned forward. "And that was it? No follow-up enquiry?"

Mercer shrugged. "It was an open and shut case as far as I'm aware," he said. "I didn't work it, but a buddy of mine did. Said it was horrific." He rubbed his temples, then looked at Hall, a pained frown creasing his forehead. "How could a mother do that to her son? Once forensics had proved she'd killed the boy, nobody really cared where she was, so long as she stayed missing."

"So, it was covered up?"

Mercer rolled his eyes. "I wouldn't go that far, Hall." He pointed a finger at her. "Don't go looking for conspiracies where there are none."

Hall held up her hands as though to assure her captain she wasn't – Marr could see through the lie. "What do we do now?" she asked her captain.

"We need to report it to command, they'll know how to proceed. I just can't believe Alexandra Moretti is 'the woman'."

"And that creep… Banks?" Hall asked. This little bitch was going to be a pain in the ass, Marr thought.

"Mercer smiled. "I'm glad you didn't mention it while that fucker was in the room. Banks and his cronies have got Reid locked up in their little hole at NewHaven. I didn't like his derogatory comments aimed at the force. We'll do this in-house."

"And command? Are you going to call them now?" Hall asked.

Mercer shook his head. "No, I'll schedule a meet. This needs to be done face to face. I'll not have that fucking spook intercept any of our mail."

Smart, Marr thought… almost.

"They can do that?" Hall asked, her naivety coming off her like Faulks' cologne.

"I'm not entirely sure they can, but I'm not chancing it."

"What do you want me to do in the meantime, sir?" she asked.

"Go home. You've done enough... more than enough, good work, Hall. I'll call you after I've spoken to command. No doubt they'll want a word with you..."

Marr switched the monitor off. He'd seen enough. He thought about calling Faulks, but after the way he'd handled Reid, he was better off dealing with this himself.

XXIII

Her eyelids fluttered. It was dark and her blurred vision came in hazy strips of grey. The only noise present in the gloom was a rasping sigh; she soon realised the sound resided from within her lungs, as her breath came in and out in strained wheezes.

She was standing on her tiptoes. She tried to return her feet to a standing position, but she found couldn't. Her body felt restricted; fixed in place. The realisation brought on a momentary bout of panic; her instincts forcing her to fight against the restraint, as she couldn't rest her feet flat on the ground. It soon dawned on her where she was. She must have slipped into unconsciousness again – she'd lost count how many times that had happened over the course of... was it days... weeks? She couldn't be sure.

The roughcast metal, which bound her wrists together, rubbed her skin raw. The shackles – attached to the high ceiling by a thick length of chain – clinked from her movements from time to time. Blood had run down her arms, eventually drying so that it became uncomfortably tacky, pulling at the hairs whenever she made any sudden movements. Her eye throbbed, but it was an improvement to the intolerable agony she'd felt when the bleeders had removed it. The thought made her want to vomit; she could taste bitterness at the back of her throat and it took all of her will to suppress the gorge, threatening to rise.

When they had dragged her into the room of misery, kicking and screaming, the two bleeders – there were always two, she noticed – had been waiting for her; their sinister instruments laid out neatly on a linen cloth. They'd watched silently as she was beaten, then hoisted onto the chain. The thugs who'd dished out the abuse had jeered and mocked her as they'd left, finally leaving her alone with the bleeders. If she was being honest with herself, she'd found the bleeders' silent indifference more unsettling than the maliciousness of her chaperones.

The bleeders had injected a serum which had rendered her immobile, but fully conscious. They'd stripped her of all her clothing; gently folding the rags of material in neat piles on a table on wheels. Then strangely, they'd washed her, using strips of wet cloth and cleaning alcohol. For some reason, she couldn't explain why, but she had the absurd notion that her pain was over.

It couldn't have been further from the truth.

They had waited until the effects of the serum had worn off before beginning. Despite the fact she was naked, there was no rape or verbal abuse. As she endured their torture, she'd quickly came to the conclusion she was naked because it provided them with a blank canvas, without random bits of clothing interfering with their task. They only saw her as a workstation, nothing more.

They asked her probing questions; questions she had no answers for. She told them as much;

screaming over and over again as they sent thousands of volts through her body; made intricate cuts on specific areas of her body; manipulated nerve endings to maximise her agony, until she began to beg them to just get it over and done with… to kill her.

At least her blue-eyed boy was safe. It was the one thought that she still clung to – it was the only thing that kept her going.

She didn't believe her torturers were human. They made no judgement on her wails and cries. They barely reacted when she'd pissed herself, or vomited – just made notes on a nearby scribe, then simply stopped what they were doing, cleaned her up, then resumed.

At one point she had even managed to find the strength to deal one of them a couple of kicks to the face. The bleeder had grunted, staggering back clutching his nose. She struggled in her bonds, fully expecting him to do the natural thing and lash out. But he hadn't. He'd quietly retired, returning sometime later – she couldn't be sure how long – as though nothing had happened.

She hadn't seen them in a while. Maybe they were just leaving her to die. She hoped they were, she didn't know how much more she could take.

Her thoughts were answered as the quiet was disrupted by the sound of grating metal, followed by a bright light. She squinted, causing her to wince from the lance of pain which erupted in her empty eye socket. The bleeders were back, but they weren't alone. They were accompanied by four men, dressed head to toe in black. Their faces were a blur, but she could make out a chuckle from one of them.

"Fuck me, you two weren't kidding when you said you'd been thorough," one of the men said. "Waste of a decent piece of ass."

"We do not base ourselves with such primitive urges that provide us with nothing but wasted time. We performed our interrogation as was required," one of the bleeders whispered.

"Almost nothing left for us to take to the boss."

"She spoke the truth when questioned," the bleeder said. "Our work is done; we shall leave her in your custody."

The bleeders turned without another word and left her alone with the four men.

They unshackled her, dropping her to the ground like a lead weight. One of them drew close to her ear. She barely had the energy to lift her head, she was so weak. "The boss is waiting; he's got a surprise for you...

~

Lex stared down at the shanty-town, leaning on the railing outside Brooks' command station. She could feel the presence of the two guards, behind her; their eyes boring into her back. They'd been debating her decision to leave for twenty minutes. Voices rose in volume every so often – from an obvious disagreement in opinion, she surmised. It didn't matter what they discussed, or what decision they finally came to.

She was leaving to finish what she had started.

One thing that troubled her though, was the revelation that Sapien-republic had saved her from a watery grave. She didn't know whether she felt relief at them having saved her, or anger as they should have left her to expire – at least then she would be with her boy.

She pulled at a loose thread on the sleeve of the itchy boiler-suit. She would need her suit. She couldn't wage her war against the Inner-Sanctum kitted out in a potato sack that was twenty years old if it were a day.

She was suddenly aware of being watched. Her senses were attuned to such things, like the pull of a magnet. She looked up. Leaning against the outer fence to the command centre was the little girl she'd seen earlier. She wore grubby looking pants, a little too short for her, and a shirt that was two sizes too big; the sleeves of which had been rolled up so much they looked like oversized bangles. She flinched for a moment, before slowly raising her hand. She waved at her. In spite of herself, Lex raised her own, returning the little girl's greeting. She could feel a smile pulling at her face.

I can't remember the last time I smiled.

A grin spread across the little girl's mouth, which made her look both cute and mischievous. Lex took a step back from the railing and descended the steps, making her way cautiously towards the girl.

"Don't wander out of our sight, not unless you want a bullet in the back," a gruff voice called at her back.

"I'm quaking in my fucking boots," she retorted waspishly, eliciting a snigger from the other guard and the little girl.

She stopped ten feet from the girl and knelt down so they were looking at each other eye to eye. "It's okay," she said. "I'm not going to hurt you." She held out both her hands, palms outstretched to let the little girl know she posed no threat. "What's your name?"

The little girl's expression twitched, uncertain about how to proceed. She glanced up at the two guards, then back at Lex, her body relaxing a little. "You're *her,* aren't you?" she said. "The one they call 'the woman'."

Lex slowly nodded her head in affirmation. "You can call me Lex."

"Mother Joan says I'm not to go near you... because you're dangerous."

Lex narrowed her eyes. "Mother Joan's right; I am dangerous. But here you are... now... only a few yards away. Why have you not listened to your mother's council?" Lex asked playfully, raising an eyebrow. She gave her a wry smile.

I haven't spoken to a child in a very long time.

"She's not my real mother. My real mother died when I was very little. Mother Joan looks after the orphans."

Lex gave her a sympathetic smile. "I see. I'm sorry about your mother."

The girl shrugged. "It's okay. I don't really remember her... I know she was nice... and kind."

"Do you think Mother Joan would like you speaking to a dangerous person?"

160

The girl looked Lex up and down, trying to make her mind up. She raised an eyebrow, apparently coming to her own conclusion. Lex decided she liked this little girl. "I think you only hurt the bad men, above us in Sanctum-One. Besides, you don't look so scary up close."

Lex's expression was sceptical. "Are you sure? You ran away from me earlier today."

The girl blushed. "I wasn't scared, I was being cautious," she declared, attempting to soothe her embarrassment.

"A wise move, you don't know me from Eve."

The girl squinted in confusion. "I don't know anyone called Eve."

Lex chuckled, finding the act almost foreign. "No... it means... never mind. What's your name? I've told you mine, I think it only fair you give me yours."

Does my laugh really sound like that?

"Kat, my name is Kat. It's short for Katrina," she said, her chest swelling with pride.

"Well, pleased to meet you, Kat."

"What happened to your eye?" Kat asked, pointing at Lex's eyepatch. Children never ceased to amaze her with their ability to call out a curiosity, regardless of social protocol.

Lex reached up and touched the eyepatch, feeling a little sad. "Bad men took it," she said, her voice almost a whisper. She could feel tears begin to well up in her eyes, which she quickly rubbed away. Kat didn't seem to notice as she was still appraising her.

Kat's lips curled in disgust. "Bad men from above? The ones who wear the masks?"

161

The little girl's knowledge of the bleeders took her by surprise – she found it unsettling. The bleeders were barely known above ground, let alone in an underground community. She thought, at least, the children down here would be kept in the dark from the knowledge of those monsters who plied their trade in torture and misery.

"How do you know of them?" she asked.

"I heard Brooks talk about them with the doctor. I think that's why he doesn't let the children venture up into Sanctum-One."

"Brooks is right," she said.

Kat pointed to her eye. "I think the patch makes you look cool," Kat said, nodding.

Before she could answer, the doors to the command centre opened. The two of them glanced in its direction.

"Off with you, Kat. Mother Joan wouldn't like it if I told her you were hanging around command again," Brooks said. His tone suggested he was being stern, but from his jovial expression, she knew he wasn't particularly annoyed with the girl. Lex sensed the hint of affection in his voice.

Lex turned to face Kat, but she had disappeared. He smiled as he descended the steps and approached her. "I'm sorry that took so long. We had much to discuss."

Lex raised herself to her feet. "What difference does it make? I'm still leaving."

"I don't think we could keep you here, no matter how much we'd like that. As I've said, we could make ourselves a formidable partnership."

Lex remained silent. Brooks gazed down at her ill-fitting garment. "That reminds me, the doctor had your suit mended; he also made some improvements. He's just gone to fetch it." His gaze focused beyond her, towards his community. "While we wait, would you indulge me if I give you a quick tour of the compound?"

He walked past her without waiting for a reply. Lex rolled her eyes and followed, but her gaze lingered on the spot where Kat had stood not moments before.

XXIV

The Halls of Truth was situated deep within the bowels of NewHaven's lesser-known locations; a dark, restricted, sinister warren of cold corridors, interrogation rooms, and surgical laboratories which held a constant aroma of chemicals and disinfectant. If the bleeders ever saw themselves as human – with the same base notions of what it meant to be alive – they would call this hive of misery home. What added to the secrecy of this particular part of NewHaven, was the fact the area had been wiped from the building's schematics. As far as Sanctum-One was concerned, the place simply didn't exist.

The place certainly existed to Marr, as he stood in one of the cells. He seethed with rage – the irrepressible emotion only exasperated by the silent indifference emanating from the two bleeders standing before him; arms clasped behind their backs, completely unaffected from the tirade of abuse spewing from Marr's mouth. Most people would be too unnerved to even comprehend hurling insults at a couple of bleeders, especially within their base of operations – but Marr wasn't most people.

"So, I ask again, how the fuck did this happen?" he asked through gritted teeth, pointing to the mass of butchered flesh that used to be Alon Reid. "Your job was to question him, not cut him to ribbons like some wet-behind-the-ears butcher's apprentice on his first day."

The bleeders slowly turned their heads in unison to the former investigator. Reid lay in a bloodied heap. What remained of his clothing hung off him in tatters, his most exposed extremities mostly devoid of skin. His eyes had been gouged out of their sockets; the raw holes stared out at the trio almost in accusation. His lips had been cut off and Marr could see that the majority of his teeth had either been drilled or pull out at the root. Marr soon averted his eyes from the horror; unable to maintain his gaze on the mess.

This was going to take some fixing, he thought to himself. He suspected Faulks had a hand in this nightmare; he'd been quite keen to give Reid to the bleeders based on piss-weak accusations. The Proxy was becoming more and more unhinged the longer this Moretti business dragged on.

The bleeders fixed their gaze on Marr once more. Their eyes peered at him from behind their surgical masks; completely devoid of any comprehension of what their handiwork had caused. For their own self-preservation, they were lucky none of their sadistic tools were close to hand, as Marr would be more than tempted to send them to join Reid in whatever fiery hell the investigator was now languishing in.

"Much to our disappointment," one of them said in that flat, emotionless voice they all seemed to have. "We did not anticipate his heart failing as it did. We had such high hopes of him lasting a little longer." They both turned to look at Reid, with as close to regret as Marr assumed they were capable of.

He laughed bitterly. "You've got to be kidding?" He approached Reid's body and knelt down beside it. He immediately regretted getting so near to the corpse; the smell of shit and blood was more prominent this close. But he chose not to rise to his feet – he would be damned if he was giving the two of them the satisfaction of seeing his discomfort. Instead, he turned his head to face them, sucking in a quick breath to help suppress the urge to vomit from the putrid stench coming off Reid like heat. "Did you try and remove his heart with a blunt hatchet – beginning at his ass – to have a closer look. I may not fully understand your craft, as macabre as it is, but I'm not fucking stupid. You were ordered to kill him, weren't you?"

"We are not at liberty to discuss the nature of our interrogation," the bleeder replied calmly.

He stood up, knowing he wasn't going to get any answers from the two sadists and made for the door. He needed to get as far away from the bleeders as possible – for their sakes. He desperately needed fresh air; the place was so thick with the reek of disinfectant; he was struggling to breathe and he was beginning to feel light-headed. Also, the mood he was in if he remained where he was, he was sorely tempted to triple the room's current body-count. Yet more problems lay on his doorstep; this new addition provided by the two scalpel-happy sociopaths in front of him, completely incapable of understanding and considering the greater good.

"Do you wish to take the body, or may we be permitted to carry out further tests on it. Though dead, he may prove…"

Marr felt something inside him snap. In a heartbeat, he rushed over, pulling out a curved blade from within his coat, and grabbed the nearest bleeder by the collar, pressing cold steel against his pale throat.

In an equally impressive display of speed, the other bleeder whipped out a scalpel, resting the small razor-sharp blade against the flesh of his neck, he knew the carotid artery lay. One quick flick of the wrist would mean death in an instant; the room quickly washed in his blood.

"Please release my colleague," the bleeder asked, in a similar tone one would use if asking a guest in your home if they would like a cup of tea. He noticed this one was female, though her dullness of tone was similar to her partner's.

They stood there, bathed in artificial light and the aftermath of Reid's misery, amidst the stench of disinfectant and blood. Marr glared at them, murder blazing from his eyes – a complete contrast to the bleeders, who merely returned his anger with expressions of abstract curiosity. The female bleeder cocked her head to the side, studying him.

Thankfully, their impasse was interrupted, as the door opened. It was Faulks.

"What the fuck is going on here? Marr, let him go," Faulks ordered.

Marr glanced over to the Proxy, then back to the bleeder. He grimaced as his rage began to subside, only to be replaced with frustration. He released his grip on the bleeder and pushed him back a few paces He concealed his weapon. The female bleeder flicked her eyes to the Proxy who narrowed his eyes in warning. She slowly drew her eyes back to Marr, as though deciding what to do. Her colleague placed a hand on her arm and gently eased the scalpel away from Marr's neck. She blinked, as though snapping out of a trance and slipped the scalpel inside her overalls.

Faulks broke the awkward silence, which had replaced the stand-off. He addressed Marr. "I see you're not happy with the results," Faulks said, stating the obvious. "I could hear you bawling like a petulant child from the elevator."

"You could say that," Marr said, dryly, still struggling to compose himself. "I knew Reid wasn't working out for you, but I didn't think he needed chopping up like firewood."

Faulks placed a clammy hand on his shoulder. He was finally thankful for the stench of disinfectant – tempering the Proxy's cologne. He thought about grabbing his scrawny arm and snapping it in two, but he pushed the thought to the back of his mind and sighed.

"You think I wanted this?" He pointed to the corpse. Marr noted there was an absence of remorse... or even disgust on the Proxy's face. "If that fucking idiot had done his job, I wouldn't be forced to take drastic measures." He waved a hand at the investigator. "At least this way, we can inform Prime Vonn Investigator Reid was a Sapien-Republic turncoat. A loose end all tied up in a pretty bow."

Marr shook Faulks' hand off his shoulder. "You think this solves everything? What about Reid's partner, Hall? She's been sniffing a little too close to our business of late. Sound familiar? Look how the last intrepid, poke-nosed cop, who got a little too close for comfort, turned out? Six months of complete and utter anarchy. All because you can't help playing with your toys, instead of pulling the trigger quick and being done about it."

Faulks' face took on a deep purple, his rage evident from Marr's short tone. "Don't you start getting insubordinate with me, you little shit. Do you know who you speak to with that mouth of yours? The Proxy, second only to the Prime." He pointed down at Reid. His eye was drawn to one of the Proxy's veins; throbbing on his temple. "Just get this fucking mess fixed before I make any rash decisions about your place within the Inner-Sanctum."

Marr had stepped too far; he knew it, but he didn't care. "Do you know where I've just come from?" he asked, diverting the subject of his 'place within the Inner-Sanctum'. "The precinct. Reid's underling, Hall, has just informed her Captain Alexandra Moretti is the woman."

The news took the wind from Faulks' sails, pacifying his rage. "Leave us," he ordered the bleeders, waving a dismissive hand to them. They complied, nodding their heads and leaving the room. The Proxy waited until they'd closed the door, then peered at Marr; his eyes bloodshot. "If she's told her captain… that makes things difficult. Is there any chance we can bring them on board?"

Marr shook his head. "I gave Hall the opportunity to unburden herself while we were in the captain's office. She decided to hold her silence until I'd left, before spilling her guts to Mercer."

"Hmm... what about the captain? Is he pliant?"

"No, not with this. In the past, we've been able to subtly manipulate the direction of some of his investigations, whenever there was a chance it could interfere with our operations. This is different. It's too big, too obvious. Besides, he doesn't hold rep's from NewHaven in a particularly bright light. He's going to take the information to his superiors... to command."

A glimmer of hope began to gleam in the corners of the Proxy's eyes. "We have creatures placed within command..." He rubbed his jaw, thinking.

Marr was beginning to lose his patience. "If we let Mercer pass this information on, we run the risk of exposure. Not every member of police command is in our pocket," he said, raising a hand in irritation. "If the web grows too large, it becomes weaker, with too many loose ends to tie up. I suggest we take this to the Prime."

Faulks stared at him, nodding. He turned away, sighing audibly. "The Prime won't be pleased with our current predicament," he said.

Marr rolled his eyes. "Really? The way things have transpired of late; I'd expect the Prime to understand. Everything is not entirely in our hands – we can't be everywhere at once."

170

"That's not strictly true," the Proxy said, quietly.

"What do you mean?"

The Proxy took a deep breath, steeling his nerves. His eyes flitted briefly to the body of Reid, before closing. He began to pace. "The Prime is a busy man, Marr. Most of his time is spent keeping our machine well oiled. I've taken it upon myself to only divulge certain aspects of the hunt for the woman to him."

This didn't sound good. He could feel what little hold they had of the situation begin to slip through his fingers. "What exactly does the Prime know?" he asked, knowing he wasn't going to like Faulks' response.

The Proxy's expression darkened. Marr detected a hint of shame and nervousness. "He doesn't know the woman is Moretti…"

Whatever fucked up answer Marr had been expecting, not in his wildest dreams could he imagine this. "For the love of fuck, you've got to be kidding me?" Marr exclaimed, his initial surprise quickly morphing into a red-hot rage. "It's been six months. Why?"

"When Sapien-Republic first reared its ugly heads – staging their 'peaceful protests' – I tried to convince the Prime to put the threat down quickly before it got out of hand. As you know, we conduct certain operations, which are necessary for the continued survival of Sanctum-One. If information regarding our activities got into the hands of those fucking firebrands, they would have a field day with it. I suggested the best course of action would be to apprehend the

171

leaders and eliminate them… but, he wouldn't listen. He just wasn't convinced they posed a threat. They are a cancer on the very civilisation the Prime created for us. If they had their way, they would destroy it all, hurtling us back to the dark days."

Marr remained silent. He glared at the Proxy, his hands balling into fists. He felt betrayed. He thought the Proxy trusted him with everything. It would seem not, apparently. The Proxy continued.

"Refused by the Prime, I was left with no choice. I couldn't just sit there and let it happen. So, as Proxy – the Prime's second – I undertook an operation, off the books, using the Inner-Sanctum's contacts within the SPD to lure out Sapien-Republic's leaders. For a time, we managed to grab a few of their lower-ranking operatives, giving them to the bleeders to play with. We obtained some information, but not enough to go on."

Faulks walked over to the far wall on the opposite side of the room, leaning his back against it. "They caught on to our tactics quickly. We began to pull in less and less of them until we were left with nothing. As time drew on, their following began to grow, their 'protests' rising in number."

There was no denying it; over the last year, Marr had noticed a steady increase in rallies by the so-called peaceful protest organisation. There weren't many incidents of violence, only a few – which was natural when a group of passionate liberals were situated in close proximity to the authorities. But it was getting more and more difficult to exact curfews when dealing with thousands of people descending on one venue at a specific time. There weren't enough officers to deal with such a high magnitude of people, crammed into such small areas and venues. Aside from this, there was one thing that was bothering Marr.

"Why wasn't I involved?" he asked.

Faulks closed his eyes, as though the question physically hurt him. "You are my brightest and best, Marr. If I'm being honest, I excluded you because I thought there was an almost certain chance the Prime would discover my off-the-book operation and punish those, especially of high-ranking authority, accordingly. I didn't want to lose my best operative."

Marr opened his arms out wide, his face contorted in a sarcastic sneer. "And here I am anyway." He dropped his hands by his side. He was begrudgingly thankful the Proxy was coming clean with him. If he'd left it any longer, who knows what irreparable damage might be caused. In spite of this unburdening of the soul – of which he had no choice – it still didn't answer the most important question. "Where does Moretti come into this?"

Faulks looked sheepish. "A few members, with knowledge of my activities, began to sense weakness in my position as Proxy, like sharks who'd caught the scent of blood in the water. When Moretti surfaced, I thought I could use her to convince the Prime to use a more militant approach to Sapien-Republic, and at the same time strengthen my position as Proxy by removing the vultures… so much has been sacrificed."

The last part caught Marr. There was something Faulks was holding back. He thought of all the Inner-Sanctum members that had been killed in the last six months. This wasn't good. "What do you mean by 'removing the vultures'? What have you done?"

The Proxy looked uncharacteristically flustered. Marr knew the man to wear his emotions on his sleeve, but it was generally bouts of controlled rage and anger. This new side of the Proxy, opening up like a flower blooming in spring, was beginning to give him cause for concern.

"I've known of the woman's exact whereabouts for quite some time. I've been using her to increase pressure on the Prime for months…to change his mind on the real threat."

Marr was lost for words. For six months, the Proxy had been using Moretti to dispose of rivals and possible threats to his position. He hadn't just used Moretti for his own ends… he'd also used Marr. He could feel the bile of fury rise up from his guts, a feeling he'd kept caged for so long.

Well, no more.

He swept across the room and grabbed the Proxy by the collar, hoisting him off his feet so that his expensive leather shoes dangled a full foot above the ground.

"You fucking idiot," he screamed. "I've been tying myself in loops for six… fucking… months."

"It was for the greater good," Faulks choked.

174

Marr almost laughed. "The greater good? Sanctum's or yours?"

Confusion reigned supreme on the Proxy's face, which was growing redder by the second. Faulks' veins bulged on his forehead, which was slick with sweat. "What do you mean? Put me down before you do something you'll regret."

Marr gripped him tighter, his knuckles going white, the bones threatening to burst through his skin. He let go, dropping Faulks to the ground. He landed hard on his ass. He remained on the ground, coughing and spluttering as Marr took a few steps back, disgusted with his boss.

Marr pointed at the body of Investigator Reid. "It's not the only reason you let Moretti murder members of the Inner-Sanctum, was it?" He wanted to hear it from Faulks' own mouth.

The guilt which flashed across the Proxy's eyes told Marr all he needed to know. He left Faulks alone in the room, slamming the door behind him. He wasn't surprised to find the two bleeders waiting quietly outside.

"Bag the body and have it sent to my cruiser," he commanded, striding away from them, his need for fresh air having never been more desperate.

XXV

On the east side of the city – three miles from the merchant district – lay the projects; a collection of ramshackle, three-story apartment complexes, built into a grid system spanning four square miles. Though hardly squalor, its occupants did lack the luxury of convenience enjoyed by their counterparts at the city centre; the market quadrant; leisure facilities; and more prominent schooling academies. For those not fortunate enough to be able to afford a vehicle of their own, the city provided a shuttle service which ran at thirty-minute intervals.

It had its obvious drawbacks; there were no local convenience stores – if a citizen had settled in for the evening, then realised they needed a few home essentials, they had to make peace with the fact it was about a two-hour round trip. It certainly wasn't a comforting thought if it was late and an early curfew was suddenly announced.

Hall slowed her cruiser to a crawl as she surveyed the door numbers. She squinted, trying to read the tiny numbers fixed above the lintels of each building. The road was bare; cruisers a rarity in these parts

It was one of the first things Hall had noticed when she'd come off the slip road and turned into the poorest district of Sanctum-One. It was also her first time venturing into its neatly-columned blocks. She stopped her cruiser in front of the apartment complex Alexandra Moretti used to live in – before her 'death'. She became very aware of her cruiser being the only one as far as the eye could see. For some reason, she felt like a target. She felt eyes on her, from a few of the locals; a couple of curtain-twitchers, peering between grubby looking blinds; a group of kids sitting on the sidewalk; and an elderly gentleman with a small dog. She may as well have 'cop' scrawled across her bonnet.

She got out, the light breeze whipping through her hair. The air was crisp – and though it was a little chilly – she found it refreshing – better than the stuffy heat of her office. She closed the door and clicked her key, arming the alarm. She took a quick look around then tried the handle to make sure it was locked; the immediate judgement sent a wave of guilt through her, much to her shame. She caught the old man's gaze and smiled. He didn't reciprocate, suddenly finding his dog more interesting as it squatted to take a piss.

She shrugged, turning around to face the building. She just couldn't imagine an investigator living here. The structure was designed to serve a purpose; no more, no less. There was no architectural ambition in its shape; no decadent balconies or fancy, garishly-lit vestibules. It was a home to exist in, not show off. She had no doubts that inside each apartment, its occupant would've added his/her touches to make it a home. Aside from this, she was baffled how a lead investigator had chosen to live here.

Hall thought of her own circumstances. Moretti had been a lead investigator, so her salary would have been more than her own. She wasn't delusional enough to believe her own salary allowed her to live in abject opulence. But it did provide her with the option to live comfortably and a hell of a lot closer to the city centre. After the rent and living costs had been deducted, she could still afford to own her own cruiser – as beat up as it was. She shook her head, internally chastising herself. She was just the outcome of two parents – overbearing as they were – who had provided their daughter with a better start in life. She had no right to judge people she knew nothing about.

"You an old colleague?" a gravelled voice asked, behind her causing her to flinch.

She turned around. It was the old man with the dog; its black, beady eyes regarded her with caution before it made up its mind deciding she posed no threat to its owner. It approached to sniff at her boots. The old man looked to his dog, then raised his head, meeting her eyes in question. "I'm sorry?" she asked, giving him a nervous smile.

This time he returned her smile; his grin spreading across his weather-beaten face. His moustache, which sat thick above his top lip, bristled. He nodded towards the apartment complex. "A colleague of Alexandra's?"

She laughed. "Is it that obvious I'm SPD?"

His eyes twinkled with humour. "Don't see many cruisers this way, my dear. When you pulled up, I thought you were either a cop or a debt collector. Then you got out and I said to myself 'she's too pretty to be a debtor'."

"I had noticed the absence of vehicles," she said. "No, I didn't know Miss Moretti. I'm just making some routine enquiries. I'm from the cold case department," she lied.

He pursed his lips, his expression losing the humour in it. "Finally found her body?"

She narrowed her eyes. As much as he was pleasant, she didn't know who he was. After her impromptu meeting with the spook, she wasn't sure who she could trust. She showed the old man her I.D. card. "Investigator Hall, and you are, sir?"

"Geno Moretti; Alexandra's uncle," he said, strolling past her. "I suppose you'll want to come in then?"

Lost for words, she followed him down the path, a few steps behind the dog.

~

Inside the complex, Hall was pleasantly surprised to find the apartments looked a lot better than the exterior suggested. The main communal area had its very own service droid; cleaning the landings, and servicing the local amenities. They skirted around one of them as it bleeped and buzzed; its internal CPU processing its current duties; oblivious to their passing. The dog stopped and growled at the droid, before catching up to its master.

Geno led her through thickly carpeted halls, furnished with potted plants; their rich scents of lavender and eucalyptus gave the interior a refreshing aroma. The walls were adorned with printed artworks, encased in tasteful frames. Geno turned his head, not failing to miss the look of surprise on her face.

"Thought it would look as shitty as the outside, huh?" he asked, amused. She didn't answer assuming it was rhetorical.

They traversed along several more corridors until they reached the Moretti apartment. He swiped his card key through a narrow slit above the door. It unlocked with a quick snap, as bolts and levers within the frame slid free. Geno opened the door and gestured for her to lead the way. She smiled politely and stepped inside the apartment, the dog bolting past her, down Geno's hallway.

The apartment was dull; the air thick with the stale smell of cigarette smoke. She looked up, noticing the once-white ceiling had a tinge of yellow to it. She reached the room at the end of the hall, then stood awkwardly, waiting for Geno who followed close behind. He removed his coat and invited her to take a seat in one of the two armchairs. She noticed one of them had an ashtray balanced precariously on one of its arms. It was obvious that one was Geno's, so she opted for the other one.

She sank into the soft cushion, expecting it to be a lot firmer than it was. It felt like it was trying to swallow her, so she shuffled forward to rest on its edge.

"I'm making some coffee, you want a mug?" he asked, making for the kitchen.

"Yes, please."

While Geno busied himself in the kitchen, she studied the room. There wasn't much; two chairs; a coffee table in between them; and a bookcase on the far wall by the window – stocked more with random junk than with books. She saw there was a couple of picture frames sitting on the middle shelf. She got up and walked over to take a closer look. The dog settled comfortably in his bed, watched her – his eyes following from behind shaggy brows.

She took one of the pictures from the shelf and used her sleeve to wipe off the dust that covered the glass, like a dirty skin. A pretty blonde, embracing a young boy stared back at her. They were kneeling down on grass, smiles adorning both their faces; pressed together in a loving squeeze. There was no mistaking the eyes of the woman looking at the camera. There was something different. Aside from the fact this woman had two eyes, they looked more human; full of life. It was hard to imagine this happy young woman was the same deranged, psychotic terrorist that had pointed a gun to her head.

"That was taken about a year ago," Geno said, carrying a tray laden with coffee and a plate of cakes. He was smiling, but Hall couldn't help notice the sadness in his expression. Geno gestured to the two chairs with his chin. She put the photo back and joined him.

Geno took a sip of coffee and then lit himself a cigarette, offering the pack to her. She shook her head. "Sorry, I don't smoke."

He settled back into the cushioned back of the chair and blew out a few smoke rings, which spun and wavered towards the ceiling. He followed their trajectory until they broke on the nicotine-stained paint, then lowered his head; his eyes sharp beneath his brows. "So, how can I help you, dear?"

Hall made a point of getting her scribe out to make notes – for appearance's sake – as she didn't work for 'missing persons'. "I was wondering if you could help me shed some light on your niece's disappearance... to possibly fill in some gaps regarding events."

Geno narrowed his eyes, the friendly expression waning a little. "My impression, given my treatment by the SPD, is that you have more important cases to work on," he said.

"What makes you say that?" she asked. "Every crime in the city is taken with the utmost seriousness by the SPD."

Geno leaned forward and took a long drag from his cigarette. He frowned, clearly sceptical of her naïve comment. "Your investigators came by for a time, taking statements, carrying out door to door enquiries. Heck, they even went to the effort of a small manhunt... but then, after they found Julian it all stopped."

"Stopped?"

"Once the forensics came back on our little Julian, they lost all interest in finding Alexandra."

"I'm here right now, Mr Moretti, asking questions on the whereabouts of your niece," she said.

Geno stubbed out his cigarette and picked up his cup, his worn fingers linking around it so tight she could see the whites of his knuckles. "Yes, but why now? It's been eight months since she disappeared... since they found..." He grimaced; the memories still raw.

"There's a lot of missing people in the city, sir. I can only apologise for the time it's taken to pursue the case. You must understand our staff are stretched pretty thin."

"After I hadn't heard from the precinct dealing with the case... I think it was about a fortnight... I began to make regular calls. It was no use though. I got bounced from pillar to post, passed from one officer to the next," he said, waving a hand dismissively. "It didn't matter who I spoke to, they all said the same thing."

"And what was that?"

He furrowed his brow, his lips curling in disgust. "They were prioritising their searches for citizens who weren't child killers."

Hall didn't have a reply, because there was none. The evidence did pin the murder on Moretti. The fingerprints on the murder weapon – found at the scene – did belong to Alexandra Moretti. As much as this proved she'd killed her son, Hall didn't think it was reason enough to quit the case. A little boy had been murdered. If anything, the evidence gave them a suspect in a murder enquiry, instead of a dead-end in a missing person case. It didn't make sense, and it certainly didn't give the SPD an excuse to treat Geno Moretti the way he claimed.

"As I've said, Mr Moretti, I can only apologise for the conduct of my colleagues. A missing person is still a missing person. I would say it was more of a priority if said missing person was a murderer."

Geno slammed his palm onto the table, startling her. "My niece is not a fucking murderer."

Hall jumped but kept her composure. She narrowed her eyes. "With all due respect, sir, Alexandra's prints were found on the murder weapon."

She could see tears brimming in Geno's eyes. He wiped them away roughly with the back of his hand. "I couldn't give a fuck, Miss Hall. My Alexandra loved that boy more than life itself."

She leaned forward and gave him a look of reassurance and understanding. "I'm not here to discuss the murder, Mr Moretti. I'm only here to find out where your niece is."

He glared at her; his face red with anger. Then he closed his eyes and sighed. "I'm sorry, Miss Hall. You don't understand what it's been like. The shit I get; judged for being related to a 'child killer'.

Hall nodded. "You're right, I don't understand. But I do sympathise. I'm not here to pass judgements. It's not my place to do so. I'm only here to get the facts."

Geno opened his arms. "I don't know what more I can tell you, other than what I said in my statement."

"If you could indulge me, I've not been privy to your statements."

He raised an eyebrow in question. "Really? Strange, I would have thought the investigator leading the search would have access to all the information."

Fuck, she thought. *Too much information.* "What I mean… is that I've deliberately not read them. I want to make my own conclusions before I take a look. Perhaps fresh eyes are what this case needs," she said, wondering if she'd laid the lie on a little too thick.

He nodded, appearing to buy it. She needed to be careful. As much as he was suffering, his grief didn't make him stupid. "Hmm, if you say so, Miss Hall. Where do you wish to begin?"

"When was the last time you saw her?" she asked, beginning with the most obvious question.

"About a week before her disappearance."

"Did the three of you live here together?"

He shook his head emphatically. "No, no. I rented one of the apartments a couple of blocks from here. I would stay over a couple of times a week to look after Julian… you know, if Lex was working late, or got called to an emergency."

"Are you living here full time now? What about your own apartment?"

"I was staying here the night she disappeared." He trailed off, his eyes becoming glassy like he was reliving the memory. "I haven't been back to my own apartment yet. I'd been staying that week. She said she was working a sensitive case and needed me here." He chuckled. "I wasn't complaining; meant I got a few extra days with…" His eyes brimming with tears; the dam threatening to burst.

"Sensitive case?" she asked, quickly moving onto another subject.

He nodded, his expression suggesting it was of no importance. "That's all she said."

185

"When did you last see Julian?"

"The day he disappeared. An Investigator came around with two armed officers. They said the boy was to go with them, as he was in danger. I told them he was safe with me, but they insisted, stating their orders had come from the Proxy himself."

The Proxy? This was getting interesting. Why would the Proxy involve himself in an SPD matter? "Do you know the name of the investigator?" she asked.

"It was Reid, Alon Reid. I was told shortly after they'd left, their vehicle was attacked and the boy was taken. The two officers were killed and Reid was grievously injured."

Grievously injured? This was the first time she'd heard this. She would have remembered her boss being out of commission due to injuries sustained whilst on duty. In the short time she'd known Reid, he didn't seem the type to put himself in the line of fire – at least not without good reason. The more she thought of it, she was sure he wasn't even part of the homicide department eight months ago. She would need to ask him when she eventually got hold of him.

This case was beginning to stink the deeper she delved. Geno continued.

"Afterwards, I demanded to know why they weren't able to keep their promise. To keep the boy safe."

"What did Reid say?"

"I never got a chance to talk to him. I persisted, but after I got a visit from some representatives from NewHaven..." He shook his head. "It

186

doesn't matter. Even if I managed to get hold of him, it wouldn't change anything. Our little Julian isn't coming back," he said, bitterly.

"I'll do my best to find your niece."

He smirked. "That's if she wants to be found…"

Her eyes widened. "What do you mean by that, do you know where your niece is?"

Panic flickered across his face for the briefest of moments, then it was gone. He waved a hand, rolling his eyes. "Look, Miss Hall, I'm tired. Could we do this another time?"

Hall wasn't letting go. He'd slipped up. He knew where she was, she knew it. He was maybe working with her, been harbouring her this entire time, she thought. "Has she been living here? Mr Moretti, might I remind you, withholding information, vital in aiding a major murder enquiry, is a serious offence?"

He slammed another palm onto the table. "Get the fuck out of my home before I do something I may regret."

Hall stood up. They were venturing into murky territory. She came here for answers, not pick a fight. "Something's not right with this case, Mr Moretti, and I'm going to find out the truth. You can cooperate now, or I can get a warrant for your arrest." She walked over to the bookcase and pointed to the photo of Julian and his mother. "I'm going to find justice for the death of an innocent little boy, whatever it takes."

A dark expression marred Geno Moretti's features. "Forgive me if I don't hold the abilities of the SPD in a particularly good light, Miss Hall. From what my Lex says, it's rotten to the core."

Hall levelled her finger at the old man. "I'm not fucking rotten, Mr Moretti. I believe in justice, whether you do or don't. I'll find those responsible for Julian's death." She dropped one of her cards on the coffee table. "Here's my card. If you change your mind before I return with a search warrant, give me a call. You're running out of time."

~

Hall stared at the apartment complex, her head resting against the window, her mind a torrent of emotions. Lex was using her uncle to stay hidden; she was sure of it. The only reason she had stayed her hand and not arrested him was the fact she'd been there under false pretences. If she was wrong, and his slip-up had been nothing more than confusion caused by his grief and hurt, she'd be kicked off the force; her feet barely touching the ground as she was slung out onto the street.

As she gazed at the drab building with the pleasant interior, she couldn't help shake the distinct feeling she was being manoeuvred like a pawn on a chessboard by hands invisible to her; a wraith hidden behind the curtain. She thought she could see Geno Moretti's silhouette at his window from amidst the gloom of his niece's apartment.

He was involved, she knew it.

She had to tell Mercer; in spite of the ass-kicking he'd dole out in her direction. She didn't care; the truth was all that mattered. She was an officer of the law and a child's murder has gone unanswered. It was her job to protect the citizens of this city and she'd be damned if anyone, superior or otherwise, was going to stop her.

Fuck it, she thought. There was no point in delaying the inevitable. She wasn't going to make any headway by moping and filling her head with self-doubt. She scrolled through her list of contacts on the dash display screen. However, before she could make the call, the screen flashed. It was an incoming call from an unknown number. She pushed the green answer box.

"Hall," she said.

"Investigator Hall, it's Banks, from NewHaven."

What the fuck did he want? "Can I help you?" she asked, barely able to conceal the contempt and mistrust from her tone.

"Cut the crap, Hall. I know you and the rest of your department can't stand me," he snapped. "Where are you?"

If she was reluctant to tell her boss where she was, the spook had no chance. "On patrol, Mr Banks."

"Oh, really?" he said, sarcastically. "I'm currently in the city centre heading for your boss' house. I have some information on Reid I'd like to share with you." He paused, his breath rasping down the line. He sounded nervous. "Look, I can't say too much, I don't trust the security on this line. I'll be honest with you, Hall, things have gone tits up at NewHaven, and I've had enough. Can I trust you?"

She remained silent for a moment, thinking. She didn't know this guy and besides, he was a spook. They lurked in the murkier areas of society; areas where lies spewed from mouths as naturally as she drew breath.

In the end, however, her curiosity got the better of her. "I'll meet you there in an hour," she said, cutting the call.

She called Mercer. He answered after the first dialling tone. "Hall?"

"Yeah, sir. I've had the spook on the line."

"That makes two of us. He called me about ten minutes ago. He wants to discuss Reid. He sounded rattled. Where are you?"

"I'm outside the Moretti apartment," she said, not bothering to come up with a lie. She knew she would tell him eventually.

He sighed in irritation. "Fuck's sake, Hall. I told you to go home." He let out a small chuckle. "In spite of your insubordination, I Can't say I'm not impressed."

She smiled at the compliment. "Sorry, sir. Thought I'd check it out."

"Your intrepid nature's going to get you into some serious shit one of these days."

"The way this case is going, sir, I think that day could be very soon."

"How long are you going to be?"

"I said to the spook an hour. I'll be at your house in thirty minutes."

"Good, I'll see you in thirty," he said, cutting the call.

Hall switched on the ignition and barrelled out of the street in a hail of dust and screeching tyres.

~

Geno watched through the fog of cigarette smoke as Investigator Hall's cruiser screeched down the street. He took a long drag as the kids, playing across the street, ran in its direction, pointing and shouting. He looked down at Bruno, his brows furrowed with concern. His little dog gazed up at him, tongue lolling from its mouth, tail wagging. "Don't think she was being entirely honest, was she, boy?"

Although the young investigator had claimed she was from missing persons, Geno had noted her badge had stated otherwise; reading homicide. He wondered what she'd been thinking of showing him her badge. Surely it must have dawned on her that he was the uncle of an experienced SPD investigator – or was, he corrected himself. It begged the question as to why a homicide investigator was poking her nose around a missing person's case. If she'd mentioned it was linked to Julian's murder, he would have understood the direction her line of enquiries had taken her. But she hadn't. Instead, she'd told him she wasn't investigating the murder, just his niece's disappearance.

He peered at the empty space where her cruiser had sat, wondering what the true motivations were for her visit to the projects. In many ways, she reminded Geno of Alexandra; they had the same tenacity; a similar attitude towards law enforcement – though, Alexandra's had soured over the last couple of years.

191

Before…

He stubbed his cigarette out, leaving it smouldering in the ashtray. He made his way to the rear of the apartment, towards the back bedroom. The room hadn't been touched since Julian. The dust had been left to settle, covering everything in a faint sheet. He stepped in, closing the door behind him. He deliberately averted his gaze to the boy's bed and toys. He didn't trust the brittle shroud of numbness he'd begun to slowly build within himself to be able to withstand the wave of grief that would surely and inevitably wash over him if his eyes lingered too long.

On the far wall sat a picture frame. Julian's beautiful blue eyes stared at him from behind the murky glass. He removed the frame from its hook, already feeling that familiar fluttering of emotions trying to rise up from his insides. He closed his eyes for a moment, composing himself, before reverently laying it down on the floor, the image facing the wall.

A small red button sat flush with the plaster of the wall. He pushed it. Clicks and rattles from several locking mechanisms released, then a section of wall, to the right of the button, slid up into the ceiling to reveal a small room bathed in red, artificial light. He stepped inside, flicking a lever situated on a stanchion. The door slid back down, secluding him inside the claustrophobic space.

The secret room was bare, save for a table which sat against the far wall. On it sat a single item; a scribe. He picked it up and placed his thumb onto the cold screen. It flashed blue before

192

emitting the image of a pretty blonde, her long wavy hair pulled around one shoulder and tied in a green ribbon. The image brought on a pang of sorrow as he began to traverse through the maze of files. After several password entries – to gain access to a secure line – he found the contact he was looking for. He knew the recipient wouldn't answer, but he pushed it anyway. It always worked this way. He waited until the voicemail asked him to leave a message.

"An investigator from the SPD just paid me a visit, looking for information regarding the disappearance of Alexandra Moretti. She wasn't forthcoming with her true motives; said she was from missing persons, but I saw her badge. She's homicide. Last I knew, the SPD doesn't give free rein for their investigators to bounce between departments willy-nilly. She'd either rogue and not working within traditional SPD parameters, or she genuinely wants to help, but has no idea what she's getting herself into… something I think you can relate to. May be worth looking into. Her name's Veronica Hall."

XXVI

Traffic had been light, which was no surprise given the route to Captain Mercer's home skirted around the city centre, avoiding the higher concentrations of congestion. The clustered, tightly-packed apartments of the projects slowly dissipated to larger, more spaciously separated homes; two – and three-story bespoke condos, tailor-made for citizens with sizeable bank accounts.

Cruisers and luxury transportation hubs began to increase in number the further she got. She also noticed the sky wasn't as cluttered with as many Zeps – a fair majority of the city's Zep owners probably lived in this quadrant – ironically, they didn't feel compelled to have their hideous monstrosities looming above their own neatly trimmed lawns and collections of expensive cruisers.

She passed maintenance crews carrying out gardening duties; street cleaning; and general repairs – the latest up-to-date droids and equipment at their disposal. As she made brief glances towards the decadent properties, she was in no doubt their occupants were a few classes above the likes of Geno Moretti – as well as herself, come to that.

"That's if she wants to be found…" The old man's words had been playing on a loop in her mind since she'd left his apartment. It hardly stretched the imagination to assume he was – or had been until her unfortunate plunge into the river – harbouring the woman. She was surprised he hadn't been hauled in before now… but then again, they hadn't known 'the woman' was Alexandra Moretti until now. The development would certainly give her a buffer when the captain gave her the dressing down, she fully expected.

She turned right, by a sizeable mall. *Prime Groceries* was emblazoned in gold above its main entrance. An image of pristine aisles; their polished floors glistening and shelves containing the very best produce, patrolled by the cream of Sanctum-One's citizenship and their snot-nosed broods. She'd once made the mistake of buying a bottle of wine from one of the wine merchants within a similar high-end mall. It had cost her four times as much as the local store she frequented, near her apartment – though, the quality was a damn sight better than the gut-rot she usually purchased.

It wasn't just the expense that she'd noticed. She'd felt the mall's regular clientele had known she didn't belong, making her feel like an interloper encroaching on their space.

She traversed the quiet streets for another five minutes before pulling up in front of the captain's home. She surveyed the clock on her dash. The journey had taken twenty-eight minutes. It was amazing how her surroundings had changed so dramatically in such a short trip.

She cut the power and climbed out. The street was like a ghost town; there was barely a sound, save for the distant hissing of sprinklers watering a few of the neighbouring lawns. She walked up the path, wondering if the spook had beaten her to Mercer's – she couldn't bring herself to believing him when he'd said it would take him an hour to reach the captain's home. She glanced back to see if Banks' cruiser was in the vicinity, then remembered she didn't know what type or colour of vehicle he drove.

She knocked on the captain's door; rattling the heavy lump of iron – shaped in the image of a dolphin – against its base. The clash of metal sounded all the louder amidst the quiet of the street. The door opened a crack... had it been left open? Maybe Mercer had seen her pull up and unlocked it so she could let herself in. But if he'd done that, why not just wait by the door?

"Captain," she called. There was no answer from within. Cold dread began to creep up her spine, as her steadily increasing paranoia worked overdrive. She pushed the door open, the hinges creaking. "Banks." Still nothing.

She reached down and unclipped the strap which held her sidearm securely in its holster. She slowly drew her gun; the weight of it reassuring. Before she even considered venturing further into the captain's home, she took a quick glance to the street, behind her; it was still bereft of activity.

She didn't like this, not one bit. Though the captain's door had been left unlocked, it wasn't really cause for alarm. This was a good neighbourhood; she imagined the crime rates in this sector of the city were almost non-existent – maybe people here weren't as vigilant about locking their front doors as they would be in her own street. She wasn't convinced; one thing the last couple of days had taught her – especially with this case – was that the unexpected could easily be closer than anticipated.

The rational part of her mind tried to provide her with a simple explanation, but each one was shot down by the paranoid part – growing stronger by the minute. Maybe he just popped out, she thought, then dismissed the suspicion as his cruiser was still parked in the driveway. She knew he didn't have a dog – even if he did, he was hardly going to go for a hike with it if he was expecting her company. The mall was also out of the question as it was a bit far to walk – besides if he wanted anything, he probably would've asked her to drop in on the way.

She stepped inside, her boots thumping audibly on the hardwood flooring. She held the gun up, peering along its barrel. Her finger hovered over the trigger, as she ventured further down the hall, step by step. When she got halfway down the hallway – making quick visuals in each room she passed – she heard a faint groan.

She closed her eyes, concentrating on its origin. She remained still for what seemed like an excruciatingly long time – and for a moment – thought she'd maybe imagined it. Then the whine of someone in pain resounded once more; this time louder. It came from the room at the very end; its door lay slightly ajar.

She pressed her back against the wall and slid along it, wincing each time a floorboard creaked. When she reached the door, she stopped, trying to listen for any sign of there being someone on the other side of it, waiting for her. There was nothing; no shuffle from agitated feet; no movement of shadows beneath the small crack of space at the foot of the door. Satisfied, she gave the door a firm kick with the sole of her boot.

It swung open violently, cracking against the wall. It bounced back, but she stopped it with the palm of her hand. She looked into the room and gasped as she spotted Captain Mercer, sitting against the far wall, his white shirt awash with blood. A rank odour washed over her, like rotting meat. She ignored it and raced over towards him, kneeling down by his side. Her knee rested in a pool of her captain's blood. It soaked through the fabric of her trousers. It felt warm and there was a lot of it, she thought grimly.

"Captain, can you hear me?" she said, cupping his face. His head felt heavy as it lolled in her hands. His eyes fluttered open, then closed again in a flash of white. He groaned, a trickle of blood spilling from his mouth. His skin was hot and clammy – not a good sign. A sheen of sweat plastered his brow and his hair was soaked through. She looked down at his torso; several gunshot wounds peppered his stomach and chest. She was amazed he was still conscious. "I'm going to call for medical assistance, sir. I'll call for back up."

She fumbled in her jacket for her scribe, then pause... where was that smell coming from? She turned her head; her eyes flitting about the room in search of the smell's origin. She soon found it. She suppressed a gag. In the corner of the room, was the body of Alon Reid... or to be exact, what was left of him. He was naked; his entire body a butchered mess. The sight caused her insides to twist in disgust. His face looked like it had been stripped by a razor. His teeth grinned from a lipless mouth and his eye sockets stared back at her; wide and black. She leant away from her boss and vomited on the rug.

In between retches, she could hear the sound of sirens as they drew closer. When she'd heaved up as much as her body would allow, she raised herself back to a kneeling position, feeling hollow and lightheaded. She took off her jacket and used it to try and stem the flow of blood leaking out from the myriad of holes which peppered Mercer's body. It felt futile, but she didn't know what else to do.

Heavy footfalls thumped down the hall. She looked up to find several armed officers, piling into the room; pointing their assault rifles in her direction. They bellowed orders for her to step away from the captain. "We need medical assistance… the captain… he's hurt bad… he needs help immediately," she cried.

"Step away from the captain, now," said one of the armed officers.

Before she could reply with a tirade of abuse towards the trigger-happy morons, another voice called out to her… one she recognised.

"Step away from Captain Mercer, Hall, before these officers rip you full of holes. You're in enough shit as it is," Banks said, pushing his way past the armed response unit.

"What are you talking about?" she cried, feeling helpless and confused. She looked down at the captain who'd stopped breathing; his chest still; his eyes wide open. He was dead.

Banks closed the gap between them. "I'm arresting you for the murders of Investigator Alon Reid and Captain Ryan Mercer. For conspiring with the woman, resulting in the deaths of several Sanctum-One citizens."

Tears streamed down her face; her features the very mask of confusion. Banks took one more step, raised his arm, and struck her across the temple with a small baton he'd been holding. Her head whipped to the side as the world began to spin.

The last thing she saw before the darkness took her, was the sly grin on the spook's face.

XXVII

Lex was alone – or alone as she could be cooped up in a huge underground hanger full of people. She could feel two pairs of eyes, boring into her back as she sat in front of an old oil drum; used as a makeshift fire. The flames flickered and danced above the rim, the wood crackled, sending puffs of fiery fragments into the air every so often. She wondered where they got the wood, then surmised it was probably from the deeper parts of the Freedom Park.

Regardless of the fire, she still felt cold.

She pulled the blanket tight around her body. She was still garbed in the boiler-suit – which wasn't designed for keeping a naked body warm. She was growing more and more irritated with Doctor Oliver, as she'd thought he would have turned up with her suit by now. For all she knew, it was still lying in a state of disrepair, or simply dumped into the nearest bin – the promise of a new outfit an excuse to prolong her stay.

She sighed, frustrated with her current predicament; waiting on the whims of others in this oversized bomb shelter was preventing her from her work up top; in the city. It wasn't what she'd envisaged would happen when she'd started her mission.

She silently observed as the compound's residents settled in for the night; huddled in their own little groups around flaming drums of their own. She felt selfish for hogging one all to herself… though it wasn't all her own doing. She'd invited a few passers-by to join her; to share the heat. But each time, she'd been politely refused – from those who weren't too scared to utter a word. They feared her, it was clear on the furtive glances in her direction; the quiet whisperings behind her back when they thought she was out of earshot. She didn't blame them, of course. As much as she'd mastered the art of indifference – her new lack of empathy – she was surprised to find herself hurt from their treatment; their reluctance to even come within a few feet of her. It was a feeling she thought she'd buried for good.

I'm Lex now; 'the woman'. That part of me died with Julian.

"Can I join you," a voice called, snapping her from her reverie.

She instinctively sprang to her feet, her posture coiled like a spring, ready to strike. *That's why they won't come near you, Lex.* She relaxed at the sight of one of the guards Brooks had posted with keeping an eye on her – the older one; the one who'd sniggered at her waspish comment to his partner. She looked past him. His partner was standing on a raised ridge of broken concrete, a few feet above her position; his weapon lingering in her direction. "Will your partner be alright with that?" she asked, a little more tartly than she'd intended.

The guard followed her gaze, seemingly oblivious to her blunt tone. "He's quite happy where he is. Me, on the other hand, I'd rather sit closer to the heat. This place gets mighty cold at night."

Lex looked up. "How can you tell? He seems to do nothing but scowl."

"You get used to it," he said, chuckling. "May I?" he asked, gesturing to the fire.

"Be my guest," she said, retaking her seat.

He nodded and took a seat next to her – out of arms reach, she noticed. She smiled.

"Something funny?" the guard asked.

"Never mind." She pointed a thumb to the guard's partner. "I suppose your partner still thinks I'm a danger?"

"Aren't you?"

"If I was going to cause anyone any harm, wouldn't you think I would've done it already?" she asked.

The guard shrugged. "I'm not sure, I don't know anything about you... aside from." He looked up. "You know... your antics up top."

She raised an eyebrow. "Or he thinks I might escape." She raised her hand to the rest of the compound. "It's not like I'd be able to find my way out of this warren."

The guard looked dubious. "I may not know you personally, but I don't believe for a second you would find it difficult to find a way out of the compound." He arced his head towards the other guard. "He's my son. He's young and keen to impress Brooks. He's just being cautious is all, don't take it personally."

"Fair enough," she said. She chose not to answer his previous statement about her not being able to find a way out of the compound. During her 'tour' with Brooks, he'd taken her through different parts of the compound. They'd traversed through the ventilation systems, water filtration and waste rooms, and finally ending the tour in the recreational halls. Several avenues for escape had become evident to her. Brooks hadn't spoken much outside of explaining details on whatever room or hall they were in. She was relieved, as she'd expected him to spend the entire time convincing her to stay. She couldn't help but be slightly impressed by Sapien-Republic's operation, her initial judgement proving premature.

She was broken from her reverie as the guard outstretched his arm towards her. "I'm Jackson," he said. "Francis Jackson." He nodded to his son. "That's Billy."

She looked down at his hand, crisscrossed with more than a few scars. She reluctantly removed her hand from the confines of her blanket and shook it briefly. "I'm Lex."

He nodded, an amused grin spreading across his face. "Pleased to meet you, Lex. I like the name... better than calling you 'the woman'."

Lex shrugged. "Makes no difference to me. How long have you and your son been down here?"

"Since the beginning," Jackson said, the pride evident in his voice. "We were one of the first to follow Brooks and the doctor."

"And how long ago was that? How did you find this place?"

Jackson blew out a breath. "Going on ten years... damn, is that right? Yeah, about ten years.

204

I didn't find this place, myself; that was down to Brooks and the doctor. Both me and my son found ourselves under the unfortunate scrutiny of NewHaven. I used to work in analysis, citizen membership and populace control. One day I put in a report to my superiors about the numbers not adding up. Thought it was a simple clerical error. The next thing I know, NewHaven spooks are banging on my door and hauling me and my family out the door."

He shuffled along the concrete block, closing the gap between them. He'd clearly made his mind up with regard to her threat, which she appreciated. "I don't want to say this too loud… you know, with Billy being within earshot. It's not good to remind him of the events that transpired that fucking day. Brooks and the doctor had just begun their purpose. We were the first citizens Sapiens-Republic rescued. They caused a distraction, enough to catch the spooks off-guard. Me and Billy got out, but my wife…" He fell silent, unable to get the rest out. He grimaced, shaking his head. "Anyway, we managed to escape. Brooks brought us down here and we've been here ever since."

She didn't really know what to say, deciding it would probably be insensitive to probe into what happened to Jackson's wife – as it was obvious. "What about Brooks? How did this all start with him?" she asked, changing the subject.

"Ah, Brooks. Well, I don't think he'll mind me telling you this. He used to work for NewHaven – intelligence. He worked a small team infiltrating possible terror threats."

"He was a spook?" she asked, unable to keep the amusement from her voice.

Jackson chuckled. "I know, the irony isn't lost on me either. It was the reason he was able to get me and Billy out." He paused, regaining his train of thought. "Tell me, Lex, have you heard of a man called Aaron Trent?" She shook her head. "I'd be surprised if you had. Trent was a low-ranking member of the Sanctum-One council, at NewHaven. He worked tirelessly behind the scenes on civil rights, slowly gaining support within NewHaven to reorganise the hierarchy of our society. In many ways he is the true father of our movement – he started it all. It was his idea that instead of our lives being governed by a Prime, it should instead be governed by a council, with each member having equal control of power."

Lex scoffed. "Doesn't sound so different to the Prime's Inner-Sanctum."

Jackson shook his head in a way he would a child who hadn't quite learned the lesson. "The difference is that the council members would be nominated and voted in by the public, only staying in office for a maximum of five years."

It was an interesting idea, she thought. "So, how does Brooks come into this?" she asked, wondering where he was going with this.

"Trent was Brooks' father-in-law."

Lex raised her eyebrows, intrigued. Jackson continued.

"Fearing Trent had a member of his family firmly rooted within the intelligence core, the Proxy began to fear for his position; becoming

206

concerned with Trent's growing influence. Having a man on the inside – privy to a lot of sensitive information – was a risk too far for our 'glorious' second-in-command. So, he tasked Brooks to persuade Trent to attend a meeting with the Proxy and several members of the Inner-Sanctum, to discuss his proposals. It was a test of Brooks' loyalty to the state over his family. Brooks succeeded in bringing Trent to the meeting. Once ensconced in the Proxy's office... things turned for the worst.

They dragged both of them down to the Proxy's secret bunker, accessed from his office, where Trent was worked on by the bleeders." Jackson shuddered at the thought. Lex, on the other hand, knew all too well what that entailed. She absentmindedly trailed a hand down her arm, knowing where each and every scar was and how she'd got them. Jackson noticed, but chose not to comment.

"After they'd got all the information they could; details of all those working close to Trent, the Proxy ordered Brooks to kill his father-in-law."

Lex slowly raised her hand to her mouth, disgusted. "And did he?"

Jackson's pained look said it all. "He had no choice."

Lex slapped her thigh. "What do you mean 'had no choice'? Of course he had a choice, for fuck's sake."

Jackson looked at her with pity. "Brooks was handed a gun and told if he didn't, his wife and two daughters would be brought to the bleeders."

Cold rage burned through her veins. She was beginning to see what drove Brooks and Sapien-Republic. The Inner-Sanctum were a disease in need of being scourged from existence. "What happened to his family?" she asked through gritted teeth, suspecting what the answer was going to be.

"After he killed Trent, Brooks was followed home by the Proxy's second – a man by the name of Marr. Brooks got home to find his wife and daughters had already been murdered. Before he could shed a tear for them, investigators from the SPD turned up, presumably called in ahead by Marr. Brooks just managed to escape, going on the run until he found this place."

Lex looked down at her hands. They were balled tightly into fists. She was starting to see this place in a new light. When she was first brought here, she assumed no one could compare their pain to her own. The reality couldn't have been further from the truth. Looking to the faces of those congregating in their little groups – laughing, talking, enjoying the solace of each other's company – she didn't see firebrands and anarchists, she saw refugees; persecuted because they didn't fit the mould imposed by the Inner-Sanctum. She suspected each and every one of them had a similar tale to Jackson's… or her own.

She suddenly felt insignificant, but at the same time, she felt a kindred spirit with these people – who'd suffered as she had.

Can I trust these people to help me rid Sanctum-one of the Inner-sanctum and its toxic influence? They may even be able to help me find Julian's murderer.

Then the face of little Kat flooded to her mind. Taking on the Inner-Sanctum was dangerous. Could she risk innocent lives such as hers, just to satisfy her thirst for blood and revenge? She grew frustrated. When she was hunting members of the Inner-Sanctum, it had been simple. The sudden intertwining of Sapien-Republic's fight with her own was muddying the waters, filling her head with uncertainty.

She looked up to the 'ceiling' of the compound, still amazed it lay beneath the city. It posed a question. "You don't just 'find' this place, Jackson. Someone must have known of this place for some time—"

"—They did, or to be specific, I did," a voice called out, interrupting them.

Lex and Jackson turned to find the doctor, standing beside Billy. He looked down at them; a sad smile etched across his features. "I'm an old friend of Jonathon's. I knew his family..." He trailed off for a moment, gently shaking his head. "I kept him hidden until the time was right to bring him down here. My father kept old maps of the previous city; the city Sanctum-One was built on." He chuckled, climbing down the ridge. "If NewHaven had ever found out my father had them in his possession... I shudder to think."

"So, what are your plans for the Proxy?" She pointed to Jackson. "I admire your tactics to get me to stay."

"All will be explained in good time, my dear." He held up something wrapped in thick blankets.

209

"Your combat-suit. I've made some adjustments. Also, I've made you a new eyepatch... well, it's more of a mask, now. It's the reason I've taken so long. If you would accompany me, Brooks and I are about to have dinner and we'd be delighted if you could join us."

Lex stood, interested. "How could I refuse?"

XXVIII

Everything was a blur when Hall opened her eyes.
Her surroundings were dull and tinged with blue,
interrupted intermittently by sudden flashes of
bright light which hurt her eyes. She jostled back
and forth as though invisible hands surrounded
her, taking it in turns to push her in different
directions; like being in a boat in a rough swell –
it did her immense feeling of nausea no favours.
Her head ached, which was exasperated by the
constant droning noise that seemed to come from
everywhere. She tried to raise her hands to touch
her throbbing temples, but found that they were
secured behind her back and fixed to the seat she
was sitting on – chains presumably, as she heard
the distinct sound of them clinking as she moved.

Her body was slouched forward at an odd
angle. She suddenly heard voices; hushed tones a
few feet in front of her. She looked up; her neck –
tender and sore – added its complaint to the
cacophony coursing through her body. She could
make out two dark shapes amidst the blue; one
was significantly larger than the other. Most of the
noise – from what her scrambled brains could
make out – came from the larger of the two
shapes; louder and more aggressive than the softer
tones of the smaller shape. She thought she
recognised them.

She tried to speak, but all that came out was an
incoherent moan. Her lips were sticky, resisting to

come apart from each other. She stretched her mouth in an effort to separate them. She instantly regretted it. A sharp pain lanced across her mouth, quickly followed by wetness which had an acrid, coppery taste to it. The two shapes ceased making their noise. The larger one drew closer. He reeked of onions and garlic; the stench causing her gorge to rise in her throat. She recoiled in a bid to get away from the putrid aroma, but she was locked firmly in place.

She felt a small prick on her arm. The veil of distortion, muddying her senses, ebbed, before finally falling away. Her whole body tensed, as what felt like electricity, passed violently through her. She screamed in agony, bucking in her fixed position, twisting uncontrollably in her chair until the pain dissipated to a tolerable throb. Her head felt like it had been squeezed into a helmet designed for a child. The sensation made her want to vomit.

"Wakey, wakey," a cruel voice called, jovially.

She sought out the sudden call, snapping her head in its direction which sent another wave of nausea to wash over her. This time she hadn't the strength to keep the bile at bay as she vomited.

"Aw, for fuck's sake," the cruel voice boomed in disgust. "It's a good thing we've not got long to go."

She remained hunched over until she'd heaved her last, her stomach spasming uncontrollably. She looked up to see the familiar face of Charlie Deacon. He looked at her with a mixture of pity and anger; his eyes boring into her own; his brows knitted. Sitting beside Charlie, was the source of the cruel voice. She finally recognised where she knew it from. It was his partner – the officer whom she'd given a dressing down to on the Freedom Bridge – though it had been merely days ago, So much had happened, to Hall, it felt more like weeks. He was waving a long tube in his right hand and smiling; his yellowed teeth showing between moist, bulbous lips in a malevolent sneer.

"Smelling salts for the new age," he said, appraising the tube with mock interest. "One jab of this could wake the dead."

"Where am I being taken to?" she asked Charlie, ignoring his partner.

But his partner wasn't finished. He drew his other hand back and slapped her hard across the face. Her head clattered against the steel-caged partition. She cried out in agony. She thought she heard Charlie shouting at his partner, but the blow had set her wits into a spin-cycle. She groaned, using all her will to stay conscious.

"...fuck off, Charlie," he said, grabbing Hall roughly by the hair and pulling her as close as her bonds would allow her. "Don't you think I've forgotten what happened on the bridge, you little bitch. I'm going to ask that spook if I can be present during your time at NewHaven."

"Melrose, let her go before I knock your fucking teeth out," Charlie growled, reaching forward and grabbing his partner's wrist.

Melrose opened his mouth, giving Charlie a belligerent glare, then closed it again – his brain too slow to retort with a witty remark, she presumed. He let go of her hair and sat back. "I don't know why you're protecting her, Deacon.

She's a fucking cop-killer, a captain *and* her partner, no less." He pointed a chubby, nicotine-stained finger in her direction. "She's going down for a long time and you know what happens to cops that go to lockup?"

Charlie ignored his partner and leaned in close. "Veronica, what happened? How were you found in the captain's house, standing over his and Alon Reid's body?"

She tried to piece together the events that had led her to the captain's house, but her mind was a mess. "He asked me to come," she said, her voice pleading.

"Mercer? Reid? Who?" Charlie asked.

"The captain... I... I didn't know anything about Reid. As far as we knew, he was still being held at NewHaven."

"Why did the captain want you at his home, Veronica?"

"She was probably fuck..."

Charlie turned around to face Melrose. "One more word out of you and I'll throw you out of this fucking van." He faced Hall; satisfied Melrose wasn't going to add anything further. "Tell me something, Veronica. Reid's body was..." He grimaced, shaking his head in disgust. "What did you do to him?"

Anger began to push through the fog her mind was languishing in. She couldn't believe he assumed she'd been the one who'd butchered Reid. "Are you fucking kidding me, Charlie? Reid was there when I arrived... I'd only been in his house ten minutes when you lot turned up and that fucking spook bashed my head in."

214

Charlie narrowed his eyes. His expression suggested he wanted to believe her, but it was fighting with the cop in him – the logical part. She had to admit it didn't look good. "I'll ask again, why were you at his home?"

"I can't tell you; I don't want you involved in this," she said, frustrated with the predicament she was now in. She couldn't tell him even if she wanted to. If they were alone, maybe, but in front of his partner, no chance.

Charlie sat back. "The spook said you're linked to the woman; that you're in league with her. He claims you're her contact within the SPD. Is that true."

As much as she liked Charlie, she'd lost her patience. "Seriously? It's me that's had the bash to the head, Charlie. The woman? Really?"

He ignored the jibe. "What were you doing on the Freedom Bridge the other night?"

"I was following a lead."

"What lead? Did Captain Mercer give you the order? Reid?"

She suddenly felt weary. She sighed, letting her head bob forward. "I can't tell you, Charlie."

He closed his eyes and shook his head; disappointed. "Have it your way then."

They travelled the rest of the way in silence, the smell of her vomit permeating the air. Charlie didn't look at her. Melrose, however, sat back, his large frame resting against the wall of the van. He remained silent. He didn't have to; in his eyes, she was guilty; her fate already sealed.

When the van stopped, they unhooked the cuffs from the bar behind her seat – Melrose unlinked the chain a little rougher than was necessary, scraping her wrists in the process. They escorted her into the precinct which, despite the severity of her current predicament, was a damn sight better than if she'd been taken to Newhaven. The image of Alon Reid's bloody corpse rose to the forefront of her mind. What had he done to deserve such a fate?

She'd never know.

It broke her heart as she was booked and taken to one of the interrogation rooms, as though she were just another common criminal. Colleagues she'd had drinks with – worked cases on – glared at her with contempt and hate; already labelling her guilty. One officer spat on her as she passed, calling her 'a fucking cop-killer'. She was in tears by the time she was dumped unceremoniously into a chair and cuffed to the desk. Charlie had watched, unable to keep the pained expression from his eyes – his partner's expression the polar opposite.

After ten minutes alone, the door was pushed open. Banks stepped into the room, smiling at her from behind a scribe he was holding to his chest. "Investigator Hall, how's the head?"

His nonchalant jest at the predicament he'd put her in was too much to take. She screamed and thrashed against her bonds – the futility lashing out forgotten in her desperation to get to the spook and tear his eyes out of their sockets. What made it worse was the pitying look he gave her as he patiently waited until her fit of rage had passed. "You fucking bastard," she roared. "You killed them."

216

Banks tutted, wagging a finger. "That is a nasty temper you have Miss Hall. I'm glad you're cuffed to that table. I wouldn't want to end up like Reid and Mercer."

She glared at him, sitting back down. Instead of sitting opposite her, he turned and poked his head out the door. "You can leave us alone, officers. NewHaven will take things from here." He paused, presumably waiting for whoever was behind the one-way glass to vacate before he closed the door. He smiled down at her, casually strolling over to a corner and switching off the camera. He waited until the red light above the lens died, before turning to face his prisoner. "That's better," he said, approaching the table and taking a seat. He pocketed his scribe. "Nice and private."

"Why bring me here? If you're going to take me to the same place as Reid, why the charade?" she asked.

He nodded, approvingly. "Good question, Miss Hall. For appearance's sake. If I just dragged you off to NewHaven, there'd be questions I'd rather not have to answer. It's less suspicious if I bring you here first, to be paraded as a traitor in front of your entire precinct, then ship you off to NewHaven." He leaned forward. "Now tell me what exactly you and that fucking captain had on Alexandra Moretti?"

Hall didn't answer. Instead, she spat in his face.

For just a moment, fury flashed in his eyes, then it was quickly suppressed. He chuckled, fetching a tissue from his pocket and wiping the spittle from his brow. He sighed, then in a fit of speed, he lunged forward and grabbed her by the hair. He smashed her face against the table; driving her forehead onto its surface. Her vision flashed white, as the inside of her cheek mashed against her teeth. She cried out as fresh lances of agony coursed through her skull. She spat blood on the table and groaned. She felt his breath on her ear. "Now listen to me, you little cunt, you can tell me here and I'll have you shipped off to the nearest prison, or tell me later at NewHaven. It's your choice. In the end, you'll give me what I need."

"It doesn't matter where you take me... I'm dead either way." She spat some more blood onto the table, surprisingly finding a defiant resolve. She screwed her face into a scowl. "I hope Moretti finds you and puts a bullet in your fucking head."

For the first time, fear flashed in the spook's eyes. "This mess has caused the deaths of a police captain, a senior investigator, and countless innocent citizens... One more cop isn't going to make a difference if it means drawing this sorry affair to a satisfying conclusion." He pulled out his scribe, placing it against his ear. "It's Banks, have my cruiser brought around the back. I'm taking her in."

XXIX

Lex sighed with relief as she climbed out of the coarse boiler-suit. She winced at the small persistent protests her wounds and aching muscles still gave her – despite the doctor's treatments. She threw it disdainfully onto a nearby table, feeling tempted to pick it up and discard it into the closest fire. She looked down balefully at the mess the garment had left her skin in. The rough material had caused her flesh to break out in angry red patches which itched like crazy – ironically, they were too tender to touch, in spite of the overwhelming urge to claw at them with her nails. Also, she'd wished she'd asked Oliver for a sports bra or, at the very least, some strips of bandage to protect her nipples from the constant chafing; each an angry red made more prominent against the backdrop of her pale skin.

Her bandages, however, had remained unmolested by the boiler-suit. She made a quick appraisal of them, thankful none of them leaked any blood. They were frayed at the edges but were clean and tightly woven. The doctor knew his stuff; he'd done a flawless job patching up her battered body.

After her discussion with the guard, Jackson, Oliver had escorted her to the compound's command centre. As they'd made their way through the labyrinth of shacks, huts, and lean-tos, Lex noted there was a significant reduction in the stares and quiet whisperings of the residents of the compound than there had been when she'd first been ushered through its grounds, to which she was thankful for. It also helped that the lighting had been dimmed – presumably to conserve the compounds energy reserves. Once past the security protocols, at the entrance gate, she'd been led to a small room – the one she now occupied – where Oliver had informed her, he had something to look into. He'd promised she wouldn't be kept waiting too long and hurried out the door, his coat flapping at his back.

She knelt down to peer beneath the door, not surprised to find a pair of boots standing on the other side. *They want me to work with them, but still don't trust fully me…* She rose to her feet and walked over to a free-standing mirror where her repaired and newly improved – so the doctor claimed – combat suit was; draped over the top. She unfolded it, appraising his handiwork. The tears and holes which had peppered it were now gone. She drew it up close for a more detailed inspection, amazed she couldn't pinpoint any exact location where it had been repaired; there was an absence of stitch marks or even the slightest hints of patchwork, which she found astonishing. Also, where the suit had been completely black before, it was now laced with stripes running down in angry-looking shards; a deep crimson in colour. She squinted in suspicion.

If this is the same suit, I'll resurface, up top, and become the next Prime of Sanctum-One.

She was disturbed from her scepticism, as a knock resounded from the door. "Come in," she said, walking behind the mirror. The hinges creaked as the door swung open. Heavy footfalls thumped on the rickety, uneven floorboards.

"Lex?" Brooks called. He sounded confused – and if she wasn't mistaken – a little uneasy from her absence. She couldn't stop a smile creeping up her cheeks. He sighed in relief as he must have spotted her bare feet below the rim of the mirror. His steps grew closer to the mirror, halting two feet away. "The doctor sends his apologies. He won't be joining us in the mess quarters. He'll join us after we've had a bite to eat." He paused, as though trying to find the right words. "Something's came up… something that might be of interest to you."

"Fine, just give me a sec," she said, pulling the suit up to her waist. She poked her head out. Brooks stood with his arms crossed; they looked a little grubby like he'd been tinkering with a motor engine. He wore the same type of boiler-suit as the one she'd been wearing, though it had been rolled down and tied at the waist. She couldn't help notice his toned torso, beneath the thin fabric of his t-shirt. "What news has come up?"

A thin smile crept across his face. "I'll explain in the mess." He nodded to her exposed shoulder, and then turned, heading for the door. "Pull the rest of that up and follow me. I'm starving."

~

Lex flexed her arms and performed the various stretches she usually did before she ventured out to hunt, in a state of shock and awe. The combat suit felt like a second skin; both light and pliant to her movements. "What the fuck is this made of?" she asked, from beneath the suit's hood. "It feels like I'm wearing a coat of paint."

"Looks like it too," Brooks muttered. He was leaning against one of the countertops, keeping a safe distance from her kicks and swings. She suspected he was deliberately averting his gaze from the way her new battle attire clung to her.

She ignored the comment. "As much as this gives me a lot more manoeuvrability, it won't mean shit if I'm more susceptible to damage." She stopped moving, eyeing him dubiously. "Inner-Sanctum thugs tend to welcome me with knives bared and guns blazing." Brooks chuckled. She raised her eyebrows. "Something funny?"

He shook his head, his eyes meeting hers. "A little. Oliver said you would say that." He turned and opened one of the drawers – stacked in rows underneath the countertop. He pulled out, what looked like, a pair of goggles. He threw them over to her, which she caught deftly. "Believe it or not, but it's more impervious to damage than it was before."

She eyed him quizzically. "Before? Correct me if I'm wrong, but I assume my combat suit… you know, the one I was wearing when you found me in the park… is lying in the trash." she said.

Brooks caught the meaning of her tone and grinned. "When did you twig?"

She gestured to herself, her arms wide. "I think I might've bought it if Oliver had put a few random stitches or patches on it. No one could take my old suit in the sorry state it was in and turn it into this. No way."

Brooks shrugged. "Fair enough. Well, as I was saying, about ninety per cent of the suit is nano-web smart-frame."

"Nano what?"

"It's a state-of-the-art diagnostic armour. It won't bounce bullets back at its recipient, but it should hold off most knife attacks, and protect your body from falls – which will be handy given your penchant for flamboyant exits."

She narrowed her eyes, but there was humour in it. "I assume you're referring to my escape from the Trammel building?"

"Which one?" he asked, a wry smile creeping up his cheeks.

She shrugged. "Good point."

He raised a hand up to his stubbled chin. "Now that we're on the subject, how *did* you manage to jump through his window without ending up with your brains scattered across the sidewalk below?"

She tapped her finger against the side of her nose. *Got to leave some mystery.* She pinched the material on her arm, making sure she got some skin underneath. She felt the nip on her flesh as if she wasn't wearing anything at all. It did not fill her with confidence. "Forgive me if I remain sceptical."

"Put the mask on," Doctor Oliver said, standing in the doorway.

Lex nodded a greeting to the doctor and removed her hood. She slipped the mask over her head. "You do realise I've only the one eye?"

Oliver rolled his eyes, ignoring the sarcasm, and stepped closer. He reached a hand towards her, then stopped as she flinched. "May I?" he asked. She nodded, feeling a little embarrassed.

The doctor has treated your wounds. Christ, he's seen you naked. What's the matter with you?

He reached up and flipped a tiny switch situated behind her ear. She was beginning to doubt him when a surge of electrical energy coursed through her body. The glass that had covered her eye ignited with analytics. Suddenly Oliver and Brooks' forms were outlined with a stream of information. She read through them, realising it was their physical attributes; breathing patterns, weak points, height, weight etc.

"Try moving now," Oliver said.

She took a step back from him, giving herself some space. She resumed her stretches and exercises, as she had done before, only this time she felt quicker, stronger. "This is amazing," she exclaimed. Oliver smiled, but Brooks had a dark look across his brow.

"There's a switch on the other side of the mask, it switches your view to night-vision; infrared; motion sensor; and security system detection," Oliver said.

Lex turned to him, intrigued. "Security system detection?"

Oliver clasped his hands together. "The mask can detect trip sensors, keypad locked doors, and camera locations."

The Inner-Sanctum won't know what's hit them.

Amidst her delight at her advanced equipment, a few questions surfaced in her mind. She turned to Brooks. "How did you acquire this technology? I mean… as much as your compound is functional and operational, the technology is nowhere near as advanced as what's in this suit."

Brooks clasped his fingers together, a look of sorrow crossing his features. "The technology and the equipment to build that suit were acquired at great sacrifice. We lost many good men and woman to get it." He grimaced, as though he were reliving whatever had transpired to ascertain the equipment.

"Where did you get it?" she asked.

"NewHaven," Oliver declared.

Her eyes widened. "NewHaven? How? When?"

"It doesn't matter now, it's done. What concerns me, is what you're going to do next. Will you join our cause?"

Lex thought about what Jackson had told her. Brooks – and the majority of the compounds populous – had been through a lot of shit – about as much shit as she had herself. Their cause was a noble one and no mistake, but it didn't dispel one of the questions she had about her current situation and the great lengths Sapien-Republic had gone to kit her out in this advanced combat suit.

"Before I decide anything, tell me why you're doing this? Why do you need me in particular?" She lowered her gaze to the suit. "Your friend, Li. She's about my size and weight. She looks like she could handle herself in a fight. Why not her?"

Oliver smiled. "We need your help to try and create a better wor—"

"—cut the bullshit, Oliver. I'm not asking for the poster-boy routine. I'm asking Brooks a simple question." She turned to face the Sapien-Republic leader. "All I'm asking for is some honesty. Why do you need *me?* I know for a fact you don't trust me." She pointed to the door. "The guards stationed on the other side of this door tell me as much, regardless of the fact that Oliver fixed me up with the suit and all." She pointed a finger at Brooks, beginning to feel a little pissed off with them beating about the bush. "You of all people should be able to relate with the shit I've been through."

Sadness, mixed with anger flashed across his eyes. "I'll presume you've been told how I ended up down here? That I had to shoot my father-in-law to save my family only to find them dead anyway?" he growled, his hands balling into fists. His gaze flicked to Oliver. "Did he tell you?"

Oliver shook his head emphatically. "I can assure you; it wasn't me. I'd guess it was probably Jackson. I found him with her, earlier."

"Then you can understand the anger and the drive that keeps me going. To see this through. I don't have time for friends, or causes… only vengeance," she said, raising her voice.

Brooks didn't rise to her anger, he merely took a deep breath and puffed it out, his shoulders sagging slightly. He looked at her with pity. "You're right, I do understand. I was where you are right now. My mind was full of hate; bitter and twisted. And let me tell you, Alexandra, it'll only lead to one place, and that's the grave." He walked past her and stood beside Oliver. He put a hand on the doctor's shoulder, an expression of affection on his face. "Oliver helped me see past it, that I could still contribute to my father-in-law's plans. To finish what he started and make my wife and daughters' proud."

Lex raised her head, refusing to believe there was a future beyond the pain and grief that coursed through her veins. *Let them have their revolution,* she thought bitterly. "I know the two of you are helping these people, and I commend you for it, I really do. They've got nowhere else to go and I've seen what this government does to citizens who don't fit the criteria for 'Vonn's vision'."

"Where are you going with this?" Brooks asked.

"She took a step towards them, her feet barely making a sound. "I want to hear it from your own lips that you're not interested in me joining your cause. You only need a blunt instrument; someone who's expendable; a grunt who can get the job done.

"Alexandra we—" Oliver began to say, but Brooks cut him off.

"—you've more or less stated to us you don't want to be saved, to join our cause, so yes, in many ways we need a blunt instrument to get the job done. What does it matter?"

"It matters plenty. If I help you, I want to know where I stand. I don't want to be put under any false pretences regarding my role in your plans. I want the truth at all times, no bullshit. The last

227

thing I want is to be in a situation where I need backup and it doesn't arrive because I've not been informed of all the details."

Brooks nodded, seeming to see her point. "When we came across you at the docks – floating face-down in the water – we were in the middle of a reconnaissance mission. As much as we'd succeeded in finding a safe haven for our people, that's as far as we got. We were trying to gain some intel on their operation; to find an opportunity for infiltration. Once we witnessed what happened to you and your son, I thought it was our way in; a gift from the heavens; finally, a key to the door.

So, we took you back here, and during your recuperation, we did some digging on your background; we found out who you were, what you could do." He turned to Oliver. "Simon?"

The doctor began to pace in front of her. "The original plan was to give you a new identity and plant you within NewHaven. From your extensive records, we knew you'd be more than capable. What made this possible was the fact that you were officially dead as far as the Proxy was concerned. It was the best chance we'd ever had to infiltrate the Inner-Sanctum."

"In the past," Brooks said. "We tried to use our own operatives to carry out this mission, but soon enough, as each and every one of them turned up on our doorstep – butchered by the bleeders – we began to suspect the Proxy held records of all those missing in the city. It's the only explanation as to why all of our operatives were blown

228

whenever they got too close – al the Proxy had to do was run their name through his list."

"With you being 'dead', the chances of discovery would be less likely," Oliver said.

"Then you escaped," Brooks muttered under his breath, but she heard him all the same.

"Then I escaped," she said, coldly, her stare intense.

"Where did you go?" Oliver asked. "We know your only family is an uncle in the projects, but for weeks his apartment was kept under close surveillance. How did you evade capture?"

Lex shrugged. "I did what I had to do. For your information, you're not the only people in this city living below the radar. Working for the SPD taught me some valuable intel; Sanctum one has a vast community of dubious individuals living in plain sight. How'd you think I got all my equipment, my fake identity."

Brooks held out his hands. "So, what do you propose we do, given our situation?"

Lex leaned forward, a thin smile playing on her lips. "Contact."

"I'm sorry?" Oliver said.

"We can work together to bring those bastards down, but that's as far as it goes. If you have a piece of intel, share it with me, I'll do the same. Once the job's done, I'm done. You can enjoy your new world, there'll be no place in it for the likes of me," she said, surprised that she didn't feel sad about it.

I'll maybe see Julian again, once the dust has settled.

"You can't mean that?" Oliver said.

She nodded, her lips pursing, her face marred with conviction. "I do. I've nothing left to live for but to eliminate the cancer which has eroded this city for far too long."

Brooks' face flashed with disgust and pity. "Fine with me, if that's how you feel." His brows crossed at the admonishing look from Oliver. "Don't look at me like that, Simon. She asked for honesty." He faced her. "How do we begin?"

Lex's gaze rested on Oliver. "Well, first off. I'd like my scribe back."

Oliver paused for a moment, his eyes flicking to Brooks, who nodded. He sighed, fishing her scribe from inside his coat pocket. She walked to the furthest corner of the room and booted it up. There was a voice mail message from her 'source'. She listened intently at the news from her uncle, switched the scribe off, and re-joined Brooks and Oliver. "So, what's this information I'd be interested in?"

Oliver glanced over to Brooks once more, who sighed, exasperated. "Tell her."

"Well, there's been a development. According to the Sanctum news broadcast, it seems you've had help from inside the SPD."

"Veronica Hall."

"How did you know that? Was she your source?" Brooks asked.

Lex shook her head. "A contact of mine left a message on my scribe. Hall's been investigating my background, outside her remit. Doctor, do you have an image of her?"

Oliver fumbled with the pockets of his coat until he found his scribe. He swiped at the screen until he found what he was looking for. "Here she is. She looks very young," he said, passing her the scribe.

Lex raised her eyes in surprise from the scared, confused face on the screen, staring back at her. The last time she'd seen that face was from their standoff at the Trammel building. It was the investigator who had blown her cover, inevitably leading to her eventual plunge into the river. "I've met her. She was at the Trammel building... the second time. She saw through my disguise."

Brooks drew closer to take a look. He smelled of sweat and engine oil – not all that unpleasant. *Never mind what he smells like, Lex. Get your head back in the game.* "So, she's not your contact?" he asked.

Lex shook her head, taking a step back from Brooks. "No. As far as I'm aware, she works under Reid – the lead investigator; one of the Inner-Sanctum's minions.

Oliver took the scribe back, secreting it inside his coat. "Well, Reid's not going to be a problem."

"How's that?"

"He's dead, so is his and Hall's superior – Captain Mercer. Hall was discovered at Mercer's residence, standing over their bodies. She's been arrested for their murder."

Lex was confused. As far as she knew, it was only Reid who'd been on the Inner-Sanctum's books. She doubted Mercer was – she would have known about it. As for this Veronica Hall, the fact she'd been pestering Geno for information on her disappearance – without orders to do so – raised more questions than it answered. The investigator's predicament was very familiar to her own origins in this sorry affair.

"Why would she murder her partner... and her boss?" Brooks said, his eyes roaming the room in search of an answer. "I mean, I'd believe it if she was working for you. No offence, Lex. But Reid was Inner-Sanctum."

A suspicion was beginning to form in her mind, and it wasn't a good one. "The only possible explanation is that they found out she'd been digging where she shouldn't. This is their way of silencing her."

"How do you know that?" Brooks asked.

She thought back to her own investigations into the mysterious disappearances in Sanctum-One. "Because the same thing happened to me." She made for the door. She knew there was a guard standing on the other side of it, but she didn't care. "I have to help her. It's happening again. To someone else."

Oliver made to block her, then thought better of it. "Alexandra, you can't—"

"—can't do what? I'll do what I fucking want." She stopped and turned to face the two of them. She unfastened her suit and pulled it down to her waist, revealing the collage of scar tissue running all over her body. The two of them turned away from her. Her breasts were exposed and she presumed they were averting their gaze out of respect. She didn't have time. "Cut the blushing bullshit and look at my body," she barked. "This is what those fucking bastards did to me. This is what awaits Veronica Hall if I don't help her."

232

Anger flashed in Brooks' eyes as he took in the mess her body had been left in. She was glad his expression was devoid of pity. Instead, a dark shadow of determination crossed his features. "She's right, Simon. We can't let that happen. She could also provide us with valuable information. Lex, what do you need?"

Lex pulled her suit back over her shoulders and fastened it. She slipped the hood over her head and pulled the door open. "I need to get out of this compound and back on the streets. It's time I gave this suit a test drive."

XXX

Hall's hands were shaking as she held them out in front of her; quivering incessantly. The chain which linked her cuffs to the large ring embedded into the table rattled – it's what her shattered nerves would sound like if she could hear them. She had chewed her fingernails down to the quick; a symptom of her dawning realisation – which also had her stomach roiling in a state of perpetual turmoil – she was well and truly fucked.

Banks had a hand in this, more than a hand, she thought bitterly. The spook had orchestrated this to cover up... what? She didn't know. There was no other explanation for it, or at least, none so screamingly obvious. He and his department had been holding Reid at NewHaven ever since Moretti had slipped through their fingers at the Trammel building. The one thing she was having trouble piecing together, was how on earth he'd got Reid's body into Mercer's home unseen? It had taken her just under thirty minutes from ending the call with Mercer to arriving at his home. Mercer hadn't given her any reason to suggest Banks was with him at the time of their last conversation.

She scrunched her face, slamming her fists down onto the table; her blood boiling with frustration. She could run through theories until she was blue in the face. It wasn't going to help her – especially not in her current predicament as there was no way she could disprove the evidence heaped against her. Besides, no one seemed to want to find out the truth of the matter.

The disgusted looks from her colleagues said as much. Even Charlie Deacon's. The memory of his expression as they'd sat opposite from each other in the back of the police transport hub – a mixture of shock and betrayal – made her skin crawl with shame and helplessness. But there was something else; something floating around the whirlwind of emotions she was feeling. It was a feeling that was causing her hands to ball into tight fists. The feeling was anger. Sure, she didn't know Charlie intimately, but enough that his reaction to her charges – his apparent acceptance of her guilt – made her want to vomit with rage. Surely, he knew she wasn't capable of this, wouldn't he?

She pushed the fury to the back of her mind. In her current state, she needed to think, to try and figure a way out of this mess. She needed to get out of her restraints and as far away from the precinct as she could before Banks took her to NewHaven. She thought of poor Alon's eviscerated corpse. The wounds he'd suffered weren't fresh – the stench said as much. The thought of ending up like Reid threatened to overwhelm her; reduce her to a blubbering wreck.

She could still feel the tears she had shed after Banks had left her alone in the room to find out why it was taking so long for his cruiser to be brought around the rear of the building. Her misery had poured out of her in great torrents; running down her face in an endless cascade of torment and distress. She glanced across to the one-way mirror, her vision still blurry from her weeping. She almost didn't recognise the bedraggled, sorry state staring back at her; eyes red-rimmed and puffy. For all she knew, Banks was standing on the other side of it, laughing at her.

Get a grip of yourself, she thought. She had to find a way out of this, a way to prove her innocence – possibly shed light on the spook's involvement in the process – before he carted her off to NewHaven. But how? She pulled at her bonds, the metal rubbing against her skin.

She was startled as the door suddenly swung open. Banks came into the room, that same self-assured smile spread across his face that made her want to rip his lips off. He wasn't alone. A duty officer accompanied him – she noted he refused to make eye contact with her. "Miss Hall," Banks said, cheerily, moving to the side as the duty officer unlocked her cuffs from the table. "Our chariot has arrived." He turned to the officer. "If you would be so kind and make sure the prisoner's hands are restrained behind her back. I can escort her from here."

The duty officer looked unsure. "Are you sure, sir? I think it would be best if you didn't accompany her alone – given her charges."

A flash of irritation flitted across his eyes for a second, only to be replaced by his aura of self-assurance. "Duly noted, Officer. Restrain her as I've commanded and leave us." The officer paused for a moment, before shrugging and doing as he was ordered. Once cuffed, the duty officer left – but not before casting a scowl back in her direction. "Now," Banks said, satisfied. "Shall we?" he asked, rhetorically, grabbing her roughly by the arm and ushering her out of the room.

They passed through several of the lockup checkpoints in silence. The officer's manning each of the desks, treating her similarly to the duty officer who'd cuffed her in the interrogation room. It wasn't until they were alone in the stairwell leading to the rear of the precinct, Banks decided to break his silence.

"You know, it doesn't have to be this way," he said, halting them at one of the half-landings, his voice echoing in the hollow, empty space. His expression was one of concern, yet there was something else, something lurking beneath the surface – was it worry? Anxiousness? "I'm giving you one last chance to open up about what you and your captain were onto. You've seen the lengths I'll go to. Though Reid wasn't my own doing, he still fell victim to the same path you're currently treading."

She narrowed her eyes. She felt confused he felt compelled to assure her Reid's death wasn't by his hands. Why go to the elaborate effort of moving his body to Mercer's home to pin his death on her. He almost certainly had a hand in the captain's death. What was going on? She was getting sick and tired of his games. "What happened to Reid?" she asked, craning her neck around to face him. "One minute we were carrying out a routine inspection of Trammel's apartment... the next, we're chasing the woman and then he all but disappears."

237

Banks sighed, disappointed in her answer. "You're in way over your head, Hall. There's a reason why our law enforcement is structured the way it is. Everyone is a cog in a machine bigger than ourselves. Reid didn't understand that and he paid the price." He leaned in closer, his lips almost brushing against her ear. "Give up what you know, and I'll make sure you're treated fairly."

It was at this point Hall realised she'd reached her limit with this hideous man. He was hiding something about the woman. Something she suspected Reid may have stumbled upon. The deaths of both Reid and the captain sounded to her like acts of desperation. The tolls of conspiracy were ringing in her head; loud and clear. In one swift motion, she brought her head forward then drove it back, connecting with Banks' jaw. Her skull screamed a protest as it crunched into the spook's teeth. He grunted and stumbled back, losing his grip on her. He clattered into the wall behind him.

Without taking a moment to look back, she barrelled down the stairs, taking them two at a time. She heard Banks curse, clambering to his feet. He bounded down the stairs in pursuit. Unfortunately, the disadvantage of having her hands cuffed behind her back was her downfall. Just as she reached the last flight, the light of the outside spilling in from the open door at the bottom, she slipped. If her hands hadn't been restrained, she could have easily reached out and grabbed the railing to steady herself. But it was not so. She fell awkwardly onto her side; the cold, unforgiving concrete floor, knocking the breath out of her. Before she could recover, Banks landed on top of her, his elbow driving hard into her ribcage.

She screamed as her vision flashed white. She was grabbed roughly by the hair and hauled to her feet. Banks roared unintelligible curses in her ear. He swung her around and drove his fist into her jaw. She was sure she felt some of her teeth loosen in her gums, as her head snapped to the side. Everything became a blur; her previous head injury now exasperated tenfold by the spook's strike.

He dragged her out of the building as blackness began to reduce her sight to a narrow tunnel. She felt certain unconsciousness loomed. Before she passed out, she thought she could hear footfalls descending the stairwell, followed by a raised voice.

Then she lost consciousness.

~

Lex stood on the roof of the building across from the precinct where investigator Hall had been taken to. She looked down at the throng of reporters who were crowded behind a cordon outside of the main entrance. She marvelled at her new 'mask', as the diagnostic software outlined each of their forms. She smiled, wondering where it had been all her life.

I would have got more of my work done undetected if I'd had this little baby from the start.

239

She began to scroll down the list of contact details logged into the mask's memory banks. She stopped when she got to 'Brooks'. Although she'd enjoyed the solitude of working alone, she was beginning to see the possible advantages of having someone to reach out to should the need arise.

That's if he's true to his word.

The doubt concerning Brooks and Oliver's intensions weren't unmerited. If Brooks was given the choice between coming to her aid or succeeding in his mission to avenge his family, it was a no-brainer which one he'd go for – she knew what choice she'd make herself.

Before she left the compound, the doctor quickly showed her how to go about hacking into the precincts internal communication system. But despite her masks impressive capabilities, he stressed to her that it had its limits. She would only be able to infiltrate the basic line – the lines used and reserved for more senior personnel were behind firewalls far too sophisticated for her new kit to break through. But that was fine. Hall's arrest would be the talk of the station. If they were moving her, lower-ranked officers would be involved in any transportation of their new prisoner. She'd programmed her surveillance to flag up when Hall's name or the names of any personnel involved in her processing was mentioned over the precinct's comms.

She didn't have to wait long as her ears were soon filled with the sound of internal chatter coming from the precinct. "Officer Morgan to front desk regarding Hall," a crackled voice announced. "The spook is taking the prisoner to his cruiser to the rear of the building. The prisoner is to be transported to NewHaven. They'll take over from there."

The rear of the building. That's where I'll be waiting.

She switched off her surveillance and strapped her rifle onto her back. She'd had to make a quick detour on the way to the precinct and pick up some of her gear. During her rampage, she'd secreted her equipment in lock-boxes and storage units all over the city – due to the fact she'd simply accumulated so much that it would have been unwise to keep the equipment and weapons in her apartment.

She made her way along each of the buildings – internally thanking the designer who'd mapped out this section of the city, as there were plenty of options to cross the street, via the rooftops, instead of below, which lowered the risk of detection. It wouldn't have been a concern if it had been at night, but it was the middle of the day and she wasn't taking any chances.

Once she was satisfied with her position and view of the backdoor. A cruiser waited, a few yards from the door. It appeared to be unmanned – which she found odd. She unstrapped her rifle, peered through the scope just in time to see Hall being dragged out by a tall man in a long overcoat. She watched as he bundled the unconscious investigator into the back of his cruiser. There was something familiar about him, but she couldn't place where from. Her inner-musings were cut short as an officer came running out of the door in their wake. The officer and the man began to argue.

As the two men continued their verbal sparring, a second officer – much larger and unfit than the first – emerged from the doorway. Then something strange happened. The larger officer pulled a gun out and pointed it at the first officer.

Now, why would an officer pull a gun on his colleague?

Intrigued, she decided the roof was no longer adequate.

~

Charlie Deacon thought of himself as a good cop; an honest cop. As he'd sat across from Hall – in the back of the transport hub – doubt had begun to settle in his fairly pragmatic mind. He knew Veronica from the academy, and though a few of his fellow students scoffed and made – in his mind – crude remarks about Hall's achievements at making investigator so early in her career, Deacon hadn't been one of them.

Give credit where credit was due, regardless of gender or ethnicity, he thought. She'd been top of the board in just about every subject. He hadn't done too badly himself. He knew, eventually, he'd make it to the rank of investigator. Unlike Hall, Deacon preferred a slow and steady approach when it came to climbing the ladder. He'd been more than happy to be seconded to his department. He wasn't one to judge his own career path by the achievements and placements of others. It just simply didn't make any sense to him.

In his short career, he'd seen some pretty shitty crime scenes. He'd worked cordons around incidents which showed what human beings could be capable of. But when he'd looked across at Hall – over the stink of her stomach contents – he hadn't seen a murderer. Instead, he'd seen someone caught in someone else's crosshairs – the details of which he had no clue. It didn't change how he felt about the situation.

His suspicions had been backed up when he'd hung back, after the spook had ordered everyone out of the interrogation area, and heard what the spook had told Hall. She was being used for something the spook was up to his neck in. What that was, he didn't know. But that wasn't the point. The point was, that he would be fucked if he was going to let a damn fine officer go down for something she didn't do.

"I said step away from that murderess little bitch, Deacon," Melrose barked at his back. "I knew you had a hard-on for her, but I didn't think you would go as far as aiding and abetting a known killer."

Deacon almost chuckled. He looked to the spook, who regarded him with calm curiosity. "Innocent until proven guilty, Melrose," Deacon said flatly.

He heard the idiot snort. "Are you kidding me, Deacon? She was found at the scene hovering over their dead bodies. Trust me, she's guilty. Step away before I do something we'll both regret, Deacon. I've already called it in. The cavalry will be here shortly. Don't make this any more difficult for yourself."

Fuck this, he thought. He was about to take a step towards Melrose when a dark shadow landed on top of the spook. It grabbed him by the collar, spun him around and dealt him a series of blows. The shadow was a blur of deadly force; arms and legs moving with violent precision as it struck again and again. The spook's body jerked and spasmed from the torrent of physical abuse, eventually dropping the ground in an unconscious heap.

He couldn't believe his eyes at what he'd just witnessed. The shadow turned its head to regard Deacon and Melrose. It was a woman; wreathed in black; with dark red stripes running down her and a hood covering most of her face. A wicked smile gleamed from the gloom of her hood. Deacon thought she looked like a fierce panther. He stood in complete slack-jawed awe as she uttered one word to him. "Duck."

He did as he was told, throwing himself to the ground. Melrose wasn't as quick. Before he could shake himself from the same stupor Deacon had found himself in at her arrival, she threw what looked like a thin pole at him. It cracked against Melrose's head. It struck his partner's head with a sickening crunch. His head whipped back as he gave out a pained whine. He teetered for a moment, before dropping to the floor, his gun clattering onto the ground.

Deacon slowly rose to his feet; his eyes never leaving the hooded woman. His heart hammered in his chest. At closer inspection it looked like the black suit with the red stripes was her skin. It clung to every part of her. There was only one person in this city who would be garbed in this type of outfit. He immediately became certain of one thing... the woman hadn't perished in the river.

"Focus," she growled from beneath the hood. "We need to get her out of here."

Deacon glanced back to the door, knowing reinforcements weren't far away. Then an idea struck him. "You're going to need some time. I can veer them off in the wrong direction. But you're going to have to hit me. Make it look like the three of us were assaulted by you."

The woman nodded. She pointed down at the two unconscious men. "They'll know the truth once those two are awake... unless," she said, pulling out her knife.

Deacon waved his hands emphatically. "No, you're not killing them. I just need enough time to veer them off, then disappear whilst they're looking for you."

"Where will you go?" she asked.

The question threw him off. He didn't actually know where he could go. The most important thing was to help them getaway. Then he would think about himself. "I'll find somewhere to lay low."

He felt as though she sensed his doubt. "Once I've got her safe, I'll find you." She pulled out a small card from a pocket attached to her belt. She handed it to him. "Go to this apartment, give the man that answers this card and wait."

He took the note, slipping it into his back pocket. "Okay, what—" His head whipped around as she punched his jaw. Before he could spit out a curse – or a couple of teeth – she dealt him a few more blows.

He watched, sitting with his back against the wall, as the spook's cruiser screeched away and around the corner. Moments later, armed response burst out of the doorway. One of them looked down at them. "Sir, what happened? Are you okay?"

Deacon spat, not surprised to find blood in it. "Fuck knows," he said groggily – a part of his act he didn't have to act out. He pointed in the opposite direction Hall and the woman had gone. "Whoever it was, took the prisoner and went that way."

The officer nodded, buying it. He bellowed orders over his comms and turned on his heel, quickly followed by his team. Deacon got up, took one last look at the spook and his partner, then ran down the street, hoping he'd given them a chance to escape.

XXXI

Marr lay on his side; brought back to reality by the tumult of orders and progress reports bellowed from the armed response unit. The noise reverberated down the narrow alleyway as they relayed information back and forth to each other; either face to face or over the comms. He felt a stickiness on his head, matting his hair to his scalp. He reached up and gently touched it. He winced from the sharp pain exuded from the wound; still wet and open. He groaned as a dull pain in his shoulder – presumably from his rough landing – arced down his arm.

He gritted his teeth and sat up. He seethed with rage; furious with himself; of his failure at letting a perfectly straightforward task – transporting that meddlesome investigator from the interrogation room to his cruiser – spiral out of his control. This sort of shit happened to wet-behind-the-ears recruits – not seasoned vet's such as himself.

One of the response team officers noticed his movements. His eyes flashed with concern as he scurried over to him. He knelt down and checked Marr's eyes for signs of concussion. "Sir, are you alright?" he asked, offering Marr his hand. "The paramedics are on their way."

"I'm fine," he groaned, accepting the officer's proffered hand. Once pulled to his feet, he glanced over the officer's shoulder to where the fat officer – the one who'd had tried to help – sat; propped against the wall to the side of the precinct exit door. From the way the big oaf's eyes darted in every direction – confused and unfocused – he surmised he was still having trouble regaining his wits – what little of them he possessed. A thin trail of blood ran down from a nasty gash above his right eyebrow; the dark fluid dripping down to his shirt, staining it in crimson splotches.

Marr scanned the area for the fat man's partner, Deacon. He was nowhere to be seen. He returned his attentions to the armed response operative. "Where's the other one?"

The officer raised an eyebrow, inviting him to elaborate. "Other one, sir?" His expression switched to one of concern. If he'd been a little older, the look might have had some weight, but he wasn't. To Marr, it just looked patronising. He placed a hand tentatively on Marr's shoulder. "Sir, you've hit your head pretty hard. Please, take a seat beside Officer Melrose and the ambulance crew will be with us shortly."

He didn't have time for this shit. He slapped aside the hand resting on his shoulder and stepped closer to the young officer. "Never mind me. Where's Deacon?" He pointed over to Melrose. "That fucking idiot's partner. He was here when I was assaulted."

If the officer was crestfallen from his help being thrown back in his face, he didn't show it. He simply nodded down the alleyway towards the main street. "Officer Deacon was also injured in the attack. He's gone to find the precinct first-aider at the front desk to treat his wounds."

Like hell he was, thought Marr. The insolent little shit had exasperated the situation; coming to Hall's rescue like some white knight in shining armour. It had inevitably led to him being distracted enough to get his underwear pulled over his head by that fucking woman he felt was beginning to haunt his every step. And now he was stuck in this alleyway with a semi-comatose idiot and an officer just off his mother's tit.

He tried to wrap his head around Deacon, and why he'd deliberately cost Marr his prisoner – his chance to fix the fuck-up Faulks had created. He cast his mind back to when he'd first come across Officer Deacon after he'd followed Hall to the Freedom Bridge. He distinctly remembered Deacon and Hall being on very friendly terms. They probably served at the academy together. And given his recent display, he probably had a soft spot for her. He was also present during Hall's arrest – so much so that he sat in the back of the transport shuttle that had taken her to this very precinct. Was there a chance Deacon had been in on Hall and Mercer's little cabal and he'd simply missed it? They worked in the same department, albeit at different levels. It was certainly possible.

He looked balefully at Melrose. It hardly stretched the imagination they could have colluded in the back of the shuttle, planning a way for her to escape, right under Melrose's nose. Whatever the method and how it was executed didn't mean shit now. They were both gone and he was left standing in this shithole alley with his dick in his hand.

"Bullshit," he growled to the officer. "Deacon's in on it. He aided in Investigator Hall's escape. Put out an APB on him. I want him found and in restraints immediately." When the young officer didn't respond, he grabbed him by the arm and pulled him close. "That's a fucking order. He helped that murderess little bitch escape." He released his hold on the officer's collar and pushed him away. "Now, fucking find him."

The officer nodded curtly and spun on his heel. Before he disappeared into the precinct, he stopped, turning back to face him. "I'll let the pursuit team know, sir. If what you say is true, it'll affect their attempts to apprehend the fugitives."

"What makes you say that?" he asked.

The officer raised a finger, pointing down the alleyway. "There's a good chance Deacon deliberately sent them in the opposite direction." He turned and vanished into the doorway.

Marr cursed. He just about slipped into despair, when a thought occurred to him. He reached into his pocket for his scribe... it wasn't there. Cold dread clawed its way up his spine. Where was his scribe? He began to search the area where that psycho had got the drop on him; dropping to his hands and knees, becoming desperate — all the while watched by Melrose, who stared at him in confusion. There was no sign of his scribe; his one piece of equipment that held everything. "No, no, no," he heard himself muttering, over and over again.

"Something the matter, sir?" Melrose asked.

"Shut the fuck up," he roared. Melrose opened his mouth but closed it at the sight of Marr's crazed expression.

Had he left it in his cruiser? No, he had it with him when he'd interrogated Hall. That meant it could only be one place. Moretti.

He ran over to the first officer he could see. He grabbed at him, pulling him away from his colleagues. "Listen, the woman has Hall. She's taken my cruiser. Contact control... tell them to access my cruiser's tracking chip. The ident is 442ZX5," he said, almost shouting.

The officer stared dumbly at him. "Sir?"

"I said, the fucking ident is 442ZX5," he screamed. "Now, fucking do it. That's an order."

When he'd woken, he didn't think the situation could get any worse. He thought of Faulks and the choice words that would spew from the fucker's mouth when he found out how much he'd fucked up — especially after the way their last meeting had ended.

He was wrong. This was worse than anything he could possibly imagine.

~

She was lying on her back; her fragile brain and battered body a miasma of pain and misery. Wherever she was, she appeared to be moving at a higher speed than the gentle buffeting her body experienced at sporadic intervals would otherwise suggest. She sensed it in the muted sounds all around her, as though hearing them underwater; a scream; the blaring of a cruiser's horn; the screeching of tyres – all gone as soon as she'd heard them. Each noise was accompanied by the constant whip of something cutting through air at high velocity. It was a strange sensation, enough to make her want to puke – a physiological act she felt she'd overdone these last few hours.

She was suddenly thrown to one side, jarring her neck and rattling her teeth. She moaned as her shoulder flared in agony. Her head throbbed as though it were trapped in a large press; whose pressure contracted and retracted, exasperating her nausea. She smacked her lips, tasting copper, the acrid tang sending her stomach into debilitating spasms. She must have bitten her tongue or cut her gums on her teeth, she thought, attempting to curl up into a ball.

Her vision was also coming in waves, playing events in flashes, like fractured memories. The last thing she remembered clearly in her mind was Banks landing on top of her, his bulk driving all air and sense out of her. Then…

She lurched forward abruptly, as whatever was carrying her slowed its speed exponentially. A small moan erupted from her lips as she gripped her head, almost certain her brains were beginning to leak from her ears. A curse roared from someone a few feet from where she lay. Her eyes darted in search of its origin, her fragmented vision clearing enough to discern where the hell she was.

She was lying on the back seat of a cruiser – possibly Banks'. She squinted, trying to see if it was the spook sitting behind the wheel. It wasn't the spook. The driver, wrestling with the steering wheel, was garbed all in black; a hood covering their head. The driver, having presumably sensed her return to consciousness, swivelled round to get a look at her. Whoever Hall might have guessed was her chauffeur, this was the last person she expected.

All words escaped her, as the woman made eye contact with Hall. She appeared to be wearing a mask, which in Hall's opinion, made her look a lot more sadistic. How the fuck had she ended up in a cruiser with Sanctum-One's most-wanted? She'd been attempting to escape Banks, then... for some reason... Charlie Deacon came to mind. Had he been there? Or was it something her scattered brains had conjured up?

She was sure, and for the moment. It was hardly relevant as she now had bigger problems to deal with. She was now alone in a cruiser – clearly on the run – with a woman who'd pointed a gun in her face... very recently.

Her mind raced with questions. Had she been rescued by Moretti? Kidnapped? Was she being taken to her death? Had Moretti discovered she'd uncovered certain elements from her murky past – scratching the surface on what had led to her son being executed and her subsequent transformation into 'the woman'? It was certainly something which had caused the deaths of people she knew. She internally winced as the images of Mercer and Reid came to mind; their blood-spattered bodies lying in Mercer's home. She had no doubt there was a bigger picture to whatever happened to Moretti – possibly a cover-up of sorts. But the fact of the matter was, Moretti herself had killed a lot of people – some of whom in cold blood.

And Hall was now lying on the backseat of a stolen cruiser… alone with this killer.

Moretti tried to reach over to her. She said something, but Hall couldn't make it out, too engrossed with the gloved hand grasping at her. She scurried back into the backrest of the seat, attempting to get as far away from her as possible.

Before she could scream, the woman turned back around and pulled the wheel to the left, sending Hall sliding to the right-hand side of the vehicle. Her head thumped against the armrest. She cried out as her surroundings swam in her vision. Gritting her teeth into a snarl, she pulled herself up to a sitting position just as the cruiser slowed to a stop. She watched as Moretti got out and pulled the door closest to Hall open. She tried to fight the hands that hauled her out of the cruiser, but it was no use – she didn't think she could match Moretti in a fight on a good day.

Then, in their ensuing struggle, Moretti stumbled back giving Hall all the opening she needed. She pushed Moretti with all the strength she could muster and made a break for it. Unfortunately, her legs were a little weaker than she'd thought as they gave out on her. She dropped onto the unforgiving concrete; the rough ground scraping into her palms raw. She rolled onto her back as Moretti reached down and grabbed her. Hall struggled, swinging punches in every direction. She managed to land a feeble punch to Moretti's jaw, but it was quickly reciprocated as Moretti dealt her a slap to the face. Her head whipped to the side in a spray of spittle.

"Will you calm the fuck down," Moretti bellowed, flipping Hall onto her stomach. She grabbed both of Hall's wrists and wrenched them behind her back.

Hall craned her head around to face Moretti; her face red with rage. "If you're going to kill me, just get it over with," she spat.

Moretti leaned in close so that her lips brushed against her ear. "If I was going to kill you, you'd be lying in a pool of your own blood in that alleyway beside two dead cops and a dead spook." She took a moment to catch her breath, then let go. She took a few steps back, giving Hall some room. "As is the case, thanks to your friend, there's only one unconscious cop and a spook who'll have a nasty headache when he comes around."

Hall opened her mouth to speak then closed it. 'Friend?' She rolled onto her back, then sat up. She inspected her bloodied hands and winced at the sight of the ragged flesh. She raised her head and glared at the hooded spectre standing before her. "You didn't kill Banks?" she asked.

Moretti raised her eyebrows in question. "Is he your friend? The one who helped you?"

Hall snorted. "Friend? I haven't got any friends. Banks is the reason I'm in this mess." She paused, thinking. "Technically, you're the reason I'm in this mess. If I'd just left well enough alone, I'd probably be behind my desk at the moment, instead of sitting here with Sanctum-One's most wanted."

Moretti bunched her fists, a dark expression crossing her features. "And I'd be spending time with my son." Hall didn't have an answer for that. A small glimmer of guilt began to climb up her spine. Moretti took a step closer and knelt down. "They'll pay for what they did... they'll all pay."

Hall gazed at Moretti – this woman gone to hell, only to return in the guise of the vengeful horror looming over her. Hall looked into her sad eyes and found that she pitied her more than anything. "Is that all you care about? Killing?" she whispered

Moretti sighed. "Spare me your pity. I'm not going to argue with you... but yes, that's all that's driving me. I want to make sure I put them all in the ground before I join them." She rose to her feet and looked up to the sky. She sighed audibly. From the small waver in her voice, Hall suspected Moretti didn't fully believe her own statement.

"Then you're no better than them," she said.

Moretti laughed; a throaty cackle which chilled Hall's blood. She placed her hands on her hips. "You think you know it all, don't you?" she asked in a mocking tone. Hall presumed the question was rhetorical, so she held her tongue. "Believe me when I tell you, Hall, you have no idea what you've got yourself into. I was a cop once... just like you. I stumbled across something I shouldn't have, just like you did. The difference between us is that I got dragged to NewHaven, to be toyed with until I lost all sense of the world. If I told you half of what they did to me, you'd piss yourself with fear. I lost my boy and my life. They made me what I am. They created 'the woman'. I find it ironic she'll be their downfall."

Hall got to her feet and faced the fierce woman; all in black, save for the red stripes running down her body. Aside from the fact her career as an investigator was finished, the intuitive part of her – the part that had to know the questions to all the answers – screamed at her to push Moretti for more information. "I know you were a cop. I know there was a coverup. But why? Why was your son found dead in an alleyway, next to a gun with your prints all over them?"

Moretti looked as though she was about to answer, when they were interrupted by the distant sound of sirens. She flinched in fear; panic crippling her insides. If she was found in the company of Moretti, it would be all the leverage they needed to pin Alon and the captain's deaths on her. And who could blame them, at the moment it didn't look good. She glanced at Moretti, who didn't look to be concerned in the slightest. "They're coming, what do we do now?"

Moretti rolled her eyes, as though the steady arrival of Sanctum-One's finest was a minor inconvenience. "I was hoping your friend's diversion would've held the cavalry off a tad longer. Deacon I think his name was."

Deacon.

In the cruiser, she'd assumed it was her battered mind struggling to grasp at reality. When Moretti had said 'friend', she was baffled as to who she was referring to. But it was Deacon's voice she'd heard before she'd lost consciousness. She took a step closer to Moretti. "Charlie? Where is he now? What happened to him?" she asked, the questions spewing out of her in a torrent of worry for her friend. If he'd helped her escape, he didn't truly believe she was responsible for the deaths of Reid and Mercer. She found his belief in her innocence a small ray of sunshine amidst the shit she was in.

Moretti held her hands up. "I can't answer those questions for certain. Deacon was attempting to stop the spook from taking you to NewHaven. The spook and his partner – a hug whale of a man – had other ideas. He gave me enough of a distraction to take the two of them out." Her eyes flicked toward the direction of the sirens. "Though, it's possible the spook woke up early and was able to provide the SPD with the tracker ident on his cruiser."

"If he stayed where he was, he won't be safe. Not after helping you."

"I gave him instructions to follow. If he goes to the address, I gave him he'll be alright."

Hall narrowed her eyes, still finding it difficult to believe she was telling the truth. "What do we do now? There's nowhere for us to go."

"You'll come with us, we can take you to safety," a voice called behind them. Hall turned. Three people stood a few yards away; two men, and a woman. From Moretti's reaction, she'd been expecting them.

"Took your time, Brooks," she said with a scowl.

"Who the fuck are they," Hall asked, which elicited a snigger from the woman who'd just

258

arrived. The man smiled, casually wiping a stray lock of hair from his eyes.

"Help. You either come with us now or," he nodded past her, "take your chances with them. Lex was adamant we came to your aid."

Hall stared at Moretti, who deliberately avoided her gaze. "You were? Why?"

Moretti looked away; clearly uncomfortable with the possibility of the conversation straying near any other emotion other than anger. "I've told you already. We don't have time for this. Go with Brooks, he'll take you to safety."

"What about Deacon?"

"I'll find him, now go. They're close."

"Aren't you coming with us," Brooks asked.

Moretti shook her head. "You have an opportunity… the one you've been waiting for since the beginning," Lex said, her lips twisting into a malevolent grin.

"What do you mean," Brooks asked, perplexed.

Lex pulled out the scribe she'd swiped from the unconscious spook and handed it to Brooks. "I had one that belonged to Trammel. On the way to the precinct, I made a detour to my old apartment, but it was crawling with Inner-Sanctum minions. It seems they know who I am. I guessed they must have taken everything of importance." She nodded to the scribe. "This belonged to the spook who had Hall. I'll bet my life he's Inner-Sanctum if he orchestrated Hall's fall from grace. It could be your way in."

Brooks remained silent, as he gaped at the scribe. He looked as though he were about to weep with joy. He stared at the small piece of hardware like it was a holy relic. He raised his eyes to meet Moretti's and nodded dumbly. "I'll get this to Oliver right away. He's waiting for us at the stairwell, near the entrance to the compound." He blinked. "What are you going to do?"

Moretti arced her head in the direction of the sirens. "I'll give you the distraction you need to escape. I'm going to find a way into NewHaven… to find out who killed my son. Then I'll finish it."

She turned to leave, but Brooks grabbed her wrist. She looked down at his hand. Her eyes became suddenly became cold. To Hall, her expression suggested she was considering whether to break his arm or not. "You agreed to help us, but to be honest, I was sceptical. You have no idea what this scribe will do for the cause." He paused, trying to find the right words. "For that, you have my trust."

Moretti looked confused, and a little irritated. She pulled her hand free from his grasp. "That's great, Brooks. But you need to go before the cavalry arrives."

He nodded. "What I mean is… I know who killed your son…"

Moretti's face lost all colour. A darkness passed over her face; her eyes like two flints of ice. That expression chilled Hall's blood. She did not envy Brooks' shoes. "Who killed my son?"

If Brooks was as scared as Hall felt, he didn't show it. "Samuel Faulks," he said.

Moretti's eyes widened. "The fucking Proxy? How long have you known?"

260

Brooks grimaced. "After we got you back to the compound."

Moretti narrowed her eyes. "The first time, or the second?"

"The first…" Brooks said.

"Why didn't you tell me?" she asked, her voice hoarse with anger.

"It doesn't matter. I'm telling you now. If you're going to NewHaven… I thought you should kno—"

His words were cut off as Lex punched him then stormed off towards the cruiser. Brooks staggered back; his bottom lip bleeding. His two companions took a step forward, to presumably intervene, but Brooks waved them off. "Leave it," He said, spitting to the side. "It's less than I deserve."

After Moretti disappeared, he turned to one of his comrades. "Li, grab your bike. How quickly can you get the EMP's"

The woman, named Li, stepped closer. "Not long, why?"

Brooks gazed down at the scribe in his shaking hand. "This can get us in so far. But we'll need to kill the power at the source if we have any chance of breaching the firewall and gaining access to the Inner-Sanctum files."

Li smiled. "I'll be in contact. I have a bike not far from here." Then she took off at a sprint.

Brooks turned to Hall and gestured to his remaining comrade. The man handed Hall a hood. Hall turned to Brooks with an expression of disbelief. "Really?" she asked. The man clearly had trust issues. Her initial sympathy for what Moretti had done to him began to subside rapidly.

Brooks nodded, rubbing his jaw. He took one last look to the spot where Moretti had vacated, then strode past Hall without a word. Hall slipped the hood over her head and was left with little choice but to wonder where she was being taken to.

~

Lex sped out of the derelict car park, screaming her lungs out in fury. She gripped the steering wheel so tight she thought her knuckles would burst through the fabric of her gloves.

Brooks had just shown her the reason why she couldn't trust anyone. He'd known the identity of her son's killer all along but only chose now to tell her. Why he'd waited until now, she couldn't begin to comprehend. Besides, it didn't matter. The audacity of it made her completely overwhelmed with rage.

He didn't know it, but she'd almost reached down for her gun. The only reason she hadn't shot him there and then was because she was so overwhelmed with fury her limbs had been temporarily incapacitated; trembling in shock. What right did he have to keep it from her?

Her mind fought through the fog of emotional turmoil; still reeling from Brooks' revelation. The Proxy...

She couldn't believe the architect of all her pain and misery was the fucking Proxy. She'd always suspected it was someone within the higher echelons of NewHaven... but the second most powerful man in Sanctum-One? The more she thought about it, the more it started to make sense. The sheer scope of what she'd uncovered could only have been suppressed this long by someone as high up as the Proxy. It was why her superiors had warned her to back off countless times. The Proxy must have been made aware of her digging and tried to use his influence over the SPD to try and dissuade her from her investigation. If she'd succeeded, it would have exposed the Inner-Sanctum for all to see.

Her mind wandered back to Brooks and why she hadn't killed him. Why she hadn't taken the scribe back as payment for his treachery, and to hell with Sapien-Republic. In the end, she found the answer was simple. It came in the guise of a grubby little face staring up at her with curiosity; innocent eyes of a girl who chose to see past Lex's terrifying reputation and gaze upon the person beneath, regardless of what everyone else thought.

She used little Kat to kindle the embers of her resolve; to keep going in spite of the shit she'd been put through. She decided she would keep going for her sake... so she wouldn't befall the same fate as Julian.

The investigator hadn't been exactly thrilled with her rescue; Lex intervening in her transfer to NewHaven by the spook – whose face she recognised, but couldn't place where from. To a degree, she understood. Hall had no way of knowing what horrors had awaited her at NewHaven. She wasn't sure Brooks would tell her once they got her to safety – maybe that was a good thing, she thought. All she had to do now was keep the cavalry occupied whilst Brooks got Hall to safety, then find a way into NewHaven… to the Proxy.

She careened the cruiser with ease through a fork in the road, deliberately heading in the direction of the sirens; their wails growing louder with each passing second. She needed them to see her. She knew they were tracking her – they had to be. Deacon had sent them in the wrong direction barely twenty minutes ago. There was just no way they'd suddenly figured out they were heading the wrong way and somehow knew the exact coordinates of her stolen ride.

The spook's awake, Lex. You should have killed him. You're growing soft.

She shook her head, relegating the cold, deadly voice that had been her very essence – up until recently – to the back of her mind… for the moment. If they saw her, their caution would be thrown to the wind caused by every cop's urge to catch the perp; to fulfil their duty. Their blood would be up and would be embroiled in a full-scale police chase. She just hoped it would be enough to lure them away from Brooks' position. One thing nagged at her. If the shoe was on the other foot – and she was the one in pursuit – she'd wonder why her target had suddenly stopped at one position for so long, to then suddenly turn around and head straight for her. In the end, it didn't matter; it was out of her hands.

She weaved through the traffic with practised expertise; soaring in and out of lanes, which merited an orchestra of horns, slammed down in aggression, and cries of anger and abuse from citizens caught off-guard by her sudden, high-speed appearance to their relatively normal day. A cruel smile crept across her face as the g-force pulled at her. Her heart hammered in her chest as she revelled in the slick handling of the spook's top of the range cruiser – she found it currently helped keep her mind from Brooks' betrayal.

I'll have to compliment the spook on his choice of vehicle the next time I see him... before I put a bullet in his skull.

The cruiser gripped the tarmac as though it were part of it as she drew ever closer to the blare of sirens. She could see their lights; reflected off the glass panes of the skyscrapers – two blocks ahead. Two more cross-sections and she'd be on them.

Up ahead, the traffic lights hanging above the middle of the junction suddenly changed to red, causing the vehicles in front of her to close ranks, blocking her way through. She was driving further to the left of the wide street. She quickly scanned the sidewalk, thanking the heavens it was devoid of pedestrians. Without taking a second thought, she wrenched the wheel around, darting the cruiser towards the sidewalk. The cruiser, not designed to drive up sidewalks at high-speed, jolted violently causing Lex to bite her tongue. She wrestled with the wheel in an attempt to recover control and passed the intersection, almost colliding with a transport-hub.

Ignoring the fact she'd narrowly avoided a collision -- one she'd almost certainly have come out second best – she slammed her foot down on the pedal; rebuilding her speed. She cursed as the SPD convoy barrelled around the corner in a hail of sirens; four heavily armoured assault vans, more than capable of reducing herself and the cruiser to pulp. She had to think fast. If her chances with the transport-hub were bleak, a head-on collision with the armoured vehicles was non-existent.

Yet, Lex decided to take a chance – not that she had an abundance of options open to her – straightening her cruiser so its course was facing dead-on with the wall of metal bearing down on her. Civilians on the sidewalks looked on in horror as the two parties drew closer and closer; their eyes transfixed on the scene playing out before them.

She turned on the auto-drive function and unbuckled her seatbelt. She opened the door, grimacing at the blur of the tarmac below, as it flowed past her like a conveyor belt. She patted the material of her suit, a dubious expression twisting her features. *If Oliver's talking shit about this suit's durability, he's going to get one serious ass-kicking… if I make it, that is.*

She took a deep breath and leapt out of the cruiser; her muscles coiled and ready for impact. Suddenly, everything seemed to go into slow motion; her short descent to the road dragging on for what seemed like minutes as opposed to seconds. Then the world began to spin at a sickeningly rapid speed. She tried to roll with the velocity, but in the end, it was just too fast. She bounced and skidded along the unforgiving terrain in a tangle of limbs. Her body felt like it had been stuffed into a cement mixer with a dozen bricks. She was thankful the doctor had spoken true about her suit's ability to dampen heavy impact damage. And though she was certain her body would be covered in a miasma of bruising; it would be nothing compared to the damage she would have sustained if she'd been wearing her previous attire.

Her trajectory veered her away from the road, towards the sidewalk where she was sent hurtling between two parked cruisers. She smashed into the steel shutter of a vacant shop with terrible force. Her impact bent the thin steel inwards, buckling it, and destroying the glass pane window the shutter had been protecting. She cried out as she dropped onto the concrete; all air and sense knocked out of her.

She slowly lifted her head off the ground, groaning as sharp pains lanced their way through her head and down her spine. Her view of the road was blocked, so she heard rather than saw the collision. A great cacophony of screams and twisted metal resounded through the street like thunder. Her optical sensors picked up a small crowd nearby, but it seemed as though an invisible cordon stopped them from proceeding closer to where she lay; their curiosity kept in check by their fear of her. It had been little more than ten seconds since she'd thrown herself out of the cruiser. A voice suddenly rang out in her head.

Get up, Lex! We'll deal with the pain later… it's not like you aren't used to it.

The sobering tones of her inner-monologue brought her back to reality. She reached up and grabbed the twisted mess the shutter had become and pulled herself to her feet. She dusted herself off, checking her suit hadn't sustained any damage – surprised to find the suit completely intact.

She cast her gaze across the street where the convoy lay in a state of chaos. Her stolen cruiser lay upside down on the roof of one of the police units – having presumably been flipped over on impact. The convoy had sustained minimal damage but was in such a state of disarray it would give her an extra few precious seconds to get as far away from them as possible. Her sensors picked up the outlines of several officers scrambling out of their vehicles, trying to regroup and salvage the situation.

"She's over here," a voice called from behind her. Lex turned to find a man pointing at her with a length of broken shutter which must have broken off after she'd smashed into it. He blocked her escape down the sidewalk. He was young – maybe mid-twenties. His hair was shaved on one side; the other dyed blonde and slicked back. He was bigger than Lex, and though his stance was intended to be menacing, Lex could see the fear in his eyes that betrayed the façade.

She turned to face him; aware the officers probably knew where she was. She drew her pistol, the sight of which caused the blonde-haired man's hand to shake; his thin piece of sheet-metal quivered in his grasp. She had to give him credit. He didn't drop his makeshift weapon and run. He remained where he was, his eyes, though terrified, held a stubborn defiance.

He nodded to her gun. "So… y-you gonna shoot me, now? In cold blood?" he asked, his voice barely a croak.

She rolled her eyes. "Not exactly," she said. She flipped the gun to stun mode and pulled the trigger. The small bolt of electricity made contact with the metal sheet, sending a few thousand volts up its length, continuing up the man's arm. He shuddered – a comical squawk escaped his lips – as he fell to the ground in a writhing, juddering tangle of limbs. She casually slipped the gun back into its holster and hopped over him. "Nothing personal," she said, before sprinting down the street.

She passed a few more shocked citizens, calling for help. Unlike the blonde man she'd shocked, the other bystanders had the good sense to stay out of her way. She took a right and sprinted down a narrow side-street, hoping it would be enough to lose her pursuers.

~

Sergeant Ortiz growled as he fumbled with his seatbelt; the thickness of his protective gloves made it more difficult than it should have been. Eventually, he managed to unclip it. He grabbed the door handle and pushed it open. He clambered out of the armoured SPD chaser and scanned the area for signs of the psychotic woman who'd caused the carnage. His partner, Martins, was nearby; assessing the scene for any casualties –

civilian or SPD. Lucky the street wasn't too busy, he thought. Otherwise, it could have been a hell of a lot worse. He caught Martins eye and beckoned him over with a nod.

"You alright, sir?" he asked, jogging over.

Ortiz ignored the question. "Where's the assailant?" he barked, his eyes flitting in all directions; looking for any signs of her whereabouts. He couldn't believe his eyes as he'd watched her throw herself out of the vehicle. Sure, he'd heard stories of her from colleagues. But hearing, and seeing were two completely different things. His friend, Gus, had been at the crime scene during her flight from the Trammel building. "She's one tough son of a bitch," his friend had said, one night over a few too many beers. "Saw her waltz out of the place like it wasn't filled to the brim with officers."

He shook his head, still in a state of disbelief. He'd watched her tumble onto the road – hitting it hard – before he'd become too preoccupied with swerving his chaser out of her cruiser's path. She had to be dead, he thought; the speed she'd been travelling at would have ripped her body to shreds.

A cry echoed from across the street, pulling him from his reverie. He snapped his head in its direction. That was when he spotted her; dressed in a black suit with red stripes running down it, and a hood covering her head. She soon disappeared from view as she skirted down a side-street.

He called his team over, who were combing the street for her whereabouts. "She's gone down that

270

side-street. Follow me, stay frosty." Then he was off, barrelling towards the alleyway, his team falling in behind him.

Martins drew alongside him. He cast a sidelong glance at his sergeant. "Sir, will I call for backup?"

Ortiz shook his head. "We're the backup, Martins. Besides, we don't have time," he said, panting from the exertion of running in full body armour. Martins looked doubtful with his superior's decision. Ortiz huffed out a sigh in frustration. "You've read the reports on this bitch. She has a knack of vanishing into thin air. If we wait for more men, she'll be gone by the time they arrive, c'mon."

The eight-man response team reached the mouth of the narrow street. Ortiz held up a gloved hand, halting his team. The street was littered with oversized bins and caged storage units – used by the retailers on the main street to store stock. Plenty of places to stage an ambush, he thought bitterly.

"Sir," Alberts called. "I've checked the street schematics. Good news; this street leads to a dead-end."

Ortiz pursed his lips, craning his neck slightly to acknowledge he'd heard. "We'll call it good news when she's in cuffs," he replied with a growl.

Knowing they now blocked the assailant's only exit, they proceeded down the street with caution; covering each man as they systematically checked every possible hiding place. Ortiz's unease increased the further they got – made worse by the fact they hadn't found her and they were running out of street.

They rounded a bend where they met with a brick wall. Confused, Ortiz turned his attention to his team. "Where the fuck is she?"

But before his compatriots could answer, his vision was filled with white light, followed by an ear-splitting boom.

Then the screaming started.

~

There were two things Charlie Deacon shouldn't have done after he'd sent the armed response unit in the opposite direction of Hall and her would-be saviour. The first was driving in the direction of the pursuit after they'd been informed of his collusion in their misdirection. He'd been on his way to the address the woman had given him when his SPD comms alerted him to the development, despite his brain telling him otherwise, he'd made a U-turn and drove towards the direction of the chase.

He pulled up a short distance away from the collision – he'd heard collide two blocks away – and killed the engine. He waited, remaining cautious as he presumed all parties – especially the response team – had been tasked with bringing him in should they spot his presence.

The street was a mess. Banks' cruiser lay on top of one of the SPD chasers; having been flipped up onto its roof on impact. The front end of the vehicle was a crumpled mess, and for a moment, he thought his diversion to the scene was in vain. Nobody would be able to survive that crash, he thought. His initial suspicion went up in smoke as he spotted several armed officers running down the street, away from his position, turning right and disappearing from sight.

He jogged down the street, passing a group of people as they congregated around a blonde guy; who was propped up against a steel shutter that had seen better days.

"She fucking stunned me, man," the man said to no one in particular. "I thought she was gonna shoot me dead."

Deacon continued on, reaching the small side street. He glanced down it to see a black blur, ripping its way through the armed response team in a flurry of devastating violence. Watching the precision of each strike was something to behold. His intention had been to provide support for the woman, but it appeared his intentions weren't required. "Who can stop that?" he said.

"I can," a familiar voice called, behind him.

Deacon froze as the cold barrel of a gun was pressed against his neck, as he realised that was the second thing he shouldn't have done...

... was get out of his cruiser.

~

Lex moved with deadly force; gliding her body through the fight like the flow of running water. She ripped through the response unit as though she were a knife cutting through wet paper. Of course, she wasn't so flawless as to avoid every attack swung in her direction, but she'd learned

273

from years of combat training that the best way to recover from a strike was not to fight against it but to use the momentum of the attack to her advantage.

She ducked a thrust aimed at her head. The baton, wielded by the officer, passed harmlessly over her head; missing her skull by inches. The officer's clumsy swing left him wide open. She replied with a chop to his throat, temporarily cutting off his air supply. He staggered back, eyes bulging, gripping his throat as though it would somehow aid in his desperate efforts to draw in a breath. With the slight distraction of being unable to suck in air to his lungs, Lex snatched the baton from his grasp and drove the end of it between the gap in his visor. His head snapped back, blood erupting from his shattered nose. He dropped to the ground in a gurgling whimper.

She gasped as a fist pummelled her ribcage. She grunted, turning to face her new adversary. It was the leader of the unit; his sergeants' badge shined brightly in the afternoon sun. His eyes blazed with fury; his mouth an angry snarl as he swung the baton at her neck. She twisted around his attack, bringing her elbow around and cracking it against his thick helmet. He fell back and paused. He tapped his headwear and shook his head; his lips spread into a confident grin. She rolled her eyes. She knew the blow wouldn't affect him physically. It was intended to drive him back and give her a little space to assess the best way to attack him. The idiot just didn't see what was coming.

They stood for a moment. Time ceased to exist as they both took in their opponent; gauging the others next move. The leader took a quick glance at his fallen compatriots, who were strewn across the alleyway – all unconscious. She smiled. Her flashbang had caused enough of a distraction for her to take out half the team before they'd realised what was happening.

"I've changed my mind," the sergeant said, his lips twisting into a snarl

Lex arched an eyebrow. "And what would that be?" she asked, sounding bored.

"I was going to bring you in." He waved a hand to his incapacitated comrades. "I'll tell the brass I had no choice… I had to kill you."

Lex chuckled. "Is that so?" she said, beginning to move around the sergeant like a cat who'd cornered a mouse. "Give it your best shot."

The sergeant roared, closing the short space between them in as close to a run as he could manage – garbed in that ridiculous armour. In his Kevlar-padded combat suit, it looked clumsy and slow. The armour the assault team were provided was good in a firefight. However, engaging in close-quarter combat was ill-advised. Especially pitted against someone as quick as Lex.

She waited until he was almost upon her, then in one quick motion, she stepped forward to meet him, directing a chop to his exposed neck. He gave out a spluttering choke, his body tensing from the blow. She never gave him time to recover as she slipped her fingers between the small gap which separated the officer's chin to the padded rest of his helmet and wrenched it free.

She pushed him back with a well-directed kick to his abdomen and swung his helmet in a wide arc towards his face, using all the strength she could muster. The helmet smashed his nose with a sickening crunch; the collision of Kevlar on flesh reaching its inevitable conclusion. Blood spurted freely from his ruined nose before his eyes rolled back into their sockets. He teetered back, finally landing in a heap to join the rest of his unconscious brethren.

She dropped the helmet and made her way back to the mouth of the alley. She could see citizens passing by the entrance of the narrow street; their eyes and curiosity drawn to the largest accumulation of onlookers congregated at the epicentre of the roadside smash to the left of the opening, out of sight. Her heart hammered in her chest; the exhilaration of the fight coursing its way through her veins.

She picked up her pace to a jog. She needed to get out of the area quickly. She stopped dead in her tracks at the surprising sight of Charlie Deacon – or more to the fact, the man standing behind him, his pistol pressed against Deacon's neck – as he was pushed out from the left-hand wall blocking her exit.

It was the spook whom she'd ambushed outside the precinct. From where she stood – twenty paces away – she finally twigged where she'd seen him before. It was one of Trammel's bodyguards; the one she'd fired at before leaping through the window. It didn't stretch the imagination as to who had killed Trammel – given the fact the SPD had turned up as she'd made her escape. Trammel had been very much alive when she'd vacated his premises but had been declared dead at the scene according to the news bulletin – with herself being named as his killer.

It was a gift from the heavens. From what she'd gathered from Trammel's scribe, Trammel was an ambitious asshole. Was it possible he'd tread on the wrong toes and the spook had been ordered to take him out? Although, they could have just left her to do it. She cast the questions aside; now was not the time to dwell on semantics. The main thing here was that she'd found her way in.

"We meet again," she said. "Banks wasn't it? I presume you're the one who killed Trammel after I left? Who gave the order? The Proxy, perhaps? I'll presume so, seeing as Trammel was becoming a pain in the ass."

"Where's my scribe?" he growled, ignoring her accusation. He looked pissed, shaking his hostage by a handful of his shirt to emphasis his feelings. "Hand it over and I'll let this little fucker go."

Lex laughed, shaking her head. Though, in her mind, she was furious. Deacon had got himself into this mess instead of doing what she'd told him to do and get to safety. "What? So you can kill both of us after you get what you want?" She clapped her hands together, mocking him. "Tell you what, I have a better solution. Let him go," gesturing to his captive, "then we can talk."

Banks turned his head to the side and spat, telling Lex what he thought of that. "You don't dictate to me, you little cunt. This ends today. You either give me the scribe, or I shoot the two of you right here and now."

She gave him a sympathetic smile. "That is an option, yet with one major setback. I don't have your precious scribe. I dropped it off with some of my new friends." She felt she had to force the last word out as she thought of Brooks.

"Veronica? Is she alright?" Deacon asked, his trembling with fear.

Lex nodded. "I told you to go, Deacon. I don't need some cop acting the hero. Hero's tend to get themselves killed."

Before Deacon could reply, Banks slammed his gun into the side of his head. He cried out as his neck snapped awkwardly to the side. The spook kept a hold of his collar, holding him upright. He was much larger than Deacon; a head taller and a lot broader across the shoulders. The act of holding Deacon up appeared effortless to him. He held him like a puppet who'd just had his strings cut. A trail of blood poured down from Deacon's temple as he struggled to keep his legs steady. "Never mind this little shit. You're fucking lying." He raised the pistol in her direction, confident Deacon wasn't going to try anything as he was still reeling from the blow. Blood began to drip off his chin and onto the ground. "I'll ask you one more fucking time… hand it over."

Lex took a step forward, growing tired of the repetition of the spook's demands. "Before your cruiser was smashed to pieces… a pity as it was a lovely cruiser, I'd wager there was a tracking device fitted within its CPU. It's the only explanation why these idiots," she gestured to the bodies, behind her, "were able to descend upon my location so fast. Now, given the fact Deacon had sent them in the wrong direction, you know, after I kicked your ass." She took a little pleasure as the comment clearly rankled. "I'd bet my life you woke up and gave the cruiser's tracking signal to the response unit."

Banks shrugged. "So, what if I did? What difference does it make?"

"A lot of difference," she said, twisting her face in an expression which suggested she was stating the obvious – which technically, she was. "From the tracker, you'll have known I'd stopped in a derelict car park for a few minutes before heading back the way I'd come to meet with the cavalry." She paused for a moment; her eyes boring into the spook. "Now, why would I do that? You're a smart man... at least, I think you are. It doesn't make any sense... unless I dropped something off to my new friends, who were waiting on me, then caused enough of a distraction so they could get away."

The spook looked dubious. "Or, you dropped Hall off to your *friends* and kept hold of the scribe." He slowly directed the guns focus back to Deacon's head. "Won't stop me putting a bullet in dear Charlie's head."

He was running out of ideas. She could see it in his eyes. Doubt clawed at his features. She had him exactly where she wanted him – off balance and pliable to demands. There was sensitive information on that scribe, information that could possibly leave him surplus to requirements with regard to his position within the Inner-Sanctum. It

279

was also a way for Sapien-Republic to gain access into NewHaven's mainframe – she surmised that was what worried him most of all. He was bluffing and they both knew it. "Do you really want to take that chance?" she asked. "Kill me and Deacon, then find nothing on me? Is it really worth the risk?" She pursed her lips. "So, here's what I propose. You let Deacon go, then we go for a little ride to meet the Proxy. Once we're all cosied up at NewHaven, I'll give you the location of your precious scribe."

"The Proxy won't go for that, I'm afraid. Try again," he said, regaining a little of his composure.

Lex arched an eyebrow. "He will if he knows I'm willing to tell him the location of Sapien-Republic's base of operation."

He looked dubious, but at the same time, a little panicked. "Your new *friends?*" She nodded, knowing they were the worst people to have access to his scribe. "Horseshit," he spat. "You know fuck all about those halfwits."

"What will the Proxy... no, the Prime do with you if he found out you killed me before gaining valuable intel on where Sapien-Republic's headquarters are situated, as well as the fact they practically had a key to the Inner-Sanctum's front door in the form of your own equipment?" She laughed. Banks looked ready to blow a gasket, whereas poor Deacon looked completely bewildered. "You have to admit our glorious Prime does have a hard-on for extricating that particular thorn from his ass."

Banks turned his attention to Deacon. "Give me your scribe," he said. Deacon glanced to Lex, who nodded for him to comply. He fished his scribe from his pocket and handed it to the spook. Banks jabbed at the screen, keeping a close eye on his captive. He then pressed the scribe to his ear. "Get me Faulks… no, I don't want him to fucking call me back, tell him it's urgent. I have 'the woman'." He waited as he was put through, while Lex chuckled at the last part of his statement. *I have you, you fucking ingrate.* He was quickly put through to the Proxy. He explained the situation, and after weathering a torrent of abuse, he cut the call.

"Your boss not happy?" she asked.

She could see the spook's entire world crashing down around him from the beleaguered look on his face. He narrowed his eyes, nodding to her belt. "Lose the hardware. I'll take you to the Proxy, but Charlie's coming with us in case you're talking shit. That way I can watch the bleeders tear the two of you to shreds."

The faint sound of sirens – resounding a few blocks away – caught her attention. Their time was up. It was probably called in by the response unit or a civilian bystander, amidst the scene on the main street. She wasn't the only one to notice, as both Deacon and Banks craned their heads around in its direction.

Lex shrugged, taking off her belt and throwing it to the side. "Fine, but we'll need to be quick. This area will be crawling with SPD in a few minutes. If we're still here when they arrive, we're fucked. Because if they spot me and rip me full of holes, the contents of your sad little existence goes viral."

Banks grimaced, his eyes flitting between Lex and the sound of the incoming unit. He closed his eyes, as though he'd come to a decision. He pushed Deacon a few yards in front of him and began to shrug off his overcoat – switching his gun from his right to his left, then back again, as he negotiated his arms out of the sleeves. He threw the coat over Deacon's head, where it landed at her feet. "Put that on and follow me," he said, grabbing Deacon and pulling him towards the main street.

Lex quickly followed.

~

Li straddled the seat of her bike; her features hidden within the confines of her helmet, as she watched the trio cross the street – surprisingly unnoticed given the fact the place was crawling with citizens strewn across the street in a state of panic and high alert. They climbed into a vehicle. Li recognised the model; frequently used by the SPD. The tall man, she presumed was the spook; Banks pushed a smaller man she didn't know into the rear of the cruiser. She was a fair distance away, but she could see the smaller man had a nasty looking gash to his temple. She wondered who he was and how he was involved in proceedings.

Moretti opened the door, then paused. She turned her head, making eye contact with Li. She winced from the woman's intense gaze. Moretti set her teeth on edge. She couldn't be trusted. She'd voiced her concerns with Brooks after they'd brought her in from the park. But her reservations were met with deaf ears. Both Brooks and the doctor were blind to the fact Moretti was only in this to avenge the death of her son.

No more, no less

As much as it was a tragedy, her reputation over the last six months pretty much told Li she'd sacrifice anything – or anyone – to get her revenge. Moretti wasn't the only one surprised by Brooks' revelation; that he knew the identity of Moretti's son's killer. He must have recognised him when they were on that boat, all those months ago, and kept the information to himself – there was no other explanation for it. She sympathised with Brooks' decision to hold back the information. He was waiting until she proved trustworthy to Sapien-Republic. She'd been sorely tempted to take her out when she'd punched Brooks. But again, her leader had chosen to let it slide.

So, why was she here? Why was she following Moretti? She'd been asking herself those very questions since she'd left Brooks in the car park. And in spite of her denial, the answer was alarmingly clear. She was jealous of what Moretti could do. She'd followed the carnage to see how Moretti would handle the convoy of armed SPD… and she wasn't disappointed.

It was also because without Moretti, Sapien-Republic had no chance of gaining access to the Inner-Sanctum – she'd given Brooks the stolen scribe, and thus provided them with their best chance against the Inner-Sanctum, as their track record shot any argument to the contrary out of the sky.

Aside from Li's begrudging respect for Moretti's abilities, she still thought the bitch had been ungrateful after all Sapien-Republic had done for her. They'd fished Moretti's lifeless body from the water, and how had the ungrateful bitch repaid them? By attacking her saviours and somehow managing to escape the compound to start her six-month reign of terror, accomplishing feats against the Inner-Sanctum she and the rest of Sapien-Republic could only dream of. After losing Moretti, morale within their organisation had reached an all-time low. They had found themselves back to square one, only this time, with a severe lack of volunteers willing to risk their lives for the greater good.

She remembered vividly, the look on the doctor's face when she'd been the only one to step up and volunteer herself. He'd smiled at her in that fatherly way that made her want to slap him and told her she was a vital member of the group and couldn't afford to lose her – which, in Li's eyes, more or less told her how confident he and Brooks were of another attempt to infiltrate NewHaven succeeding.

She'd pulled up as the officers had clambered out of their vehicles. She'd watched them pursue Moretti into the alleyway. She'd glanced at her GPS monitor and discovered Moretti had ventured down a dead end. She'd fully expected Moretti to be escorted out – cuffed and safely in police custody, or in a body-bag – when the distinct sound of a flash-bang going off resounded from the area.

Strangely, there had been no sounds of gunfire – despite the unit being armed to the teeth and out-manning Moretti eight to one. Then the two men had entered the alley shortly after the response unit; the smaller one, quickly followed by the larger one. A few more minutes had passed before Moretti and the two men came back out.

Moretti gave Li the briefest of nods before climbing into the driver's side and pulling away from the scene. Li cast her gaze to the mouth of the alleyway, reluctantly impressed with Moretti's skill at clearly having dispatched the unit without drawing a single gunshot in response. She shook her head and quickly sent Brooks a progress report. She revved her bike and took off.

Her destination: NewHaven.

XXXII

Hall followed the small group in a weary state of silence; her mind struggling to deal with the ever-rapid changes to her circumstances. They descended down a set of steel steps built into the side of a derelict water filtration plant. Their footfalls boomed with each step, reverberating through the metal structure. It didn't help Hall's feelings of unease concerning the structural integrity of their walkway. Hall winced each time there was a sudden sound of something breaking, or falling apart – always out of sight, but nevertheless feeding her growing paranoia that she was only moments away from falling to her death.

She wondered how old the stairwell was as it creaked and whined from their progress; threatening to disengage itself from the dilapidated building and hurtling them towards their deaths.

"Is this safe?" she asked, to which no one answered – presumably not wanting to tempt fate by talking about it.

If her chaperones were worried, they never showed it – or, more accurately, didn't show it as much as she did. They led her to God knew where at a casual, if not leisurely pace; unperturbed by the stairwells obvious state of disrepair. She guessed from their air of nonchalance this wasn't the first time they'd used this route. From what she could make out, they appeared to be leading her to some underground hideaway – it would make sense as they were clearly enemies of the state.

She flinched, as the sudden blare of a cruiser horn rung out from above. To Hall, it sounded close She gripped the handrail tightly and whipped her head around in panic. Her eyes scanned the area for signs of the armed response unit she was convinced were right behind them; weapons drawn. She breathed a sigh of relief as there was no one there. They were alone.

The one called Oliver – who was directly in front of her – caught her apprehension and tried to give her a reassuring smile. "You're quite safe, my dear. These old stairs are sturdier than they'd have you believe. We're nearly at our destination."

"And where is that, exactly?" she asked, as she had no idea where she was. After she'd followed Brooks – led by his comrade who was mostly silent – over rough ground for ten minutes, the course piece of cloth had been pulled away from her eyes and she was met with the kind face of Oliver – she surmised was one of Brooks' closest confidants – who'd smiled warmly to her, before gesturing to the death-trap she was currently climbing down. There were a few more who had been waiting with the doctor, but he'd simply chosen to introduce himself and not the others.

Oliver smiled, turning to resume his progress. "Do keep up, Miss Hall."

With little option but to 'keep up', she was left to ponder the reality of her predicament with each treacherous step. She thought of her parents. What would they think of their only daughter – now labelled a murderer and an enemy of the state? She choked back a sob. She was sure Oliver had heard her poor attempts of hiding her pathetic snivelling, but thankfully had the common decency to ignore it.

She pictured their horrified expressions in her mind's eye as they were told what she'd done – spoon-fed lies with complete disregard for the truth, or their feelings and the impact it will have on both their lives. She felt like throwing up. She shivered with revulsion the more she pictured the scene she'd created in her head; of her parents' world being shattered. Would that devious bastard, Banks, use them to get back at her? It was entirely possible; he certainly had no qualms with murdering a police captain or a senior investigator.

Her life wasn't going to be the same again. It was now thrown into uncertainty – that was if she managed to make it down this fucking stairwell in one piece. Her career was in tatters, there was no doubt about that; everything she had envisioned for the future gone in a puff of smoke. She felt tears gently rolling down her cheeks. She was tempted to wipe them away, but couldn't summon the energy, so just left them to trickle down to her chin – what was the point.

But amidst her crippling fear, there was also rage, simmering just beneath the surface. She was angry at Moretti; if it wasn't for the shit-storm she'd wreaked over the last six months, she wouldn't be in this nightmare. She was furious with the SPD for being convinced of her guilt – their complete lack of loyalty for one of their own was like salt in an already festering wound. But most of all, she was angry with herself for being too rash and ambitious with her investigation, which made it easy for that fucking spook to play her like a fiddle.

So lost was she in her inner-turmoil, she hadn't noticed the procession had stopped. She bumped into Oliver, who oddly apologised. She looked over his shoulder. They'd reached a long stanchion which ran into the structure from a small platform, perched at a slight angle. Brooks quickly checked there were no stranglers then made his way into the structure.

He'd barely uttered a word since they'd left the carpark. When Moretti had punched him, she was sure everything was going to descend into chaos. She couldn't believe the Proxy of Sanctum-One had personally killed Moretti's son. It was possible Brooks had been lying to her as a means of manipulating her, but he'd seemed genuine. She hasn't been on the force long, but she knew a liar when she saw one, and Brooks wasn't lying – to her eyes, at least. The fact he'd kept it a secret from her, given he'd had opportunities in the past to tell her. It didn't shine him in a particularly good light. For the moment she decided she'd make her own mind up as she hasn't been privy to the whole story.

It made her think about Moretti; the woman who'd shoved a gun in her face and dragged Hall to where she was now. Despite the anger she felt towards 'the woman', she was beginning to understand her frame of mind. She'd been a cop, and something had happened that had caused the death of her son. There was a good person hidden beneath all the rage and the violence. There had to be – why else would she risk her neck by rescuing her from a NewHaven spook outside an SPD precinct?

She gazed up at the sky, mottled with cloud, wondering if this was going to be the last time – if at all – she'd see its beauty. One thing she did notice about this part of the city, was the distinct absence of Zeps – which she'd always thought spoiled the skyline. She understood why the group used the abandoned structure as a means of slipping in and out of civilisation. It was completely devoid of surveillance.

With one baleful glance over the rusted railing, down to the broken concrete thirty feet below. She took one last breath of fresh air and entered the structure.

~

Marr gripped the handle of his gun so tightly it was beginning to hurt the joints in his knuckles. His trigger finger trembled; the urge to fire barely suppressed as he kept it aimed at the hapless cop sitting across from him. The temptation to decorate the cruiser's interior with both his captive's brains was almost overwhelming – though, 'captive' was used in the loosest of terms. His control of the situation had slipped from his grasp the moment that little bitch had ambushed

290

him outside the precinct, absconding with Hall, and most debilitating of all, his scribe.

The moral high ground he'd had over Faulks – ironically caused by the Proxy's recent inability to keep things under control – had disappeared in a puff of smoke. In the end, he was just as much a fuck-up as his boss, the reality of which grated on his nerves. His head throbbed as he was sure he could feel his blood pressure sky-rocket the more he dwelt on the most catastrophic failure of his career. But it was all he could do. He was known to be a man of precision and purpose; always several steps ahead of those foolish enough to cross his path and he'd lost it; lost all that defined him as Sanctum-One's best. The way he felt vulnerable and helpless; completely at the mercy of someone else's agenda was presumably what his enemies felt when they knew who hunted them.

The cop, Deacon, looked as miserable as he felt. He knew a gun was currently trained on his head, but he chose to face the front, head down slightly. Blood dripped off his chin and onto the fabric of the seat between his legs. He seemed not to care, as the idiot looked to be too preoccupied contemplating his doom in defeated silence. It helped a little to know he wasn't the only one in this shit-heap of a cruiser miserable as he was.

The woman, however, was a different matter. He directed his eyes to the rear-view mirror. She was staring at him; her eyes seeming to read his every thought from behind that ridiculous mask she wore. Her new *friends*, as she'd called those fucking firebrands, had clearly gone to great expense providing their new ally with some new equipment and battle attire. He could see the mad joy crinkling in the corners of her eyes. It was enough to make him want to scream. She really was fucking psychotic.

When he'd surprised her in the alleyway – during which time he'd been convinced he'd steered events back to his advantage – he'd noticed her new attire and how pleasing it was to the eye; the way it had gripped her every curve. His pleasurable appraisal of her figure was soon soured by the revelation she'd handed his scribe to Sapien-Republic. The only thing he'd wanted to do to her after that was rip her to pieces, burn her corpse, and piss on the ashes.

They steadily climbed a slight incline in the road; the buildings beginning to rise in height as they approached the heart of the city. Above, the numeracy of Zeps increased exponentially, looming over Sanctum-One, emblazoned with images ranging from political messages – usually an effigy of the Prime in all his fatherly splendour – and advertisements of products varying from household droids to lap dancing club offers. Amidst the hubbub of business and leisure opportunities flaunted by the city's elite, the white monolith that was NewHaven stood proud at its centre, its magnificence second to none.

Faulks had been less than friendly given their last encounter, but his frosty demeanour had been tempered when he'd told him the news that he was in custody of the woman – negating to mention the full facts, of course. Faulks had brightened at the prospect of finishing what should have been dead and buried months ago. He gave Marr instructions on where he would be; telling Marr to lead their happy trio to the rear of the building.

"Where to?" Moretti asked, waving her hand out towards the white structure.

"Round the back, I'll direct you. The Proxy has relieved security to the rear of NewHaven. He seems quite excited to be reunited with you." He found the cruel smile that spread across her face very unsettling.

~

Lex followed the spook's instructions as she wound her way through the centre of the city. It wasn't even dark yet and still, this part of Sanctum-One was lit up like a Christmas tree. Garish billboards flickered their trinkets of the day. Neon lights were already lining the busy nightlife in a multitude of colours which, if she hadn't been wearing the mask – whose optical sensors dimmed their obtrusive light – would be giving her a headache.

She glanced back to the spook now and again, to make sure he was still going to play ball and not decide to put a bullet in her or Deacon's head. She didn't trust him, and she certainly wasn't going to underestimate him. She knew a man like that didn't get to his position by playing fair. The moment an opportunity arose that gave him a chance of turning the tables, he'd take it – she'd bet her life on it.

She shifted her gaze to the cop. He looked tired and completely out of his depth. His face was chalk-white and she could see beads of sweat peppered across his anxious features. He wouldn't have known what they'd been talking about with regards to the 'Inner-Sanctum' – in her eyes, it was better he remained in the dark. She just had to find a way to get him out of this. It was a problem she wouldn't have had to deal with if he'd just did as she'd asked. She had no doubts the spook had already decided Deacon had heard enough to not let him get out of this alive.

They passed by security checkpoints which weren't manned; the barriers were raised and the guard-boxes were absent of armed personnel – the Proxy's doing, she presumed. He'd want this little meeting to be nice and private. Unbeknown to him, that was exactly what she'd been hoping for. She was finally going to be face to face with the man who'd killed her little blue-eyed boy.

"It's just passed this last blockade. Pull over to the side, under that canopy," the spook said. She complied, directing the cruiser under a large canopy which she surmised was used as a smoking shelter. Black smudges, edged in grey, pitted the ground on one corner, near the gate; remnants of countless cigarettes extinguished by footwear. In spite of dusk being an hour or so off, the area was unusually dark.

She killed the engine and climbed out. Her muscles tensed; her mind alert for an ambush. The spook and Deacon vacated the cruiser. Banks searched for signs of his boss.

"Where's the Proxy?" she asked.

Before the spook had a chance to reply, a shot boomed out from the darkness. Charlie Deacon staggered back, his expression one of bewilderment. A sheet of blood cascaded down his face from the gaping hole which had appeared on the top of his head. He raised a hand up to the laceration. His mouth worked but no sound came out. His outstretched fingers got as far as his chin before his legs gave out on him and he collapsed to the ground.

The spook's eyes darted in all directions, in search of the shot's origin. Confusion and surprise had him at a loss on how to react. Lex, not prepared to be next in the firing line, had no such problems. She threw herself over the bonnet towards Banks, who didn't expect her speedy reaction to the sudden gunfire and dealt him a chop to the throat. He gargled a choked protest, gripping his throat with both hands. Lex slapped his hands away and wrapped her arm around his neck, using his body as cover.

She glanced down at Deacon's prone form; her teeth clenched in a snarl. He was sprawled awkwardly, blood pooling from the top of his head, staining the concrete black. "What the fuck is this?" she hissed into the spook's ear. "Deacon was ignorant in all of this… just a stupid cop," she roared.

"But a part of this all the same," a voice called out, reverberating across the area. The sound of boots thundered in the quiet as a dozen armed guards – garbed in heavy Kevlar with the seal of NewHaven emblazoned across their chests – emerged. They formed a line in front of her and Banks. "Let Marr go," said a man in his fifties, emerging from the gloom. *Marr? How many names does this fucker have?* He held a pistol, lowered casually at his side. She had no doubt it was the weapon who'd killed Charlie; she could see tendrils of smoke seeping out of the barrel. He wore a dark suit, white shirt, and a blood-red tie. He smiled at her with too many teeth, which to Lex, made him look reptilian. It was a smile she'd only seen once before – the rest of his features wreathed in shadow – but it had been enough to brand her dreams ever since; grinning down at Julian before he pulled the trigger.

She could feel her inner-demon – the one the Proxy had essentially created – try to fight for supremacy within her; to take over. For the moment, she pushed it back. She had to stay in control. "Tell your men to stand down," she said, nodding to the flunkies wielding their automatic rifles in her direction, "or I snap his neck."

The Proxy chuckled. "Like I care what happens to him," he said, waving a dismissive hand towards his man. She felt Marr tense at his boss' lack of concern for his wellbeing. "The way I see it, I could give the order to gun the two of you down and rid myself of two pains in my ass for the price of several rounds of ammunition. Those fucking *terrorists*, as they've been ridiculously labelled, can keep sending me lambs to the slaughter. We'll find them eventually."

This wasn't going how she'd intended. It looked as though the Proxy wasn't as enthusiastic in bringing down Sapien-Republic as his superior. Her mind raced with an alternate plan other than getting herself killed. The Proxy clearly wasn't feeling as pressured into cooperating with her as

296

his subordinate was. But then again, he could be bluffing. She needed something to call him out with… That was when it hit her. She thought back to Marr's conversation with the Proxy in the alleyway. Not once had the spook mentioned she'd passed his hardware to Sapien-Republic. He'd only mentioned he'd lost Hall and that he had 'the woman' in custody.

"That is a shame," she said, keeping her voice level. "I'm not surprised by your lack of worry. A man in your lofty position is untouchable to the likes of a few firebrands waving their banners for attention."

He nodded and waved his hand; his expression suggesting a point had finally been grasped by someone intellectually inferior. "Exactly… now if you're ready to die, shall we?" he said in the same tone one might use when asking if anyone wanted the last piece of pizza.

She ignored him. "On the other hand… if said 'terrorist' organisation had the means to gain access to the very heart of the Inner-Sanctum's dirty little secrets, you know… like the one I stumbled upon back when I was a cop – which then led to my boy being murdered in cold blood, you fucking cunt, then I wouldn't be so carefree now, would I? Those banners would certainly begin to have an opportunity to chip at the foundations our gracious Prime created."

The Proxy looked perplexed. The spook struggled in her grip, but she tightened her hold on his neck. "What the fuck are you talking about?" The question was for her, but Lex noted he only had eyes for Marr – and they seethed with rage.

She drew her lips close to the spook's ear. "Tell him."

"What the fuck have you done?" the Proxy asked his man.

Lex loosened her grip on Marr when she realised, he couldn't speak through the tightness of her hold. "She took my scribe," he croaked, "gave it to Sapien-Republic."

Lex took great delight in watching the smug, self-satisfied confidence drain from the Proxy's face. "You fucking idiot," he screamed. "Do you realise what you've cost us?"

Lex retightened her grip once more. She glared at the Proxy; her eyes promising unspeakable violence. "So, I would advise you to stand your minions down and relieve them of their duties before I do something rash. If I die, Sapien-Republic will gut you from the inside out – and I'm the only one here who knows where they're based."

She watched the Proxy. He glared at her with such malice, she could almost see the things he wanted to do to her. Then his expression of panic subsided, replaced by the look of a man at peace and in control of the situation – which was odd as she had him over a barrel.

That was when he heard the scrape of a boot on the concrete behind her.

She turned just in time to see a bleeder plunge his taser-rod into her neck. The interruption was enough for Marr to break free. He pushed her back, taking a few steps away from her, just in time to avoid transference of voltage. She tried to stay upright, but her body spasmed and wracked

298

uncontrollably. Her legs went from under her, her vision blurring. She was then grabbed roughly by the arms and dragged into NewHaven.

~

Li watched them drag Moretti into the building, senseless and incapacitated. While she'd been talking to the older man – she presumed to be the Proxy – a tall figure wearing a white coat that fell to his ankles, and a surgical mask covering the majority of his face had emerged from the shadows, sneaking up behind her and sticking her with the taser-rod.

She waited until they disappeared into the building, leaving two guards to stand sentry outside. They chatted to each other; their rifles held casually at their sides. One of them pointed to the body of the man Moretti had called Deacon, the cop; the dark silhouette of his prone form a few metres from their position. They showed no sign of empathy towards the dead cop or any interest in moving the body.

Li gritted her teeth as she thought of Deacon's family being told their loved one was nothing more than a common criminal; gunned down for his treachery against the city, when in fact, he fought – albeit unknowingly – for its freedom. She thought about leaving the scene and making for the power grid situated to the rear of the building. But the sound of the sentries cruel, derisive chuckling was more than she could take.

Li was far enough away and hidden within the shadows, to move unnoticed as far as the guards were concerned. She'd chosen that specific spot to keep an eye on proceedings unmolested. She unstrapped her sniper rifle from her back, unzipped its carry bag, and levelled its barrel; aiming towards the two fuckers stationed at the door. She peered through the scope, steadied her grip, and fired. The bullet whispered through the silencer, barely making a sound, and ripped through the furthest guard's jugular, replacing his raucous giggles with a panicked gurgling. She smiled as he fell to the ground like a rag-doll, clutching his throat in a fruitless attempt to stem the flow of blood which spurted between the gaps in his fingers. His colleague had just enough time to glance – open-mouthed and horror-struck – in her direction before she sent a bullet through his eye, staining the wall behind him in a spray of blood. He fell back and remained still. The guard she'd shot through the neck, slowly turned his head in the direction of his comrade's corpse before finally going still himself.

She dismounted from her bike and replaced the rifle back in its bag. She crossed the small courtyard, her boots crunching on the coarse terrain, closing the gap to the dead cop. She kept her helmet on, aware there may be cameras situated nearby. She assumed there were, so she didn't have a whole lot of time to loiter in the vicinity.

She approached Deacon and knelt by his side. She inspected his corpse; her eyes creasing with pity. The wound to his head – a few inches above the contusion above his temple – was slowly leaking blood onto the cold ground. "Poor bastard," she said, her voice muffled within the confines of her headgear. She grimaced as she quickly searched his pockets. She didn't want to do it, but the thought of Inner-Sanctum goons indignantly fleecing him of his belongings forced her hand. She was surprised to find the spook hadn't relieved the cop of his scribe. She pocketed it along with his SPD badge.

She got up and quickly ran over to the two dead guards and searched them for anything that may prove of use. She was in luck; they were in possession of a comm's receiver – presumably to check-in with their comrades on the inside. She swiped it, along with their I.D. badges.

Using her own hardware, she patched into their security channel. Her earpiece immediately filled with chatter as she made her way towards her bike. When she passed Deacon's body, she heard a groan. She stopped and dropped to a crouch, unholstering her gun; ready for a fight. There was no one there. She shook her head, convinced the noise must have been her imagination... when Deacon coughed.

For a few moments, she stared dumbly at the cop, half-convinced it was all in her head... before he groaned once more. She scrambled over to him, placing two fingers to his neck. There was a pulse. It was weak, but there was no denying the cop was miraculously alive. She couldn't leave him where he was. He was in a bad way, and if she left him, he'd surely die – either from the severity of his injuries or by a NewHaven lackey when confronted with his two dead comrades.

As carefully as she could, she dragged Deacon over to her bike and positioned him so he was seated in front of her; his head resting on the space between the handlebars. It wasn't ideal, but it would have to do. She started the engine and made a call.

Brooks answered before the first dialling tone had finished. "Li, progress report?"

"Brooks, I'm at NewHaven. Moretti's been taken by the Proxy." Brooks paused for a moment, clearly not expecting this in her progress report. "Moretti? What the fuck is going on, Li? I told you to go directly to NewHaven with the EMP's."

"I took a detour. You won't believe it, but that crazy bitch took out the convoy that was headed our way. She rammed her stolen cruiser at them. She tried to escape down a side street, but it led to a dead end. They followed her and she took all eight of them out," she said. "Then she got in a car with Hall's friend, Deacon, and another guy who works for the Proxy."

"The spook?" Brooks asked.

"I would assume so. She probably used the information about his stolen scribe to wrangle a meeting with Faulks. It's the only explanation as he surely would've killed her."

"And what about Hall's friend, Deacon? Moretti said to Hall she told him to get to safety?"

"He clearly thought he could help. I followed their cruiser to NewHaven. They shot Deacon and took Moretti," she said.

He needs urgent medical assistance. I don't know how long he'll last," she said.

Brooks was silent for a moment. "That complicates things somewhat. I'll contact our closest reconnaissance team and send them to your location."

"I can bring him in after I've destroyed the cells. There's no need to jeopardise any more of our people."

"It's a bit late for that now, Li. Proceed to the power grid. They won't be long," he said, cutting the call.

She sighed, accepting her superior's orders. She looked down at Deacon. "If you die, don't blame me," she said, taking off towards the power grid.

XXXIII

Within the steel structure, Hall trailed at the rear of the group as they made their way through walkways, corridors, and a multitude of doors. With each step, she traipsed further and further into the unknown; the space between her old life as an SPD investigator, and her new one as a disgraced fugitive growing larger. Though it was dark and hard to pinpoint her position, she felt as though she was being taken underground. Their course was cast mostly in darkness – save for the scant number of lights which littered their way – and the air around her felt colder. She was on the verge of asking one of them where the fuck she was – for the umpteenth time – when they pushed through a set of double doors much larger than the rest. Her surroundings suddenly opened up exponentially as she gazed at what could only be described as a ginormous compound.

Its entire space was filled with huts and tents scattered across its entirety. Smoke billowed from a number of cooking fires, where big steel pots hung from thick metal frames; their bottoms hovering a few inches above the flames. People nearest to them stopped what they were doing to gawk at the new arrivals. Eyes peered at her from dirty, dishevelled faces, like refugees from some bygone war-zone. She noted their expressions weren't as oppressed as was customary for refugees – though she was sure there was a pain in them all the same.

The rest of her party seemed oblivious to the stares as they moved through the shanty-community towards the largest structure at the compound's centre; a steel panelled monstrosity which looked in better shape than the shacks surrounding it. A fence ringed around it, cordoning it off from the rest of its neighbours. Armed guards were posted at its one and only gate. Her eyes were drawn to the semi-automatic rifles slung over their shoulders. The sight made her nervous. The sentries nodded to the group, allowing them to pass the checkpoint. She was barely given a second glance.

They climbed a set of steps which led to the main entrance of what she surmised was their headquarters. Once inside, Brooks' scribe began to ring a comically jovial tune. He dismissed all the party, except the doctor, and excused himself, leaving her alone with his comrade.

"Would you like a drink or something to eat?" Oliver asked. "I don't suppose you've had much since you were arrested."

Hall shook her head in spite of her stomach's disagreement. "What I want, is to know what the fuck I'm doing here?" she asked.

The doctor smiled. He nodded, as though expecting this reaction. "Well, if Moretti hadn't intervened and brought you here, I would assume you would be currently hanging from a hook, in some disinfected room at NewHaven, at the mercy of the spook who set you up."

The thought made her shudder. He did have a point, but she felt she was still due an explanation. "Who are you? Why are all these people down here? What's your involvement with Moretti?"

The doctor chuckled. "No one could mistake you for not being SPD, Miss Hall.

"Cut the 'Miss' bullshit, it's Veronica," she said, growing tired of his patronising tone.

"Very well, Veronica. We are Sapien-Republic, I'll assume you've heard of us from the Sanctum-One media; mindless anarchists with a penchant for troublemaking and social disorder." He rolled his eyes, clearly finding the Sanctum-One mantra amusing.

She snorted. "Something like that."

"Yes, well, what we really are, are freedom fighters with aspirations of setting the people of Sanctum-One free from her bonds, placed upon by our 'glorious' Prime."

She gazed towards the exit. "Who are all those people?"

The doctor followed her eyes. "Like myself; enemies of the state. Each and every one of us surplus to requirements with regard to Sanctum-One… or more specifically, the 'Inner-Sanctum'."

She raised her eyebrows in question. "The Inner-Sanctum?"

"They are the real government of this city, secreted within the darkest corners of NewHaven, controlling every aspect of our lives. Veronica, we are not part of a glorious new age. We are, in fact, lorded over by a tyrant, obsessed with control," he said.

"There are so many people out there... why hasn't their absence been noted? Investigated?"

He sighed, taking a seat. He gestured for her to do likewise, but she shook her head. "Isn't it obvious? Their names have been deleted from the rolls. That's where Moretti comes into things."

"How? What has she got to do with secret cabals and conspiracy theories? From what I've picked up, she stumbled across something she shouldn't have and her son was murdered for it. Then she went on a six-month rampage, seeking revenge, I'll assume. I was just starting to get to the truth when I found my captain and my partner dead and got screwed over by that fucking spook for it."

Oliver leaned forward. "Moretti's son was murdered because she stumbled upon the truth, Veronica. She found out something that, if it got out, would flip the government on its head. You'll know, from your tenacious police work, she's ex-SPD."

Hall nodded. "I found a trace of blood at the Trammel building and ran it through the SPD database."

Oliver narrowed his eyes. "So, you'll know which department she worked for?"

His question snapped something into place in her mind. Her eyes roamed towards the door once more. "Missing persons."

~

Through the gaps of the chain-link fence, Lex watched the shuttle-pod pull up outside of the department of citizen relations; a drab, dilapidated building that looked in serious need of some restoration work. Its windows were fitted with bars, awash with rust. The once-smooth exterior was covered in cracks and gaping holes, exposing the brickwork underneath. At face value, it was uninteresting in every sense, save one: the armed personnel manning its doors and waiting for whoever was inside the pod. It struck Lex as odd because the purpose of the building wasn't military or financial – basically anything that would require armed security. It was a station house for the poorest of Sanctum-One. A personal project of Prime Vonn, no less, used as a rehabilitation centre; treating those unfortunate enough to seeks its sanctuary and help them kick whatever habit they were into, or lift them from financial ruin – self-inflicted or not.

She watched as a group of people – varying in age, sex, and ethnicity – emerged from the shuttle-pod. Aside from their many differences, they all had one thing in common; which was their state of cleanliness and general dishevelment. An elderly woman stumbled as she disembarked, meriting a kick to the midsection by one of the guards. A young man – no older than twenty – tried to intervene. He grabbed at the guard laying into the woman. The guard stopped his assault and swung his baton into the young man's face. He fell to the ground, curling into a ball as the guard hit him again and again. All the while, the elderly woman screamed and begged for him to stop. But he didn't. He pushed the woman back, sending her crashing against the side of the shuttle as he resumed his beating. Lex could hear the crack of bones and the squelch of blood slapping against the metal of his weapon.

She felt sick; an impotent bystander, unable to prevent the horror before her. The voice of her captain, ordering her to stand down and drop her investigation into the multitudes of missing citizens ignored by the authorities, clawed its way to the forefront of her mind. "There's nothing going on, Lex," he'd said. "All you're doing is stepping on toes you don't want to be stepping on. Please, for the sake of your family, desist from this obsession. Down and outs go missing all the time. You know why? Because they don't want to be found."

Her captain's words had troubled her. His superiors had clearly been made aware of her activities and were putting pressure on him to veer her off her current path. Gazing across the courtyard – helpless at preventing a young citizen's murder – she resolved to find out the truth and bring those to justice no matter how high up the chain of command it went.

~

"When we found Moretti – floating face down in the water of the harbour – we wondered why the Proxy had personally risked killing her son, and almost her. I suspect he actually thought he'd killed her that night. Through underhand techniques, and a little technological ingenuity, executed by yours truly, we ascertained information on her SPD activities on the run-up to that terrible night, and why she'd garnered such wrath from as high up as the Proxy."

Hall's brows furrowed. She thought of Moretti, the image of her punching Brooks in the derelict car park. "Why didn't you tell her you knew the identity of her son's killer?"

Oliver had the good grace to look ashamed. He grimaced. "It's complicated. Brooks was the one who'd actually recognised him at the harbour. He told me, and only me, after we got her back to safety. For years we've been unable to infiltrate NewHaven. We've barely been able to cause any damage outside organising 'peaceful' protests. We took Moretti's lifeless body out of the harbour and back here, where I personally treated her. As you're no doubt aware, her mental state isn't exactly stable. She escaped and for six months..." He trailed off. "Well, I don't need to tell you what you already know about that. After she leapt off the bridge, we found her and took her in. We were just beginning to gain her trust. Without her, we have no chance of exposing the Inner-Sanctum. In truth, we were scared that if we told her we knew all along, she'd run."

Hall laughed, bitterly. "I think that happened anyway. You still had no right to keep it to yourself."

Oliver looked as though he was about to argue, but in his heart, he knew she was right. "I know. It was stupid. You must understand, we're desperate. You've seen the people out there. We care what happens to them. And we share Moretti's resolve for getting justice for her son."

He closed his eyes, as though attempting to banish the memory from his thoughts. "They took the poor child's body and dumped it in an alleyway, as though it were trash," he said, slamming his fist onto the table. "I can almost stomach the deaths from either side of this conflict, as most who participate know the risks. But when children are slaughtered in its name..." He grimaced, unable to finish as he choked on his rage. "If only there'd been some way our paths could've crossed before they got to her..."

Looking down at the doctor, who suddenly looked tired and weary, she felt for him. She took a seat opposite him and placed a hand over his. "It wasn't your fault and I can see that you and Brooks are up against it." As if the last few days had been hard to process, Hall felt as though the rabbit hole she been hurtling down, since her stand-off with Moretti, had become that little bit deeper. "What did she find out that had the Proxy so worried he had to deal with her himself?"

~

Using the darkness, and sparsely lit courtyard to her advantage, she'd pursued the procession into the building. When she'd slipped through the front door, gun raised, expecting to be met by armed guards, she was surprised to find the small vestibule devoid of human activity.

She followed the sounds of voices – a cacophony of complaints from the group of vagrants, and barking commands from the armed men – and thumps of footfalls, making her way

311

further into the building. It soon ceased to be replaced by a metallic scraping which resounded to her position, quickly followed by the steady hum of what sounded like an elevator.

She pushed through a set of double doors and was met with said elevator. It was the biggest elevator she'd ever seen; the doors spanned twenty feet across and ten, or fifteen feet high. Above it, a display board showed numbers running down in the minus. Seventeen, eighteen, finally halting at nineteen.

She turned back the way she'd came; her mind conflicted. She considered calling for backup, but the captain's reproachful tone sprang back to mind dissuading her from making the call. She waited ten agonisingly long minutes before pushing the call button, situated on the left-hand side of the doors, and waited as the numbers began to creep back up to her floor.

The doors slid open – quicker than she'd thought for being so far down – and she slipped inside. She pressed nineteen on the keypad. As the doors closed, she was unaware of the double doors opening slightly.

The neon numbers – a vibrant shade of red – on the internal display descended to minus-nineteen, all the while, her heart raced with fear and anticipation of what she would find when she reached the bottom. Where were those poor, wretched people being taken to? Death... or something far more sinister? The image of the young man being beaten to death didn't fill her with much hope. After the guard had finally ceased his onslaught, his comrades had dragged the bloody body back into the pod.

As much as she was fearful of what those men could do, she had to keep going. Besides, she had the years of training to deal with combat, should the need arise. She'd been relentless in her pursuit of the truth for months, but at the same time, hadn't fully prepared herself emotionally for the outcome when she found it. She'd lost count of the amount missing. She was astounded, troubled, and suspicious by her superior's apparent lack of interest with so many citizens having vanished off the face of the earth. She felt alone, but if she was able to provide her boss with some concrete evidence, it may change things. It had to…

She was brought back to reality by the loud clang doled out by the elevator as it slowed, then gently stopped with a creak. She pulled out her sidearm, aiming its barrel towards the doors, as they slid open. She breathed a sigh of relief as the only thing awaiting her was the acrid stench of disinfectant. She placed her free hand to her mouth in a futile attempt to stave off the disgusting aroma from invading her senses.

She slowly stepped out of the elevator, where the stench increased tenfold. She tensed as the sound of the procession suddenly emanated from the other end of the corridor. She slowly put one foot in front of the other and followed the noise, her investigator's curiosity giving her focus and spurring her on. Her personal negligence – brought on by her need to see this out – made her unaware of the elevator doors closing and ascending back up to ground level.

~

"So, what did she find that started all this mess?" Hall asked. From what she'd heard in the last few hours, her initial hatred - mixed with fear - of the woman had subsided considerably. The fact Moretti had saved her from the clutches of the man responsible for her partner and captain's deaths certainly played its part.

Oliver rose from his chair and beckoned her to a bank of monitors to the back of the room. She scraped her seat back and got up, following him. She stopped by his side as he pointed to a list of names on one of the screens which ran from the top to the very bottom. Beside these names was a brief log of basic information; sex; age; ethnicity. She also noted, from the size of the scroll box on the right-hand side, that these names were but a few.

"What am I looking at?" she asked, not sure she wanted to know the answer.

"If you went into NewHaven and typed in any one of these names into the city archive search, do you know what you would come up with?"

She glanced back to the front door, then looked Oliver in the eye. "I take it these are the names of everyone who reside within this compound?"

He shook his head, a sad smile creeping across his features. "I wish it were so, Veronica. If all of the people on this vast list were crammed in here, we'd struggle to breathe, let alone move." He sighed, suddenly looking tired, but at the same time, she noticed there was a deep resolve set in his eyes as he gazed at the screen. "A small fraction is under our care. The rest..."

She didn't like his ominous tone. "What happened to the others?"

~

The procession stopped in front of what looked like a wall of smooth steel. The armed men fanned out and herded the group so that they were huddled a few feet from the wall. One of the men began to bark commands to his comrades, who then began to separate the people into three groups; old, young, and children. Parents screamed as their children were wrenched from their arms. The sight made Lex sick to her stomach. She thought of her Julian and felt glad she had taken the precaution of getting him to safety before she'd set out to this terrible place.

Suddenly the claustrophobic tunnel filled with an ear-piercing whine as the wall of steel began to rise. A cold wind blew into the tunnel, howling towards where she squatted.

Beyond the door was a barren landscape. An old battered road led away, flanked on either side by hard soil patched with tufts of pale grass. It was the outside. Wasn't the outside steeped in radiation? Disease? She involuntarily covered her mouth with her sleeve.

Once the door had stopped its ascent, the area was filled with the ear-splitting boom of automatic gunfire as the armed men spent their ammunition on the elderly group. Bullets ripped through them; the vacuum of the outside world blew the stench of blood and misery to her position.

She tried to cry out, but a course hand clamped over her mouth, stifling her screams. "Be quiet, Lex," a familiar voice hissed in her ear, "or we'll be discovered. I'm going to take my hand off your mouth. Stay quiet. Nod if you understand."

She twisted her head around to be met with the face of her captain, Malcolm Jacobson. She nodded and he let go. "Captain, what are you doing here?" he whispered.

"I've come to get you. I told you to drop this, Lex," he said, barely concealing his anger.

She ignored the rebuke. "Julian? Is he safe?" she asked. She'd fed the captain a pack of lies about one of the local triad leaders gunning for her blood and had asked him to get Julian to safety. She wasn't surprised he'd saw through it.

"He's fine. I'm a bit disappointed you couldn't trust me enough to tell me the real reason why you wanted your son hidden," he said, sounding genuinely hurt.

Lex turned back to where the people were being forced through the threshold of the giant door. "I had to, Captain." She pointed to the group. "They're being sent outside, why?"

"You're a good Investigator, Lex. But this is necessary," the captain said.

"What's necessary..." She turned to face her superior, noticing he was holding a stun-baton... held inches from her neck. She lowered her gaze to the faint glow emanating from its tip. "What's going on?"

316

"I'm sorry, Lex. I like you, but this is greater than you or me," he said, nodding to the carnage beyond them. "If it were up to me... but, you've seen too much."

She tried to back away, but the captain was too close. He drove the tip of the baton into her neck, sending a bolt of voltage through her body which reduced her world to agony.

Then blackness took her.

~

"Watch his fucking head, you idiots," Li snapped, as Morgan and Tullisa carried Deacon into their van. They held him by the legs and his armpits like they were hauling a sack of potatoes. She knew she wasn't mad at the pair of reconnaissance operatives, but there was no one else she could take her ire out on. "Is there a doctor at the safe-house?"

"Yeah, boss," Morgan said, as he hefted Charlie Deacon's limp form up to the floor of the van.

Li nodded to Deacon. "Is he still breathing?"

Tullisa hovered a hand over Deacon's mouth, cursing as some of his blood spilt onto her trousers. "He's breathing," she said, waving her hand in disgust. "Fuck, how's this guy still alive? There's blood everywhere."

Li stepped into the van, helped them get the stricken cop into the makeshift gurney, then turned and struck Tullisa across the jaw with the back of her hand. "There's gonna be a shitload more than this before this is over, so get used to it."

Tullisa looked at Li as though she were about to protest, but thought better of it - presumably knowing Li's reputation. Morgan was quite happy to concentrate his attention on Deacon; pulling a stained blanket over him and placing a rolled-up coat behind his head.

"We good?" Li asked.

"Good," Morgan said, Tullisa muttered her acquiescence and stomped round to the front of the van and climbed in.

Li returned to her bike, the sound of the van growing fainter as they sped off to the safe-house. She crouched down to the large box, fixed to the underside of her vehicle. She removed a long tube, along with its trigger, scope, and round from its foam housing. She quickly assembled it - having done it so many times before.

From the panel she'd rested Charlie Deacon's head on, she removed an EMP grenade and slid it into the chamber. She rested the launcher over the seat of her bike and peered down the scope, aiming the crosshairs over the power cell boxes. The distance across the screen read one hundred and twenty-seven feet.

She was ready. Now, all she required was the green light. She clicked the call button on her earpiece, patching her through to Brooks' line. He answered after a few seconds.

"Li, the recon team have confirmed they've got Deacon on-route to the safe-house. They should arrive shortly. Tullisa had a few choice words to say about your conduct," Brooks said, sounding slightly amused.

"If the bitch has a problem, she knows where to find me. Are you ready with the spook's scribe?" she asked, not surprised at Tullisa's little complaint. The cause didn't have time for little assholes like her. She was convinced she'd lose her shit at the first sign of trouble – when the real fight began.

"I should be in fifteen minutes. Hang tight. I'll send you a message when you're good to go."

"Affirmative," she said, cutting the call.

~

Her eyes snapped open, her body jolting from the adrenaline that had been pushed into her veins by the pen. She barely had time to compose herself before a fist struck her hard across the face.

"Wakey, wakey, you little cunt," the Proxy said, before hitting her once more. "You have no idea how much this delights me," he said, striking her once more.

She was in a familiar place. It was the same dark room she'd inhabited not so long ago. She looked down; thankful she still had her suit on. The Proxy caught her gaze and laughed.

"Don't you worry, my dear. We'll get you out of those soon enough. You're gonna be fucked so hard, you'll think a cruiser has ripped through you," he said, grabbing a hank of her hair. His cologne was absolutely disgusting.

She took in her surroundings. The room comprised of the Proxy, two bleeders - with their tray of medical equipment. Two guards, and the spook, Marr. Her hands were tied with coarse rope - not really a problem, given what she still carried.

In spite of the apparent severity of her predicament, she was exactly where she wanted to be. She chuckled. "You know, Proxy, I'm going to leave you until last," she said as though she were choosing which order of chocolates she was going to eat from the box. "Think I'll fuck you with your own little dick, once I've ripped it off."

They all laughed. Even the bleeders chuckled as much as their lack of human emotion allowed them to... all except Marr, who took a step back towards the door. He knew first-hand what she was capable of. She was fortunate they'd left the suit on her, though she would've figured something out if she hadn't. All she needed was the Proxy to come a little closer...

...then the bloodbath would begin.

~

Brooks smiled as his monitor told him the spook's encryption codes - stolen from his scribe's software - had been accepted. He was - digitally - staring at NewHaven's main firewall. The firewall that had been their biggest stumbling block – the revolution would begin here, he thought.

He picked up his scribe and sent Li the green light.

~

Green blared in her peripheral vision. It was all Li needed. She steadied her aim and fired. "Game on, fuckers."

~

The lights went out in the crowded room, descending it in darkness. For a few tense seconds, silence reigned supreme. Then a set of fierce red stripes lit up all over the woman's suit, casting the room in a red, almost neon hue – it was the most frightening thing he'd ever seen.

Marr edged towards the door as the woman began to laugh. It was a terrible, maniacal cackle which froze his blood. The sound of metal scraping from its sheath resounded, followed by the snap of her bounds being cut. Marr looked at her in horror as two wicked-looking blades had appeared from a hidden part at her wrists.

The moment the woman had been woken by the adrenaline pen and calmly told the room what she planned to do; Marr realised he'd been played. Her words chilled him. Gone were the wisecracks and defiance. In its place were the chilling words of a complete and utter psychopath.

Thinking back to the Proxy's words outside – knowing Faulks would drop him without a second thought – spurred Marr into action. He needed time to escape, and from where he now stood - furthest from this spectre of death - he saw an opportunity.

He turned and swiped his card on the reader which unlocked the door. He slipped through and closed it. The others barely noticed; too busy taking in the neon striped psycho in front of them. Once the door clicked, to signify it had automatically locked, he shot the electronic reader on the other side, rendering it permanently out of action. The Proxy, his two guards, and the bleeders were trapped inside with Moretti.

He glanced through the window and caught the Proxy's fear-stricken gaze. He mouthed a silent 'fuck you', before disappearing down the hall, leaving cries and screams behind him.

~

Lex was finally getting what she had strived for these last months: locked in a room with the man responsible for Julian's death.

She had drawn her blades and sliced through her bonds with ease. She watched the spook leave the room and sabotage the locking mechanism. It was an interesting development, but it hardly mattered. The Proxy wasn't going to get a chance to pay the spook back for his insubordination. She sighed out a deep breath, allowing the dark essence, that had been her constant companion since she'd lost her blue-eyed boy, consume her.

There was no holding back now.

The Proxy pushed past the two bleeders – who themselves drew razor-sharp scalpels. The first one whipped the small blade, aiming it for her neck. She pivoted to the side letting the blade pass her; missing by inches. She grabbed the bleeders' wrist and rammed her elbow up, snapping the joint. The bleeder barely made a grunt of complaint before she cut his throat, slicing so deep she felt her blade scrape against his spine. Blood drenched her as the bleeder dropped to the ground, clutching his neck and gurgling his last.

The second bleeder had swapped her scalpel for a syringe – obviously wanting to subdue her with hypodermics rather than take her chances with one-to-one combat. In the end, Lex's focused rage rendered the choice moot. She dodged a flurry of jabs until the bleeder ironically slipped in her partner's blood. It gave Lex the opening she was looking for. She broke her arm in two places. The severed bone of the bleeder's forearm ripped through the material of her medical overalls, staining the white material crimson. Lex took a hold of the bleeder's fist, still holding the syringe. Unlike her partner, she was wailing like a banshee. Lex twisted her wrist and drove the needle's point into the bleeder's eyeball. The soft tissue made an audible squelch, the bleeder's screams becoming more and more high-pitched until the syringe pierced into her brain. The wailing stopped as though a switch had been flipped and she dropped to the ground.

She'd dispatched the two bleeders in less than ten seconds. Nothing was coming between her and her prey. The two guards had already drawn their weapons by the time the female bleeder had hit the ground, but they were clearly reluctant to fire in close quarters as there was a good chance of a stray bullet ricocheting off one of the walls – they looked unsure how to proceed.

The Proxy was screaming at his two henchmen to fire as he kicked and scraped at the door. Lex ducked into a roll as one of the guards finally decided to take his chances with his own bullets rather than the knife-wielding, blood-spattered, Neon wraith approaching them.

She sliced through the tendons of their ankles in a blur of steel; painting the floor in their own blood. They both dropped their weapons, writhing on the gore-spattered tiles in agony. Lex opened their throats, silencing their cries.

She stood up to face the Proxy. He held his hands in front of him, shaking like the pathetic, child-killing worm he was. "Stop... wait... it was the Prime's idea; you have to believe m— "

She kicked him in the balls with everything she could muster. "I'm sick to death of your fucking words," she growled. He dropped to the floor in a heap; both his hands covering his injured pride. She took a step back and picked up a thin knife from the medical table.

She picked him up by the hair and drove her forehead into the bridge of his nose, revelling in the satisfying crunch it made. She stopped him falling by grabbing him by the throat. She pulled him so close she could smell the coppery tang emanating from his ruptured nose. "I did my duty to this city... to the ideals set out by Vonn. I served NewHaven to the best of my abilities and how was I repaid?" She paused for a moment, wrenching his mouth open and slicing out his tongue.

She dropped the bloodied piece of flesh to the blood-smeared floor as the room filled with the gurgled screams of the Proxy. "My son," she screamed, so loud she thought her throat would burn. All her grief came out in those two simple

324

words. She repeated them as she eviscerated him where he stood. Tears streamed down her face at the same rate as the Proxy's intestines spilt to the floor.

When there was nothing left to pull out of the highest-ranked citizen - second only to the Prime - she dropped to her knees and wept. Amidst the carnage, she only had thoughts of Julian... her blue-eyed boy. "It's done, my love," she whispered to the ceiling, her voice cracked and hoarse; her body covered in head to toe with the blood of her enemies.

She looked down at the body of Samuel Faulks. His eyes were open in a permanent expression of horror. The front of his torso had been reduced to pulp. Amidst the mess, something shiny caught her eye. On the Proxy's lapel was the badge of his office. It was similar to the pins she'd taken from her previous victims. She hadn't known it until a few hours ago, but this trophy was the one she'd sought above all the others. She unclipped it and secreted it into a pocket, not bothering to wipe the blood from it.

Suddenly loud crashes resounded from the other side of the door. She could see at least a dozen heavily armed NewHaven soldiers through the window. She sighed, rising to her feet. She looked up as though she could see the face of her beautiful son. "I'll take as many of them with me as I can," she said. She approached the nearest of Faulks' dead guards and took one of the grenades from his belt.

Then the door exploded off its hinges...

~

The firewall was down. Oliver and Veronica Hall looked on as Brooks uploaded the Inner-Sanctum's biggest secret to every server, every scribe, and every Zep screen in the city. The isolated world that was Sanctum-One was blown wide open. There were citizens on the outside – beyond the city's walls – cast out because the truth was Sanctum-One had run out of resources to satisfy its population and the Prime's solution was to expel thousands to hold back the inevitable tide.

Sanctum-One was a dying ideal in which control over the populous was at risk due to the lack of natural resources at hand to sustain Prime Vonn's idea of the perfect society. Known as Operation Exodus, it provides information on the structure and existence of the Inner-Sanctum; its purpose and how everyone's lives aren't truly their own. Knowledge of Aaron Trent's attempts to change the structure of society to one of democracy and his subsequent murder.

Hall saw tears running down Brooks' face as they watched thousands of citizens descend on NewHaven; angry and in search of answers. Oliver placed a comforting hand on his friend's shoulder. "Your family would be proud of you, my friend." Brooks sniffed and nodded.

"So, What now? Where do we go from here?" Hall asked.

Brooks nodded to his friend and then looked Hall in the eyes; a steely resolve etching his features. "We finish it."

"And Moretti?" She asked.

"There was an explosion from within NewHaven. The Proxy's dead, along with several others. The firewall's back up, everything's on lockdown. The small amount of information we have, gathered by Li, is that she took out about a dozen soldiers before a grenade went off in the vicinity. She's dead."

Hall couldn't believe it… Moretti was dead. She opened her mouth to speak but was interrupted by a sob coming from the doorway. A little girl stood, tears streaming down her face. "She's not dead… you're lying," she shouted.

Brooks took a step forward. "Kat…"

Before he could get any closer, Kat turned and ran, leaving the three of them alone to contemplate their next move without the aid of 'the woman'.

Epilogue

Geno Moretti wiped a tear from his eye as he stared at the happy photograph of his niece and her son. He drained the last of the scotch and got up from his chair He staggered slightly and took a moment to steady his drunken legs. The room was gloomy. He hadn't even noticed it get dark, so deep in his cups and grief to care.

He made his way through to the bedroom to the rear of his apartment, his mind a fog, and entered the secret room he'd used to correspond with his niece. He sat in the only chair in the room and picked up the scribe.

No messages.

She was dead. He'd turned off his tele-screen when the media had reported his niece's involvement in the terror attack at NewHaven. They'd claimed the information spread throughout the city was an elaborate ruse; a falsity conjured up by Alexandra and Sapien-Republic to spread unrest and chaos throughout the city. He knew it was a pack of lies, but he still felt like putting his boot through the screen all the same. He'd opted instead to switch it off and climb into a bottle of scotch.

Things were going to change. Already there were flyers being passed around the neighbourhoods, and throughout the city centre inviting citizens on protest marches, and take part in business boycotts. But in spite of the growing change, Geno didn't want anything to do with it. His niece and his little Julian were gone. His eyes began to brim with tears.

That was when he noticed a glint of something shiny coming from the far end of the table. He hadn't noticed it before, as he hadn't bothered to turn on the light. But the glow, emitted from the scribe, had revealed it. It looked like a badge or a pin.

He reached over and picked it up. It was a pin. It was charred on one of the corners, but he could still make out the one word, emblazoned across its centre.

It read: Proxy.

His hands began to shake. He whipped his head round to the door and began to weep with tears of joy. Then he just about jumped out of his skin as the scribe vibrated in his grasp. His trembling fingers desperately pawed at the screen. He opened the message.

G,

It's done.

L.

Authors Note

And here you find yourself at the end of my novel. I hope you've enjoyed reading it as much as I've enjoyed writing it - because the idea of a dystopian trilogy came out of nowhere.

After I finished my last book, The Fall of the Hour, I had every intention of writing its sequel (which is well underway, in case you're wondering). But I sort of got side-tracked by this scene I had in my head — the scene where Lex is chasing Trammel through the market precinct.

I've always been intrigued by dystopian novels, movies, and tv shows. I think they bare a certain truth that there's a slight possibility that the human race is about half a dozen bad decisions away from descending into a world similar to the one I created (don't worry, I haven't crafted my very own tinfoil hat).

So, I wrote the scene and then soon began to ask questions. Why was he being chased? Who hunted him and why? That was where the story of Sanctum-One and my heroine's quest for justice began to take shape.

I wrote a quick outline and decided I could maybe do a novella trilogy. I sent a rough excerpt to my good friend, Ryan Mercer (not Hall's boss). He liked it and encouraged me to see where the story took me (he's honest enough to tell me otherwise). For that, I'd like to say thanks, Ryan.

So, I soldiered on. When I got to about twenty thousand words, I soon realised I couldn't fit my story into a novella trilogy. So now I'm in the middle of writing a fantasy series and a dystopian trilogy. I'm not complaining, as I spent my twenties trying to come up with one idea, and now I'm saddled with several... long may it continue.

During the course of writing this book, I couldn't have done it without the help of my wonderful wife, Karina (my head beta-reader). Over the months, she's listened to me ramble on about theories and plot ideas, returning with suggestions and critiques that have helped make the book what it is. I couldn't have made the book any better without her and feel lucky to have someone so beautiful in my life.

I would also like to thank Jeanette Lawson, for her invaluable advice. Nik, for the tremendous cover art. Fraser, for enduring the "second draft meltdown". Mum and Dad for giving me the courage and confidence to pursue new challenges. My brother, Scott, who's always there for me. And to all my friends and family, who've provided me with nothing but love and support throughout my writing.

And last, but not least, my little Millie, who inspires me in everything I do.

Graeme J Greenan 2019.

Further Reading

The Fall of the Hour
Book One of The Knights of the Hour

For centuries the kingdoms of Grunald and Helven have enjoyed a fragile peace, overseen by a mysterious order known as the Knights of the Hour, after a long war with men lost to the world and their demonic allies.

In the court of Oakhaven, capital city of Grunald, news of the order's destruction throws the peace into uncertainty, giving rise to factions within the nobility to see their ambitions realised.
Lord Kerr, last Knight of the Hour, finds himself in an impossible position. Caught between the kingdom's eagerness for war, and the search for answers with regard to his Order's fate, he walks a treacherous line in which all options seem to lead to danger and mortal peril.

Within the depths of the Great Forest, tragedy throws Lana into the sights of two men. One hell-bent on watching the world burn. The other, a mysterious exile returned to prevent it.

Amidst the search for truth, dark forces await the perfect moment to strike and descend the world into war and bloodshed once more.

~

For more news and updates on future works by Graeme J Greenan, visit him on his Facebook and Twitter pages:
www.facebook.com/graemejgreenan
www.twitter.com/GraemeGreenan

30963288R00190

Printed in Great
Britain
by Amazon